Only Betsy can get him h
bring her back before it
original if you think it bet

A grief-stricken candy-striper serving in a VA hospital following her brother's death in Viet Nam struggles to return home an anonymous veteran of the Great War against the skullduggery of a congressman who not only controls the hospital as part of his small-town fiefdom but knows the name of her veteran. A name if revealed would end his political ambitions and his fifty-year marriage. In its retelling of Odysseus's journey, *Revenants* casts a flickering candle upon the charon toll exacted not only from the families of those who fail to return home but of those who do.

"Like the best of literature, *Revenants, the Odyssey Home*, is difficult to categorize. It's a mystery, a love story, a coming-of-age story, an historical novel, a story of political intrigue, a war novel. Its richness is the richness of life. Its intention is to be compelling entertainment and to evoke timeless and universal truths. As such, *Revenants* will not fade quickly as less substantial novels do but will resonate in the reader's heart and mind for years to come."—*Mark Spencer, Dean, School of Arts and Humanities, Professor of Creative Writing, Master of Fine Arts Program, University of Arkansas at Monticello.*

"The true damage of war isn't the war-racked towns and cities, nor is it the military losses. It's the damage done to the survivors and their families. As Scott Kauffman elides past one war then another we see this damage portrayed movingly in his characters. This is a book you must read to see the truth of war."—*Robert Mustin, Sam's Place: Stories.*

"... *Revenants: The Odyssey Home* is a beautifully written novel which embraces the harsh realities of life, encompassing the reader with the rough and genuine emotions of the life altering choices made by our protagonist. Scott Kauffman tells an intriguing story which will linger in the reader's mind far after the final page has been turned."—*Florentine, Readiculously Peachy Blog.*

"In his compelling new novel of the Seventies, *Revenant - The Odyssey Home,* Scott Kauffman takes the reader on an odyssey towards recovery. With skillful character development the author makes us see just exactly what it is like to be wounded, in soul and spirit, and not at all sure you will ever recover. But one person can change all that by simply applying the universal antidote of life: love!"— *Brian Francis Heffron, Poet/Filmmaker, Author of Award Winning Novel Colorado Mandala.*

# Revenants – The Odyssey Home

## Scott Kauffman

**Moonshine Cove Publishing, LLC**
Abbeville, South Carolina U.S.A.

All rights reserved. No part of this book may be reproduced in whole or in part without written permission from the publisher except by reviewers who may quote brief excerpts in connection with a review in a newspaper, magazine or electronic publication; nor may any part of this book be reproduced, stored in a retrieval system or transmitted in any form or by any means electronic, mechanical, photocopying, recording or any other means, without written permission from the publisher.
This book shall not be lent, resold, hired out or otherwise circulated without the publisher's prior consent in any form of binding or cover other than that in which it is published. For information about permission to reproduce selections from this book, write to Moonshine Cove Publishing, 150 Willow Pt, Abbeville, SC 29620.

ISBN: 978-1-937327-81-1
Library of Congress Control Number: 2015920273
Copyright © 2015 by Scott Kauffman

Cover design by Thomas Bentley, Bentley Printing, Garden Grove, CA; interior design by Moonshine Cove staff

# Dedication

As always, for Elizabeth

# Acknowledgment

With my deepest appreciation for their numerous and close readings of earlier drafts to Angela Rinaldi, Angela Rinaldi Literary Agency, Beverly Hills, California; Mark Spencer, Dean of Arts & Humanities, University of Arkansas, Monticello, Arkansas; and Clem Cairns and Mary-Jane Holmes, Fish Publishing, West Cork, Ireland. Could not have done it without you, guys. Thank you.

## About The Author

Scott claims his fiction career began with an in-class book report written in Mrs. Baer's eighth-grade English class when, due to a conflict of priorities, he failed to read the book. An exercise of imagination was required. Scott snagged a B, better than the C he received on his last report when he actually read the book. Thus began his life-long apprenticeship as a teller of tales and, some would snidely suggest, as a lawyer as well, but they would be cynics, a race Oscar Wilde warned us knew the price of everything and the value of nothing. Scott is the author of the legal-suspense novel, *In Deepest Consequences*, and a recipient of the 2011 Mighty River Short Story Contest and the 2010 Hackney Literary Award. His short fiction has been appeared in *Big Muddy*, *Adelaide Magazine* and *Lascaux Review*. He is now at work on two novel manuscripts and a collection of short stories. He is an attorney in Irvine, California, where his practice focuses upon white-collar crime and tax litigation with his clients providing him endless story fodder. He graduated *summa cum laude* from Ohio University in Athens, Ohio, and in the upper ten percent of his class from Lewis & Clark Law School in Portland, Oregon, where he was a member of the Environmental Law Review and received the American Jurisprudence Award in Conflict of Laws.

## Preface

My late wife played the role of dark muse in my writing of *Revenants*. Strings of memory spliced one to another with her twine of tenacious insistence revealed in our rose-garden talks as we looked out across the black of the Pacific to where her Uncle Bunkle, Captain Richard Rees, United States Special Forces, died twelve miles southwest of a city then called Saigon in a country fated but to be for another sixteen months and fourteen days before it self-immolated atop that ever ascending gray ash heap of history. Died amidst a too-tentative truce while he and his unarmed men searched for Americans yet missing. Searched so they too might journey home. The first, and perhaps only, United States serviceman killed in action while deployed on an MIA recovery mission. Likely the last American combat death in our first war that even now only a few begrudging officials will admit where America was defeated, fewer still will confess as a mistake to have been waged at all, and none has yet conjured a credible explanation of what possible imminent threat its loss posed, beyond impairing their own political ambitions, to a vital United States interest justifying the slaughter of the lives of 58,220 Americans who had but begun to live theirs.

You may think you have a memory, but those black-night revelations taught me it is memory that has you for it is only remembrance that can render dignity to death. Remembrance that haunts you and holds you and will not let go. Not ever.

Also by Scott Kauffman

*In Deepest Consequences*
*Last Call at Last Chance* (forthcoming)

**Revenant** (REV-ih-nunt) - *n.* a person returning after a long absence or death; a ghost. a*dj.* 1. ghostly; returning, 2. remembering something long forgotten.

> Then let the fortunate breathers of the air,
> When we lie speechless in the muffling mould,
> Tease not our ghosts with slander, pause not there
> To say that love is false and soon grows cold,
> But pass in silence the mute grave of two
> Who lived and died believing love was true.
>
> —From Fatal Interview
> by Edna St. Vincent Millay

*To Charlotte,*
*All the best!!*

# Revenants - The Odyssey Home

To Charlotte,
All the best !!

# ACT I
# CHAPTER 1

January 1984

*Just twelve more days to Christmas and I was totally jazzed. Exams ended on a Wednesday, and I absolutely knew I'd aced all of them, even that stupid head cracker in geometry that Lisping Larry Lehman threw at us. Now I was done until the new year that I knew – absolutely knew – would be my greatest ever.*

*Even better, winter came early. Like it was God's special reward for a job well done. Almost never did we get much snow and it didn't get super cold before at least January, but on the day after exams it snowed over a foot, and then the temperature dropped below zero at night so we could go sledding and ice skating at Hanna Park where I'd get to see Billy Hufnagel every day just like if we had classes except without the Gestapo hall monitors eyeballing us to make certain we weren't holding hands. I mean really. I dare you to name me one girl who ever got herself knocked up while holding hands.*

*My fuddy-duddy parents wouldn't let me go steady with guys until I turned seventeen, but Mom said that year I could invite Billy over on Christmas Eve for hot spiced cider and caroling around the piano. Who knows? Maybe he'd slip me a friendship ring, but if he did I'd have to wear it* on a chain with my lucky locket so Mom wouldn't have a cow and make me give it back.

On the first day of Christmas my true love gave to me...

And I knew — absolutely knew — under the tree on Christmas Eve would be a pink cashmere sweater from Fitzpatrick's I'd been drooling for since September and a silver ID bracelet with "Betsy" engraved on it and maybe because it'd gotten so cold an ice-skating skirt so I could show off my thighs I'd toned up from cheering. But the best presents were on their way. The best presents year-in-year-out came in a box from my brother Nathan.

Nathan was the best. A grownup who hadn't quite gotten the hang of growing up. When he came home we cruised the neighborhood in his cherry-bomb Barracuda convertible with Tavo his poodle who he never once duded up at the groomers but let his fur grow and grow until Tavo looked like this disembodied Afro waddling about on four legs. If Nathan needed to be somewhere, he'd pay me five dollars to watch him. I would've watched him for free, but I didn't turn down the cash either because when you're a kid you've never sufficient operating capital for necessities like hot chocolate when ice-skating and you can only hustle so much babysitting. Then me and Nathan would go to the Dairy Queen, sometimes twice in the same day, and afterwards, when I was smaller, he'd drive us over to Hanna Park where he'd carry me to the playground shrieking on his shoulders or when I got older if it was summer and sometimes even in winter he'd drop the top down and crank up the radio, and we'd belt out the lyrics, getting these weird looks from other drivers.

Be-be-be-Bennie and the Jets.

Nathan's boxes, like him, were the best. They didn't arrive with little-girl stuff anymore but for the woman he saw me becoming. Like the year before his box had this gold watch that Mom said I couldn't wear every day but only for weddings and the spring prom and stuff. With it came this dozen-drawer jewelry box hand crafted out of ebony, and inside one of its tiny drawers was a pair of half-carat diamond earrings, but Mom said I still had to wait until I was seventeen – what was it with her about me turning seventeen – before getting my ears pierced?

Nathan's boxes were just so boss, but I always worried they might not make it. No need for me to have worried that Christmas. The one holding his Distinguished Service Cross came with a commendation telling us that on December 13, 1973, his helicopter, part of the Joint Casualty Resolution Center and identified by three orange stripes, took off before dawn from its base in Thailand to search for MIAs at a crash site in Bin Chanh, twelve miles southwest of what was then Saigon. Nathan and his men, all Special Forces veterans, wore fatigues emblazoned with orange pockets and insignia identifying them as members of the Four-Party Joint Military Team. There was this sort-of-ceasefire in place, and an American delegate to the Paris Peace talks informed the North of the mission a week before. They'd no more than touched down when a Chinese B-40 rocket exploded inside the cockpit, and he and the handful of survivors came under intense machine gun and small arms fire from thirty-some Viet Cong concealed in a row of palm trees. Though pinned down, Nathan stood up, hands raised.

Không có vũ khí. Unarmed. Không có vũ khí.

Three days after the American delegate to the Paris Peace talks threw Nathan's bloodstained jacket across the negotiation table and the day after the honor guard lowered his casket into the frozen earth at the cemetery overlooking Hanna Park, his Christmas box came. The doorbell rang, and I ran stocking-footed downstairs where Mom slumped against the front door, crumple-faced and still dressed in her flannel nightgown because she slept a lot now, the night's snow wisping over her pale legs, Nathan's white-dusted box on the porch behind the postman who knelt beside her.

Ma'am? What is it? Ma'am?

## CHAPTER 2

*December 1973*
The florescent hands pointed to where they had stopped at a minute past midnight ten days before. Nathan's alarm clock had kept her awake, and even after Betsy buried it beneath a mound of clothes at the bottom of the hamper in her closet and shut the door, she heard its *tick, tick, tick*. Her father must have put it back when he did laundry that week, but she never wound it again.

Tree branches scratched the frost-garbled windowpane behind the clock but not until the *Hanna Morning Journal* thumped on the downstairs porch did she push back the covers. She showered in less than a minute so as to leave hot water for the others who would soon be up and returned wrapped in a towel to her room. A full moon shined through the window, and she left her light off as she dressed.

The night before she laid out on a chair the clothes she would wear to her brother's services. She owned nothing in black, her mother insisting whenever they went shopping that she was much too young, so Betsy had decided on the indigo shift and powder blue stockings she would have worn tomorrow to Midnight Mass. She pinned a scarlet poppy above her heart and found her shoes beneath the bed, pairing them left and right. The shiny quarters slipped into their wedges for luck winked in the moonlight, and she sat on the floor to pry them out, cursing *Goddamnit* when she broke a thumbnail. She dropped the quarters in a wastebasket then sat looking at the bedroom door. Her brother's casket waited downstairs.

The smell of wood polish overlaid by paraffin hung in the air at the top of the stairs. From the living room where a votive candle burned at the head of the casket, her father's thin shadow pointed up the steps. He was still dressed in his pajamas and the ratty bathrobe Nathan gave him on Father's Day a dozen years before, twisting his wedding band, head bowed and his bed-slept hair ruffled in thin tuffs. The four rows of folding steel chairs behind him that Billy drove down from St. Paul's in his pickup the day before possessed about them in the pre-dawn a disquieting emptiness as if guests had already stood and left or those invited had suffered a change of heart. She glanced at the closed door to Nathan's room before going downstairs to seek comfort for the hundredth time from her father.

Two white roses leaned from waisted vases on either side of the burning candle. Betsy stood thumbing the pooled wax, behind her the whispered prayer of her father. *Dear Christ Jesus, take onto you our beloved son . . .* She sat beside him, folding her hands over the catechism Bible she found on her bed after Nathan left for the airport. A rosewood casket mirrored the dark visages of father and daughter.

"Honey."

Her father's gray cloud eyes shone, but he was trying to smile.

"I've finished." He placed a hand over both of hers. Thin streaks of shop grease lined the rims beneath his fingernails. "I like your dress."

"You bought it for me at Fitzpatrick's."

"It makes me a little sad, though."

"Why sad?"

"It reminds me you're growing up. Tells me time too soldiers on."

"Where is it time goes when it goes?" She leaned her head to his shoulder. "Where does it hide when it gets there?"

He smoothed away a strand of chestnut hair and kissed her temple. "You're up early."

She nodded.

"Did you think we'd begin without you?"

"Maybe you should."

The bay window behind the casket rattled.

"Do you want to tell me?"

"I'm ashamed now."

"Because of your quarrels over his re-enlisting?"

"No. I'm not ashamed over anything I said. I should've said more. I should've never shut up."

"What then?"

"Because when you drove him to the airport, I didn't go."

"You had a game to cheer, honey."

"I could've gotten one of the reserves to fill in."

"Didn't he tell you he didn't want you getting him weepy eyed in public?"

"I don't care if he would've cried. Nobody would've noticed him because I'd be bawling my eyes out."

"Farewells can be difficult. Nathan understood that."

"I wasn't even home when you left. I was hanging out at Sandy's. Playing dumb Elton John records. He had to leave his Bible — this Bible — on my bed instead of handing it to me like he wanted."

"Your brother understood. Let it go."

"He knew he wasn't coming home, and I wouldn't say good-bye to him."

"Honey, don't. I made six beachhead landings, and before every one of them I knew I wasn't coming home."

The tall-case clock out in the hallway tolled the hour.

"Guess it's time for me to shave and shower. Get Bartholomew up."

"You can't sit with me for a while longer?"

"I'd like to, honey, but Matt McLain is coming early to do a big write-up for Sunday."

"Will Mrs. Hanna be coming do you think?"

"I think she's still with Sarah Anne in Chicago getting tests where her son's on staff. The Congressman may be here."

"Daddy?"

"Yes, honey."

"What's to become of poor Tavo?"

"Tavo will be fine. A captain from Fort Bragg called. Asked if it'd be all right if they made him the company mascot. I told him I thought it'd be less traumatic for Tavo since they're more family to him than we are."

"I guess. Still . . ."

The door to Nathan's room opened and closed.

"I should see if your mother needs help."

He went upstairs. Voices murmured. A dead leaf cart wheeled down the street outside the bay window. When the telephone rang, Betsy rose, touching two fingers to the casket, and went into the kitchen of their old Craftsman bungalow. Grandpa Addison and his new bride had ordered it out of a Sears Roebuck catalog in 1913, and he built it after hauling the precut parts up from the railway depot in five wagonloads on a lot sold to them the day before by Mark Hanna, Sr. Not all the wood had been thoroughly kilned, and over time the bay window warped in its frame. A winter wind whistled in. The candle flame twisted and righted and twisted again before dying, its curling smoke rising like a lamentation.

* * *

"Amen."

Yet Betsy's head remained bowed even as those seated around her stood, their voices hushed, save that of her father.

*Will you talk to her, son?*

*Yessir. I was just going to.*

The chair beside her creaked.

"Hey there, Sweet Pea."

Betsy squinted one eye open. Beside her sat a smiling soldier with a napalmed face that resembled a Tupperware bowl a careless cook had left on a stove burner and forgotten about.

"Hey there, Randy."

"Didn't think you'd remember me."

"Sure I do. You're Randy Brindle. Nate played forward and you played guard, and you were on the diving team too. He took me to watch when you almost made it to the state finals."

"Besides turning into a heartthrob, you're a smarty too."

"He said you were recovering out at the VA."

"Nurse Baker cut me some slack, so Mom come out and drove me in."

Betsy twisted in her chair.

"She's settin' out in the truck. Mom's not much one for funerals."

"I've about had my fill for a while too."

"I hear you, Sweat Pea. You hangin' in there?"

Now jagged candle stumps burned at the head and foot of her brother's casket.

"Yeah. I guess."

"Nate was a good buddy. I'll bet he come out near ever day when he was last home to see what tree I'd climbed to see if he couldn't coax me down for a game of chess."

"What were you doing up in trees?"

"Sniper scouts is always hangin' around in trees."

Shoes stomped out on the front porch. A liver-spotted head poked through the cracked-open door.

"Daddy said he might come but what's Congressman Hanna doing here? He hardly knew Nathan."

"Same thing he does holdin' ceremonies out at the hospital with an election comin' along in November. Picking up votes. I've knowed back-street Saigon hussies with more shame than he can lay claim to."

Hanna tossed his cigar out into the snow, chucking his chin for a dark-suited figure behind him to follow. They crossed the living room to where Father Kaplan stood at the foot of the casket speaking to Matt McLain who was writing in a spiral bound notepad. When Betsy had opened the door for him that morning, she found herself at a loss for words other than to thank him for coming and to say she was looking forward to reading his article. He looked to be twenty, athletic and slender with dark brown hair stylishly long and a Pepsodent smile. At first glance wearing his wire-framed lenses he could pass for John Lennon. Hanna's aide raised a camera as the congressman leaned to Father Kaplan's ear with the casket in the background.

"Of course, Mr. Hanna."

The musk of Jade East cologne snaked the air as the three passed the front row of folding chairs. Randy shook his head. "Asshole congressman."

Hanna pawed both hands of Betsy's father in both of his.

"I only met him once, Randy, but he's a weirdo. Weird, weird, weird."

"Weird don't cover the half of it, Sweet Pea."

Her father nodded to where Betsy's mother stood with her two sisters, a tissue balled in each of their three fists.

I'll just have a short word with his mother before we must leave.

The aide again raised his camera. Hanna clutched Betsy's mother in a bear hug, lifting her heels from the floor. She flailed her hand at her husband, her face wrecking, but he was speaking to McLain with his back to her. Betsy rose and circled to behind her mother.

"Hello, Mr. Hanna. Remember me? I'm Nathan's sister. I saw you once when I was over for my piano lesson from Mrs. Hanna. You must've just gotten up because you were still in your pajamas."

Hanna released her mother, who fled up the stairs with her two sisters in pursuit, and turned to Betsy. "I'm so sorry for your deep personal loss, but I beg you to be comforted in knowing you have our country's deepest thanks for your brother's supreme sacrifice in its defense and its honor."

The aide again raised his camera as Hanna leaned to give Betsy a hug as well, but she skipped a step back so that he lost his balance and grabbed only air. The aide lowered the camera, hiding his smile.

"I remember Nathan followed you around Washington one summer and writing it up for the paper."

"Yes, he did, and a fine article it was. A fine boy. I wish I could've known him better."

"You must go to a lot of funerals now of people you hardly know."

"Why . . ."

Hanna's aide whispered into his ear.

"Oliver reminds me of another pressing engagement." He glanced around the living room. "Where's your mother, honey?"

"She ran upstairs."

"I wanted to thank her once again for her supreme sacrifice."

"I think she's been thanked enough this week."

"Yes, of course. Well, Oliver, shall we? McLain!" The hushed conversations in the room stilled. McLain looked up from his notepad. "You'll be in your office tomorrow?"

"I can be, sir."

"About ten say?"

"Yes, sir."

"Good lad."

He turned to Betsy. "Please give your sainted mother my most sincere condolences on the loss of your Nicholas."

"Nathan."

"What?"

"My brother's name was Nathan."

"What did I say?"

"You said Nicholas."

"Stupid of me." Hanna forced a smile. "This is a young man's job. I need to be thinking about moving on. Maybe next election. Oliver."

"Yes, sir."

Frigid air flooded the living room as Hanna stood in the threshold with raised hand, his aide to the side holding the door open.

"Goodnight my friends. Know that God is with you, and he is with Him."

Betsy crossed to the bay window. The two men from Washington stepped with care down the icy driveway as Hanna gestured with a newly lit cigar and his aide nodding as he held an umbrella over him. Randy came up behind her.

"You ever seen such a horse's ass?"

Betsy shook her head.

"Don't let Hannahole fool you. What you witnessed was an act he puts on. Seen it a hundred times out at the hospital. The patients know him for the clown he is, but their folks eat this up with a spoon when they come visiting. Most voters do too because they don't know no better, but he scares me. Scared Nate too. That's the reason he wouldn't go back to his paper no more after the one summer. Tell you what, Sweat Pea. You get a gaggle of 'em together in Washington and by God if they need to fathom a reason for why somebody else's brother needs to be pushing up the petunias so they can hoodwink their next election, they'll finagle one."

Oliver handed the umbrella to Hanna and trotted to the street where the Lincoln Continental sat, exhaust from its engine graying the twilight. He pulled into the driveway and got out and opened the rear passenger door. The limousine backed again into the street and continued on, its tires scarring the fresh snow. Betsy turned away. Her eyes circled from mourner to mourner.

"Everything's changed for us."

"In ways you can't begin to imagine, Sweet Pea."

# CHAPTER 3

Betsy skipped her basketball games for the Fridays before and following the funeral, but she cheered the second weekend after. They won, seventy-eight to seventy-seven, but came close to losing when a Saint Paul's player charged a Leetonia player with a second left on the clock, skidding him across the floorboards. His team's supporters chanted as the bloody-nosed boy dribbled at the foul line: *Naaaathan, Naaaathan, Naaaathan.*

Betsy's arms dropped to her sides. Her face bled white, her wide eyes searching the stands, but her parents had given away their season tickets. From where he sat high up in the bleachers, Father Kaplan hurried down the steps. Sandy Jackson raised a hand to her mouth, but none of the girls on the squad came to Betsy's side, only stared at one another with the same stolid faces as had the Casualty Assistance Officers when Betsy opened the front door.

She fled off the court and into the night, the crowd behind her drowning out Father Kaplan.

*Please, Betsy.*

She ran until her lungs burned in the January cold and the spit on her tongue tasted of pennies and she could run no more. She doubled over, gasping beneath a street lamp with hands clenching her knees. Tears froze in her eyelashes and as snow fell through the antumbra of light she cursed, *Goddamn you, God.*

\* \* \*

She found the squad's advisor after classes on Monday.

"I'm quitting, Miss Fillmore."

The first-year teacher studied the girl's vacant eyes as she tapped a pencil on the stack of papers before her.

"Why don't you think your decision over a little more, sweetie? Maybe take a leave of absence for a month?"

"I can't. Mom needs me at home."

"Please, Betsy. You've a gift. Young as you are, the only sophomore on the squad, yet you're the one who brings life to the others. We can't afford to lose your Betsyness."

"I need to be going." Betsy stepped back from the desk. "I'm sorry, but Mom needs me at home."

She fled the school by its back door. In the alley behind Reash's Newsstand a semicircle of school hoods hung out where they always did as they shared among themselves a single cigarette. They wore gray trousers and skirts with white shirts and blouses that bore the patched knees and stitched elbows of hand-me-downs from their brothers and sisters. Betsy hurried by with her beret head down and no word passing between them. When she reached the corner, though, she turned to look back, the hoods guffawing at some joke. The smoke of their laughter plumed over them. She returned, walking up to Randy Brindle's sister who sat in the back row of their home economics class. Because Mrs. Brindle spent her evenings and paychecks at Perry's Tavern, Darlene had to have her younger brother trim her hair, but this last time he was half watching *Happy Days* and cut one side a half-inch shorter than the other, leaving Darlene's head lopsided. Betsy held out two fingers. The hoods fell silent. Darlene snorted.

"Since when did Junior Miss America with her hand in the air for every single question degenerate into a fagger?"

An acne-scarred boy snickered.

"I've been smoking a while."

Darlene held up the drawn-down nub. "My last toke, honey."

"Wouldn't want to jack your last toke."

"Why don't you go into Reash's. Herman don't care how old you are so long as you can get your money up on the counter."

Betsy thumped her purse. "Busted."

"Me too." Darlene drew on the nub before flicking it into the gutter. She winked at Betsy. "Come along anyway. You can flirt with Herman while I'm discount shopping. Nothin' grabs his attention better than tryin' to talk a pretty girl into his storage room."

Betsy's eyes darted to Reash's back door. "I don't know."

"It'll be okay. You'll only be talkin.' Even Junior Miss America's allowed to shoot the breeze."

Betsy didn't answer, but when Darlene started to walk away, she followed.

"Too bad Herman don't carry no pot."

"Yeah. What I wouldn't give for a hit."

"Have to wait 'til Hudson's party on Friday. You comin'?"

"Maybe. Think Neil might have some acid there too?"

Darlene twirled in a quarter circle, squeezing Betsy's elbow.

"Ow, Darlene!"

"Don't go there, girl. Don't you remember Allen was dropping acid last year when he was walkin' a train rail on his way out of town like he thought he'd turned into a tightrope walker who'd joined the circus? They had to hose what was left of him off the tracks. Dogs was lunching out there for months. Think about your folks. Your little brother. They've gone through enough."

Betsy shook off Darlene's hand and continued up the parking lot to Reash's back door.

* * *

A month following Nathan's funeral, Sister Francesca dragged Betsy by the wrist into Father Kaplan's office. She had caught her and Darlene smoking in the restroom, and when she snatched the cigarette from between Betsy's fingers, Betsy called the nun a goddamn bitch.

"Thank you, Sister. I'll take it from here."

He nodded at one of two straight-back chairs before his desk, and Betsy sat, staring at her hands folded on her flannel skirt. He recognized that look; saw it in the mirror every morning after another sleepless night. He had served as a padre in Korea at dressing stations stretched across the front a half-mile behind the lines where some weeks he bore witness to the deaths of more boys than a run-of-the-mill private might during his entire tour. When the Chinese resorted to one of their thousand-man human-wave attacks, he would be up thirty-six hours straight and more, giving child soldiers their last rites as life seeped from their terrified eyes. Once he fell asleep in the middle of delivering a boy's sacrament, and when he woke the boy laid gaping-mouth dead. He made the sign of the cross, slapped himself sensible, and moved on to the next litter.

*The 3:30 bell rang out in the hallway.*

"You know I can't let this skip by with a talk and sending you home for three days."

"Yes, Father."

The priest waited. Betsy turned a hand palm up as if she was about to offer an apology, but she said nothing.

"I also received a report you were spotted running out the back door when Sheriff Durkin raided Hudson's party, and you didn't make honor roll this term. When was the last time you pulled a B let alone a D?"

Betsy shook her head.

"I've got to stop this now. Nathan would be livid. Destroying your life won't bring his back."

"But it will join us together again."

"Wouldn't Nathan want you to live your life for both of you?"

Winter-barren oaks swayed outside the window.

Okay, Betsy. Your call, your choice. You can go home and come back next September to take your sophomore year over."

Girl's passing voices laughed outside the door.

"You said I had a choice."

"I know Nurse Baker out at the VA. Worked there myself when I came home from my war. If anything saved me, it was ministering to the lost in that hell of a hospital."

Betsy's head snapped up.

"Helping those boys helped me come to terms with my grief."

"I don't want to come to terms."

"I told myself I didn't want to either, though I really did. I just didn't know how. You must. After classes and on Saturdays you can work out there as a candy striper. During the summer you'll work full time, six days a week. They can't afford to pay you."

"You mean I work for free!"

"And I'd better see you at Mass every Sunday."

"I have to work all the way to September for free?"

"You can continue this year and return in the fall as a junior. If not, you'll start over as a sophomore."

"It's not fair."

"It wouldn't be fair if this were punishment. It's not. This is all I know to do. It's what saved me. Please give it a chance, Betsy. You have so much to live for."

She looked down at her hands, shaking her head.

"Give me your decision in the morning."

\* \* \*

Betsy got her varsity jacket from her locker, pulling it on for the last time, and left the building. Darlene waited for her at the alley corner and offered Betsy her cigarette. The two walked, Darlene silent until Betsy finished telling her.

"Well, I guess you won't be hangin' out in the alley with us no more."

"Not until September. Do you ever come out to see Randy?"

"He don't like me to."

"Too bad. I could use a buddy now and again."

"Maybe it's all for the best. Ain't no future hangin' out in alleys."

"Might as well. Haven't got one anyway."

## CHAPTER 4

Betsy never even considered lighting up before Nathan came home on his last leave. She crossed the hall to his room every evening when he was not out with Sarah Hanna, spooning or worse she imagined, and after their parents went to bed. If not reading he would be filling the pages of his PX journal. They talked, and he smoked while they talked. He looked so sophisticated, so Paul Newman. So one night she reached across his desk and without asking told him she was bumming a cigarette.

"You smoking now, Sis?"

"Sure." She hacked. "All of us in the Gang do."

Nathan picked up his habit only after he left for basic training. When their drill sergeant told the squad to take five, he permitted them to smoke 'em if you got 'em, girls, and as all the others seemed to have them, Nathan got them too. They made a miserable nine weeks less so. He told her at times all that kept him going was the smokes with his buddies and letters from his sister.

She mailed him one each day, sixty-three in all, writing the first letter and walking it down to Mr. Crawford at the Post Office the very afternoon they came home from seeing him off at the Greyhound station, her letter no doubt arriving before he did. As she was going to be on the junior-high cheerleading squad that autumn, she filled them with breathless accounts of their tough summer practices and all the killer routines they were learning. She wrote about the weather they sweltered through and how impossibly hard it all was.

Probably twelve times harder than your goddamn basic training, I'll bet.

Spending so much time that summer with older girls, she started to swear, and she looked for excuses to test it out. Since Nathan was in the Army she mistook him as someone safe. She wrote back when he chastised her that for a killer-in-training he seemed to be a bit of a prissy butt, yet added in a postscript that she missed him. Her adolescent-tough-ass attitude she carried only so far.

Their mother early on labeled them kindred spirits. They both played the piano, though Nathan claimed she performed with a finesse never to be his. Because they shared the same taste in reading, she sometimes sneaked into his room to borrow the anthologies he brought home from college with stories like "Soldier's Home" and "Barn Burning," and after she had gone through most of his books she started working her way through his magazines. He snagged her one afternoon sitting in his closet with the door closed and giggling at the *Playboys* she discovered under the stack of *Boys' Life*.

"Those boobs can't be for real."

She was looking down the neck of her own yet-to-be-well-endowed T-shirt when he opened the door.

"Got a ways to go, don't you, Squirt?"

Not about to let that one slide its way past her, she tossed her head and gave him one of her I-don't-care-what-you-think smiles as she dog-eared the Saul Alinksy interview and dropped the *Playboy* on top of the magazine pile. She walked around him to his bed where she had stacked the books she was taking without asking.

"I'll get there."

"You think so, do you?"

"Just you wait. I'll drop them dead in their two-toned saddle shoes. I'll have a dozen — no, make that two dozen — beaus rapping on my door at all hours, day and night. You just see if I don't."

Nathan glanced across the bedroom to his ever-emptying bookshelf.

"You've been reading Gatsby, haven't you?"

"What makes you say that, Old Sport," and shut her bedroom door, collapsing to the floor in a conniption of giggles. That spring she suffered from a serious affliction of the giggles.

She tried to talk him into deserting to Canada when he came home on his last leave and got so mad when he only flashed his Cheshire grin she stopped talking to him. If at the supper table he asked her to pass the peas, she ignored him, and she made no effort to make up until two nights before he shipped out when she stepped into his doorway and found him sitting cross-legged on the bed as he wrote in his journal, her shadow darkening his words.

"You talking to me now, Attitude-Meister?"

"I guess, but it's still a stupid-ass war."

"Name me one that wasn't and watch your cussing."

He reached around to the lamp table and held his alarm clock out to her.

"Appreciate it if you kept this wound so the spring won't be rusted up when I get back."

"Aren't you going to need it?"

"Nope. It's so wet where I'm headed it'd get rusted, wound up or not." He turned his wrist to her. "Besides, I got me this swell Hamilton at the PX."

"Thanks."

"Wait until you hear the question that goes with it before you go thanking me. One to keep you awake as you listen to its ticking while I'm away."

"Don't even start in on me with your questions."

"You know your birth date, right?"

"That's not much of a question."

"Have you ever thumbed through one of those calendars Noony stuffs in our mailbox every December, admiring the prints of, say, the Holstein heifers of Wayne County, before dropping it in the trash and for a second — just a second —

wondering which of those days is destined someday to be your death day?"

She smoothed out the bed blanket before him and sat.

"Of course I haven't. Now I have a question for you."

"Shoot."

"Do all you Army jocks get weirded out before you leave for combat duty or is it an affliction curious to you?"

"Was Mrs. Hanna's question, not mine."

Betsy groaned for while Mrs. Hanna held no bias against questions she lacked sympathy toward those possessed of the audacity to believe they knew the answers.

Nathan stopped in to see her that afternoon after he returned from visiting Randy. She had raised Sarah and been one of his teachers at Saint Paul's as well as their first piano instructor. She retired some years before, and with her arthritic fingers no longer able to play she devoted her days to the poetry of Edna St. Vincent Millay and fading memories, searching her way down remembered back roads. Betsy in summers sometimes spied her as she tended her potted geraniums on the widow's walk that circled over her second story.

"So you're blaming Mrs. Hanna for weirding you out?"

"Only for providing me with words to ponder. When I said something about missing Sarah's birthday next month, she reflected on how it was she knew the birthday that Sam Wilmer would engrave on her headstone, but what would be the day he'd chisel below it?"

"Weird. Totally weird."

"The question came to her Sunday with the passage from Chronicles that Father Henderson drew upon at Mass. 'For we are strangers before thee, and sojourners, as were our fathers; our days on the earth are as a shadow, and there is none abiding.' "

"That passage gave me the goose-egg shivers."

"It recalled for her the leaving of another boy for war."

"The congressman?"

"I don't think so. We sat, dead quiet in her parlor save for her mantle clock ticking. I waited for her to explain, but her eyes closed, and her chin drooped to her chest. I let myself out and walked home." Nathan opened his journal again. "Tomorrow I'll stop by to ask her to tell me more."

The next evening Nathan left after he and her father finished talking out on the porch. He came home late with his shoes muddied, walking past her as if she was not there and went upstairs. She returned to her room where she lay awake with the door cracked open, a penciled light falling over the floorboards. When it did not go out, she crossed the hall and peeked into his room where he sat at his desk, again writing in his journal, a hand to his brow and a pianist's concentration in his eyes. She went back to bed, again leaving the door open so she could hear him if he went downstairs for a glass of milk, but she dozed off.

A minute past mid-night the metallic click of the lock to his footlocker woke her. All in the house was quiet save for rustle of sheets in his room, the tick of the clock on her lamp table. She pulled the bedcovers tight around her and sunk once more into sleep, into her dreams of the world to come where she believed life and death were memorized. A world that failed to include a nine-month sentence to a VA hospital.

# CHAPTER 5

After he punched out from the shop at the end of his shift late Saturday afternoon, her father drove her to the Veterans' hospital. They took the Barracuda because beginning on Monday she would be driving it back and forth.

"It's a lot of car under the hood for you, honey, plus I want to be certain all cylinders are hitting since it's been gathering dust back there in the shed for fifteen months."

"Sixteen."

"What?"

"Nathan's been gone for sixteen months."

They passed the village limits into farm and dairy country.

"You know, except for the time I spent in the Army, I've lived in Hanna all my life. Ashamed to say this'll be my first trip out here. Island hopped from Guadalcanal to Okinawa, and all I know about this place are the rumors handed down to me since I was a kid."

Trees five months yet from budding blurred past Betsy's window.

"Most folks in Hanna will claim they're patriotic to the bone. Line up along Park Avenue for our Memorial Day parade. Always get a big turnout on the Fourth for fireworks. The hospital, though, is a different story altogether. Folks wish it was somewheres else. The boys who don't come back dead and don't come back whole, they'd rather not think about. You'd suppose the Legion or VFW would have some goings on from time to time for them. Bingo or a checkers tournament maybe, but we don't. Never so much as heard anyone suggest such a thing except for me when I first come home. After the looks the old timers give me, I didn't raise it again. I don't know what it is about this place. About its history." He wiped away the condensation clouding the windshield with the cuff of his Mackinaw. "What goes on out here might just as well be happening on the moon as far as the village is concerned. Say what you will about him, at least Congressman Hanna hasn't forgotten them. Makes certain there's pictures in his paper that maybe not everyone will ignore. Guess it helps him out with his elections more so in the other towns making up his district than in the village itself."

"Nathan went out to visit Randy when he was last home. Almost every day."

"He was a good boy. Far better than his old man."

Her father eased the car off onto the shoulder outside a wrought-iron gate and rolled down his window. A quarter mile back from the gravel-paved road stood a four story Neo-Federalist structure, common during the first decades of the century, built of brick with a wide front porch which wrapped along its length with a turret at one corner. A cupola rose in the middle of the roof and atop the cupola a weathercock, bent over and almost severed clean from its base that spun crazily in the January wind.

"Bet this'll be pretty in the spring when the leaves come out."

Betsy opened the glove box and slammed it shut. Her father's eyes winced, but he kept his voice soft.

"In the fall, too, after they turn."

"Won't matter what they'll look like because by then this girl will have served her time and gotten paroled out."

They drove through the gate and down a rain rutted drive that wound through woods and past a frozen duck pond, following the signs that directed them to the employee parking lot. He pulled into a space and sat looking up out the window.

"Doesn't appear to be such a bad place."

"If you've got to pull time somewhere, I'm sure it beats hell out of Lucasville."

He turned to her.

"I wish you wouldn't cuss, Betsy. It would grieve your mother if she heard you, and her cup right now is overflowing."

Betsy looked out her window down to the frozen duck pond.

"Think I'll take a look-see to satisfy my curiosity." He lifted the door handle. "Want to keep me company?"

Not saying whether she did or did not, Betsy got out. They crossed the parking lot to the fence with their hands buried into coat pockets and the wind tearing their eyes. On the other side of the fence was another tree-filled ground. Because of its park benches, from across the parking lot it did not appear to be a cemetery, the simple white markers cut from limestone and sunk into the earth from a distance looked like patches of snow, the inscriptions on those closest to the fence weathered clean. Six-inch tall American flags speared the ground next to the newer markers, but most had beside them only rotted sticks with stapled red, white, and blue bits of cloth. Betsy's father fisted his coat closed around his neck.

"Norther sure has a nasty bite to her, don't she?"

Betsy scuffed her shoes in the gravel.

"How 'bout we swing by Pete's Truck Stop on our way home. Get us some hot cocoa. Maybe split a piece of pie."

Betsy shrugged and started back to the car, her father looking after her.

\* \* \*

On Monday after classes she drove to the hospital, stalling out at the first five stop signs until her foot got the feel of the clutch.

"God damn this worthless piece of junk anyway."

Nurse Baker gave her a tour of the hospital before taking her up to the third floor and Ward 7.

"Will Randy Brindle be there?"

The nurse eyed her. "How do you know Randy?"

"His sister's a friend of mine."

"Randy's a Ward 4 patient. When he's not off wherever it is he goes off to."

Betsy froze a half dozen steps down the twin rows of cast-iron beds. Five patients in back had a poker game going in full swing on four pulled-together beds with a pile of kitchen matches stacked in the middle. One lacked both arms and the player beside him held his cards for him by only his thumb and small finger because he was missing his fingers in between. When the patient next to him raised his head from studying his cards, all of his remaining upper teeth gleamed in the fluorescent light overhead because he had no jaw. Nurse Baker clapped her hands.

"Listen up, people."

The poker player missing three fingers dropped his cards face-up. "Oh, man."

"This is Betsy, our new striper. You know the drill. She's here to help you when you don't need a nurse or an orderly. So please, let's see if we can keep her for more than a week, shall we?"

Betsy stood looking openmouthed. A boy with a stumped left leg limped by on crutches, his stained shift slightly parted and exposing his emaciated pale buttocks.

Nurse Baker leaned and whispered to her. "Say *hello*, sweetie."

Betsy's lips quivered. She gaped from patient to patient, and they, their hooded eyes sunk in washed-out faces, stared at her until the boy with missing fingers grinned and jostled with his elbow the patient with no arms.

"Welcome, Betsy. Welcome to our happy home."

Betsy stepped back. Her eyes swept the ward once more before she found herself running into the hallway.

*Bingo!* the patients shouted in unison.

# CHAPTER 6

Betsy circled the village on back country roads until her gas needle flickered on E. She pulled into Pete's Truck Stop, but her purse held only a quarter and two dimes. When she drove into her driveway, not a single light burned. She lowered her forehead to the steering wheel.

"I can't go back. I just can't."

She stooped under the half-open garage door and entered the house through the kitchen. A saltshaker on the table served as a paperweight for a note from her father that she read by the light cast by a corner streetlamp.

There's a plate of meatloaf and scalloped potatoes and green beans in the refrigerator. You'll be tired. We'll talk in the morning.

She took out the plate and poured herself a glass of buttermilk and stood eating in the dark. After rinsing the dish and glass in the sink, she went upstairs where she stood at her window. A moon as red as a bloodied dog's eye hung in the sky.

"I can't go back. I won't."

She opened her closet door and took out a suitcase and began to pack. Jeans. Denim jacket. Change of underwear and socks. She shut the lid, snapping closed the brass locks inscribed with Nathan's initials and went into his room where she rummaged through the desk drawers until she found his McNally atlas and took it back across the hall. She traced a route south. Kentucky, Tennessee, Texas.

"Maybe I can find a commune of draft dodgers who'll take me in."

Her finger migrated to California and north to Oregon and up into Canada. She fell back on her bed. "They'd probably accuse Nathan of killing babies and turn me in for the reward."

The door to her parents' bedroom closed with a metallic click. Her father shuffled into her room wearing his too large Snoopy slippers that Nathan had sent home for Christmas in his box. He looked at the suitcase, the atlas atop it. He leaned against the doorjamb.

"Father Kaplan stopped by after Amy Baker called him. First days are always tough, honey. Tomorrow will go better for you."

"I don't want to go back. Not tomorrow. Not ever."

"I know it's hard."

"It's a hundred times harder than hard."

"You have to if you want to return as a junior."

"I don't give a good god . . . I don't care about being a dopey old junior. I don't want to go back."

"What do you want?"

Betsy's eyes searched the swirled patterns etching the ceiling. "To disappear. Disappear to wherever it is that time goes."

"One child disappearing from my life is one too many. I don't think I could bear to lose another. I know your mother couldn't."

"I don't want to go back."

"It's only until September, honey. Eight months. Two hundred-forty days. You can do it standing on one foot with both hands tied behind your back."

"I don't want to go."

"Were they mean to you?"

"No."

"What is it then?"

"They're awful to look at. Perfectly awful."

Her father nodded.

"I remember. It's not just boys with casts on their legs they broke while playing football."

"I feel sorry for them, but I can't bear to see them."

He sat beside where she lay on the bed. "You see them, and you see Nathan."

"His funeral was closed casket."

Her father sat looking down into the well of his folded hands for a long time before he could again look into his daughter's forget-me-not blue eyes. "It could have gone the other way, you know."

"What do you mean?"

"I saw time and time again that whether a soldier made it home had nothing to do with his courage. It's all luck, random and indeterminate, like the lights we see at night passing each other out on Old Salem Road. Nathan's was bad. For the boys you saw today, theirs, believe it or not, was better. There's no reason why they came home and Nathan didn't. It had nothing to do with what you said before he left or that you didn't see him off at the airport. I only wished I had found the words."

"You're telling me I have to go back."

"Nathan could have ended up in just such a ward."

"I hadn't thought of that."

"We would want someone trying to get him home to us."

Betsy scooted off the bed and walked over to the window. Her finger ran down the curtain.

"I could be the thread by which one of them manages to hang on. Manages to go home."

"I'd be surprised if you weren't."

Betsy looked out into the night. She nodded. "Okay."

"That's my girl."

She raised a hand to her mouth.

"I better let you turn in."

She crossed to her father, kissing him on the cheek. "Thank you, Daddy."

"No. Thank you." He started for the door. "There's a package that came today. Nathan's effects. It's in his closet. Look when you have a chance. If there's anything you want, I don't see it posing a problem."

"What's in the box?"

"Some clothes. His watch. Pair of psychedelic sunglasses. A few paperbacks."

"Did you or Mom take anything?"

"Not yet. It may be a while. Bartholomew claims he has dibs on a shirt and the glasses."

"Can I go look now?"

"Of course but then get under the covers."

Betsy sifted through the contents of the box until she knew for certain his journal had not come home. She thumbed the smudged crystal of his Hamilton watch and wound it, holding it to her ear. She took with her only the watch and the copy of the Odyssey he had read at night when he was last home on leave.

* * *

She drove back to the hospital the next morning before classes where she found Nurse Baker outside Ward 7 behind the nurses' station with a hand raised to her brow as she notated a patient's chart.

"It's my fault, sweetie. I've been around them for so many years I forget how they appear for the first time to someone who hasn't."

"I messed up bad, didn't I?"

"No, not really. No real harm done you can't undo with a little TLC. Start over when you return this afternoon. Walk down bed by bed. Ask them if there's something you can do. Sometimes all they need is for someone to talk to. Someone to listen."

Betsy looked through the doorway into Ward 7.

"They need you, Betsy. You can be the one to help get them home."

* * *

When she re-entered the ward that afternoon, she stood for a moment inside the door. Beds again were pulled together at the back of the ward. A boy on her right lay counting ceiling tiles on missing fingers. The one on her left maybe a year older than she with pimples yet rose-budding his chin played solitary Scrabble, the bandaged stump of his leg sticking out from under a sheet. She walked over to his bed and cleared her throat. She tried to smile.

"Is there anything I can get for you?"

He pretended to concentrate on the misspelled words before him. "Decided to come back to us, did ya?"

Betsy pursed her lips. She glanced over her shoulder to the door.

"Now, don't go runnin' out on us again, Sis." He lifted his eyes from the board. "Least you come back. That's more than the rest done we've had in here."

"Really?"

"Mighty decent of you to be askin' too." He winked at her. "Since you did, there is something I could use some help with gettin' ahold of."

"What's that?"

He nodded at his stump. "Maybe a parrot to go with what's left of my leg."

The temples behind Betsy's eyes crinkled. "Maybe I can find a bottle of rum for you too?"

"Hey, now you're talking, Sis."

\* \* \*

That afternoon and each day after, Betsy walked down between the twin rows of beds. She talked with the patients who could talk, each day picking up one or two new friends. She wrote letters for the boys without arms, and she read to those who had lost their sight. She talked on the telephone to the families of patients who had been throat shot, and they in turn wrote their end of the conversation out on blackboard tablets tied around their necks. Sometimes when they brushed their eyes with chalk dusted fingers, gray tears streaked their cheeks in ashy streams, and she would reach up with her apron hem before giving the boys a hug.

"It's all right. Don't worry. It's all right."

Father Kaplan allowed her to rearrange her classes at the end of April so her study halls all fell at the end of the day, which allowed her to leave for the hospital at noon, and she was glad to be quit of Saint Paul's. When she walked away from the cheerleading squad, she was no more a rising star. The postman stopped delivering party invitations. Billy Hufnagel, who sometimes stole glances of her as he dribbled from the foul line and whom she once told the other girls in the Gang she hoped would ask her to the spring prom, instead asked Bonnie Brown. Members of the Gang stopped calling.

The Gang was what they called themselves after the Our Gang shorts they howled at. Since junior high the girls without fail gathered at the house of one or another on Friday nights to watch David Cassidy and over Pepsis and popcorn talk about boyfriends, those real and those dreamed about. Discussions they deemed deep and thoughtful concerning makeup and clothes. A girl only months later now years older. After discarding her evenings with the Gang, Betsy joined the patients' poker game on Friday nights, though not as a player at first.

The patients, like CB trucker jocks, bestowed themselves with singular handles. Captain Kidd was the pimple-chinned boy with half a leg in search of a full bottle of rum and a parrot to perch on his shoulder. Quick Draw lacked arms below his elbows. Johnny Handsome refused to look in the mirror. Hawkeye and Stud. Betsy at first only helped out the players in need of her assistance. She held up the cards for Quick Draw to see or whispered to Hawkeye what cards he held before his bandaged eye sockets. After her second Friday, though, Betsy thought she had picked up the game's strategy, and the next week she brought her allowance money. Quick Draw shook his head when she asked them to deal her in.

"If we lets you in, honey, who's goin' to be helping me out with my hand?"

She found a yoga book at Reash's Newsstand, and after a few weeks of practice, Quick Draw could pick up the cards using his toes without any of the others seeing his hand or, as they called it, his foot. She recruited Sally, the candy striper who worked Ward 4, to sit next to Hawkeye, notwithstanding her dyslexia that sometimes caused her to confuse his twos and sevens. Hawkeye told her not to worry about it.

"Don't mean nothing, darlin'. I got used to being crapped out and busted long 'fore the Army ever got their hands on me."

"Luck's bound to change," Quick Draw said.

"Changes all the time. Problem is it keeps changin' for the worse."

They played through the week, betting only with kitchen matches as they practiced for Friday, their big stakes night with the interns who regularly got their clocks cleaned. Their losses paid for the patients' pot purchases from Filbert, the floor orderly who supported a mother and seven siblings who would never make ends meet sharecropping cotton and cane sugar in the Mississippi Delta.

Betsy proved to be not much of a card shark the first few Fridays, and her patients had to be certain she went home with enough gas money to come back the next week. Their chivalry, though, lasted for only a couple of weeks after which she had nights she did so well she was the one who had to return her winnings so they could pay Filbert, though they dissembled.

"Gotta have my smokes," Captain Kidd said. "Otherwise I'll be comin' down with them nicotine fits."

"Are they bad?" Betsy asked, reaching into her purse.

"Oh, they's ugly, Sis. Out and out ugly. You don't never wants to see a body get connipitioned with 'em." He folded the bills she handed him into the pocket of his hospital shift.

"Thank you, Sis. You ain't seen that Filbert wandering about anywheres, have you?"

# CHAPTER 7

Winter passed to spring and then into summer. On the morning of the first Saturday in July, Betsy filled in for a chef's assistant who had shown up red-faced drunk and querulous. She boiled lime and cherry Jello in thirty-quart pots into which she sliced dozens of browning bananas. After she and the kitchen crew finished their cleanup, she returned to Ward 7, dropping *The Last of the Mohicans* on the chair next to Hawkeye's bed.

"That be you, darlin'?"

"It be me bearing a book. I'll bet you'll get a kick out of this one. Nathan read it at least once a year."

Reaping Mennonite tractors droned outside the ward windows, and flecks of seed floated in the cut-hay scented air. Betsy read for fifteen minutes before she yawned.

"Sorry."

Hawkeye lay open mouthed, his breath shallow and rasping like the rustle of fallen leaves. Because bandages hid his eye sockets, it was difficult for her to tell if he slept, and she went on reading aloud only to stop mid-paragraph. Metal on glass clinked out in the corridor. Faint at first then louder until Filbert pushing an IV unit halted beneath a burned out light in the corridor. When Nurse Baker came up behind him, she leaned to his ear. He nodded, and the two continued on.

"Where do you think those two are going?"

Hawkeye snored.

She laid the book on the floor and walked to the doorway. The two stood whispering at the elevator. Nurse Baker had pushed the up button, but the only floor above theirs was the attic where there would be no need for a fully loaded IV cart because there were no patients. Or where she had more than once been told there were no patients. The elevator doors shut. She hurried up the stairs, laying down at the top, and peeked above the last step. Nurse Baker at the far end of the corridor was taking out her ring of keys. Stubby and tarnished except for a long-necked silver key. The door screeched when she gave it a hard shove, but before going in she glanced toward the stairs. Betsy snapped her head down. She counted to ten before she again risked looking up over the top step. Filbert had the IV unit halfway out of the corridor. Betsy rose from the steps after he pulled the door closed behind him and walked down to the door where she squinted through the keyhole. Nothing. She put an ear to the door. Not so much as a murmur.

"Damn."

She took the stairs to the second floor and went in to Ward 4. When she asked Sally where she could find Randy Brindle, Sally cocked her head at the window.

"Settin' up in one of them trees yonder, I reckon."

She returned to Ward 7 where she read to herself as she waited for Nurse Baker and Filbert until 6:30, a half hour past her shift, and still neither passed in the corridor.

\* \* \*

The house stood dark when the Barracuda rumbled into the driveway. An American-Legion friend of her father's had loaned them the use of his Lake Erie cottage, and after he punched out from his half-day Saturday the rest of the family drove up to spend the Fourth-of-July weekend. He told her they could wait for her to get home or he would even drive down in the evening. Betsy, though, said it would be nice to loaf around the house. Peruse the catalogs from Penney's and Sears the postman had just delivered and start thinking about putting together her outfits for when classes started since the coming school year would be the first they would not be required to wear Alcatraz gray on Fridays. Besides, he would only have to driver her back on Monday evening as Tuesday was a workday for her, the holiday notwithstanding.

After she brought a TV dinner from the refrigerator to thaw, she went out to retrieve the mail. She stood on the front porch, shuffling through the envelopes, until she came to the last letter. Her hands started to tremble. It was from Nathan. Addressed to her.

"No. Please no."

Her name and address tear dropped in streaks so smudged it took the Post Office seven months to guess its recipient. She went inside and only after a long while did she open her brother's last letter.

21 December 1973

Dear Squirt,
Flying out on a milk-run mission in two days time so we're getting some well earned R & R tonight and before morning we'll all be rolling drunk as Siamese monkeys including yours truly who is still waiting for his get-out-of-jail-transfer-home papers to show up. Maybe they'll be here when I get back. They're two weeks late already. The major says the word out of HQ in old Bangkok (for what it's worth, which never is much) is that some bumbling bureaucrat back in the Pentagon sent them to Frankfurt of all places. I think they must be swimming them here around the Horn of Africa.

Thanks for the birthday present. How did you know I was running low on condoms and how did you get Baptist-Deacon Wallace to sell them to you? Or did you just save up your quarters and send Barto into the men's room out at Pete's Truck Stop?

Glad to hear you're writing your term paper about the Nam. Outstanding! So, as we say in the newspaper trade, here's the scoop. The weather's hot and wet in winter and hotter and wetter in summer. The people where I was stationed before they transferred me to Thailand, at least the ones not snipering at you from behind trees, were pretty darn nice. My life was and is fairly routine, even boring. For the most part nothing much happens now with the war winding down.

It's chow time, Squirt, so I've got to go. Hamburger night. An apt meal for a soldier. Posting this on my way to the mess and hope they can keep it dry with all this rain we're getting deluged with. Will read your term paper when I'm home in a few weeks. Maybe even before you get this. We'll see. Ace it for us!

Love,
Nate

    Betsy traced her finger under each word as she read the letter again. She laid it on the table. Lightning bugs outside the bay window torched the Dutch elms and sugar maples lining their street. She read over her brother's letter a third time.
    "Oh, Nate."
    She returned the letter to its envelope and put the envelope in her apron pocket and walked over to the piano. Since the morning when the two Casualty Assistance Officers knocked at their door, she had played only once, practicing her finger exercises for but a minute before her mother fled up the steps. The score resting on the music desk, a fourhanded arrangement of a Chopin nocturne that Nathan wrote for them in a composition course, she had left open and unplayed since December.
    She had wanted her part to be perfect for the day he came home. While Nathan double majored in music and math at Ohio State, he told Betsy he saw himself as forever doomed to sitting in with amateur chamber groups. She was the one who possessed the talent to gig some day at Carnegie Hall. Neighbors stood in doorways on summer evenings when she

practiced with the blare of their television sets for once silenced or gathered out on the sidewalk in twos and threes whispering to themselves. Cars sometimes cruised by with their windows rolled down and radios off. Nathan once looked out from his bedroom as she played Mendelssohn's *Songs without Words* only to see old-man Nichols — so grumpy he wouldn't even hand out bottom-of-the-barrel apples on Halloween — stop in the middle of mowing his front yard, snub out his Dutch Masters cigar in the sole of a boot, and sit in the grass beneath his front elm with eyes shut and head bowed. When she completed her practicing an hour later, he did not restart his mower but pushed it into the garage and went inside without turning on the lights.

She flipped through the score before she tested the keys, her fingers remembering their action, and began to make her way through her part until she missed a note on the third line. She hesitated but played on. Then she missed another note on the fifth line. Notes she never missed when she practiced two and sometimes four hours a day. On the next line, she missed a third note.

"Goddamnit!" She held up her hands. "What's wrong with me?"

She smashed her knuckles into the keys, pounding over and over, the fractured chords thundering the house. She pounded so hard flecks of blood speckled the keyboard, and she kept pounding until a key popped over her shoulder. She looked down at the carpet, her breath rifling in and out of her chest, but let it lay. She paced the living room, cursing herself, the world, again cursing God. She stopped before the liquor cabinet. "I need to get rolling drunk as a Siamese monkey."

Save for the summer before when she slept over at Sandy Jackson's and Sandy sneaked into their pup tent a can of her father's Rolling Rock, Betsy had no experience with liquor until the death of her brother. She returned from the kitchen with a three-quarters empty carton of Minute Maid into which she poured in a smidgen from each open bottle her father would not miss.

"The old kamikaze."

She carried the half filled carton upstairs to Nathan's room where she sat on the floor with her back against his footlocker. She took a too-large swallow and gagged. Her eyes watered. She waited until the burning in her throat passed and shuttered only a little with her second swallow. Mile-off headlights outside the window beaconed through the coming darkness as semi-trucks rolled down Old Salem Road. She raised her carton again. The dolent whistle of the Penn Central mourned from across town.

For we are strangers before thee, and sojourners, as were our fathers; our days on the earth are as a shadow, and there is none abiding.

Maybe her old piano teacher was now better and had come home from Chicago.

She stumbled downstairs with her carton and out the door, reeling along the empty sidewalks. Outside the darkened Rutherford mansion, she studied its empty widow's walk but where she sometimes saw Mrs. Hanna tending her flower-box geraniums at odd hours. When she came to the Penn Central crossing, she followed the tracks down to the abandoned depot and sat on a step fissured from a hundred winters. Wild poppies struggled from its cracks. She raised her carton. She listened. From the machine shops lining the tracks, the wind carried a hammer-on-steel ring as though craftsmen of an earlier era, grown restless in their eternity, had returned to ply their trade. She wrapped her arms around her shoulders and studied the shadows of the night. Watched goblins of fog cross up and down the tracks. A whistle from the trestle crossing outside Mechanicsburg pealed through the valley, and a bloodless eye soon slit the dark. Clanging guardrails dropped at Court Street. She walked out to the tracks and stepped onto a shuttering rail and raised her arms, wavering back and forth like a lark descending. She waited. The alabaster eye caught in its bore of light a white silhouette on the rail ahead of her.

Don't go there, girl. Don't you remember Allen was dropping acid last year when he was walkin' a train rail on his way out of town like he thought he was a tightrope walker who'd joined the circus? They had to hose what little was left of him off the tracks. Dogs was lunching out there for months. Think about your folks. Your little brother. They've gone through enough.

Betsy threw back her head and howled. Only when the alabaster eye had all but swallowed her did she lose her footing, and the deafening train-rush of wind knocked her to her knees. Sparks flew within arm's reach. She pushed herself up, screaming into the wind.

"You'll be back, you bitch. You'll be back, and I'll be waiting."

She followed the disappearing red lights of the caboose into the woods where they passed behind the village cemetery. For some minutes she searched before finding her brother's marker. She sat in the dewy grass before it, the tombstones gleaming gray in the misty moonlight. Fog eddied through the trees, and from within the fog the shadows of thousands of boy-soldiers walking in mile-long lines passed her in silence. Some smiled. One pointed behind him. In the last line walked Nathan between two others, his arms falling from their shoulders as she stumbled to her feet. He mouthed something to her, but it would be almost ten years before she saw the words he spoke to her that night. The three continued on out of the cemetery. He turned back after they crossed the tracks, his hand raised. She took a step toward him, but he shook his head. Then he too disappeared into the dark of the woods.

* * *

Faint bars of morning light latticed the cemetery trees when Mr. Baxter came to lay a pot of pansies for his wife on his way to sunrise services. As he cornered the one hundred-fifty year old oak, he tripped over Betsy head first and landed beside her. He lay a moment regarding her white-stockinged legs. Horseflies buzzed at his ears in the tall grass. He picked himself up off the ground, nudged her ribs with the toe of his shoe, and ran to his opened-door Ford. After he made certain all his house doors were bolted and windows latched, Baxter called up to the county jail.

"She looks deader than hell to me, Sheriff. You think it's one of them goddamn psychotic lunatics that got loose from your state hospital over there in Massillon?"

Durkin break-necked his squad car the half-mile down Friend Street, cruiser lights bubble-gumming and early-morning churchgoers gaping after him. When he found Betsy, he knelt, putting his hand to her shoulder.

"Hon, can you hear me? Hon?"

Betsy blinked open her eyes. A walrus-mustached sheriff wearing his Smokey-the-Bear hat bent over her. She pushed herself up, groaned, and collapsed back on the grass.

"What's your name, Hon?"

She told him.

"You ain't Nathan's sister, are ya?"

She turned her head and dry-heaved into the grass.

"You're not fixin' to expire on me?"

She shook her head.

"That's a relief." He picked up the empty juice carton and put it to his nose. "Well, now I know why you smell like a god . . . a gosh-darn distillery. Shame on you. Why ain't your daddy called you in?"

"They've gone up to the lake."

Durkin glanced over at his squad car. "Well, I can't be leavin' you layin' out here, feeding our stray dogs to say nothing of crippling bereaved mourners come to pay their respects. Folks'll be wondering what kind of a county it is I'm a running."

"I'll be okay."

"You've got a lesson or two to learn about the evils of liquor, Hon. Maybe tomorrow you'll be okay, but you ain't goin' to be feeling okay today."

He scooped her up in his arms and drove to the jail where only the dispatcher was on duty. He forced her to drink three cups of midnight-brewed coffee while the dispatcher crossed an alley to the Country Kitchen, convincing their cook to donate a can of tomato juice after making inquiry as to the whereabouts of their Health Department license. When he returned, Durkin fed her two aspirin. He stood thumbing his gun belt as she washed them down with the juice.

"I do feel better. Thank you."

"Don't go a thanking me yet. Not 'til we hear what all your daddy has to say when he finds out where I found you and what all it was I smelled in your carton."

"Don't," she said to Durkin's boots. "Please."

"Got to, Hon."

"He has enough to worry about with Mom. He doesn't need any more with me."

"Can't do 'er."

"It won't happen again."

Durkin crossed to the desk, shaking his head. "Can't."

"Please."

"Tell me where'd you get your booze?"

She told him.

"Do you *truly* promise? Word of honor?"

"Yes, sir."

Durkin raised his eyebrows at the dispatcher. The dispatcher shrugged. "Your call."

"Ain't they all?"

"Just the ones you get dead wrong."

Durkin drummed his fingers on the war-surplus desk. Static crackled over the radio.

Okay, Hon, I'm a givin' you a break. This once and this once only. Use it well 'cause you ain't goin' to sweet-eye no second out of me."

"Thank you."

"I'm gonna to be a keeping a double lookout on you. Mind what I said."

"Yes, sir. I will."

Betsy cracked open the station door. She looked both ways and turned back, raising her hand before she shut the door behind her. Durkin grinned over at his dispatcher.

"I seem to recollect pullin' a stunt just as dumb assed when I was 'bout her age."

"Haven't we all."

Durkin reached for his hat. "I guess I need to be goin' too. Hung up on Oliver right before Mr. Baxter called us."

"Where you off to?"

"I've been *invited* out to the hospital."

"On a Sunday?"

"Sunday, hell. Don't matter to Hanna none. If he ain't a heathen, I ain't never sided up to one."

"What's he want to see you about?"

"Damned if I know except there's an election come November and startin' six month before ever one of 'em he gets as fidgety as my old-maid aunt. Always seems to have somthing to do with his hospital."

"You think instead it's got something to do with Thomson catching Garfield with his hand elbow-deep in the cookie jar?"

"Might. It were Hanna who snagged Garfield his position to begin with. Might be something else altogether, though. Fourth-of-July's day after tomorrow so there's speeches for him to be making, medals to be handing out, but whatever it be, I'll wager you dollars to donuts it's got somethin' to do with his hospital."

"I'll pass on takin' the other side of that bet."

"He's done a lot of good for this county. A lot that's gone unnoticed, but I pity the poor bastard who ever gets sidewise with him over his goddamn hospital."

## CHAPTER 8

Betsy hurried across the parking lot early Tuesday morning and ran upstairs past the empty nurses' station to the attic where she jiggled the locked door. She stooped to the keyhole.

"Hellfire and damnation."

Quick Draw and Johnny Handsome were sitting on their beds across from one another in Ward 7 as they debated the National League pennant race with Johnny holding up his end of the conversation by nodding or fanning a finger. Betsy walked down the twin rows of beds and stood sideways between them.

"Either of you two characters know anything about a patient upstairs?"

The two leaned sideways, looking around her. Johnny shook his head.

"Well, she might as well know, J.H. Ain't goin' to do nobody no harm." Quick Draw straightened. "He's sort of a secret patient they've got here, honey."

"Secret? Secret how?"

"As in highly classified and for privileged eyes only. Only two people who knows much about 'im is Filbert and Nurse Baker, and they ain't talking."

Johnny zippered closed what remained of his mouth.

"Randy Brindle told us he saw 'im one time and one time only. T'was in the wee morning hours when they were wheel chairing him down the hall as Randy was coming in from wherever it was he'd got to. Light wasn't much good but looked to Randy like the codger went way past WW II. Maybe as far back as *numero uno.*"

"That'd be over fifty years."

"I knowed you to be a math wiz. You've got that first-in-the-class look in your eye, don't she, J.H?"

Johnny nodded.

"Randy says he wouldn't be surprised none if Congressman Hannaho . . ."

Johnny fanned his finger.

"Yeah, yeah, yeah, I know. Randy says it wouldn't surprise him none if Congressman Hanna were in on keepin' him a secret."

"Why would he?"

"Because Hanna's in on anything that goes on out here. A mouse can't f –."

Johnny again fanned his finger.

"A mouse can't sneeze in this joint without Hanna gettin' on the phone to Nurse Baker about it. Saw him stalking the halls here yesterday with that wimp of an aide kissing up behind him."

"What were they doing out here?"

"Lord knows, honey. Went into Nurse Baker's office with that scum-bag of a sheriff and didn't come out 'til two hours later."

A Negro built like an Ohio State linebacker swished a mop down the corridor past the ward door. "Filbert's my buddy. I bet he'll tell me."

"Tried that route. Couldn't get him to tell us nothing." He winked at Betsy. "Then again, none of us was a pretty girl neither."

"Me?"

"You. Tell you somethin' else. Just on account he don't talk white, don't let 'im fool you. It's a act they learn when they's children so's white folks don't go stretching their necks for being uppity. Filbert's a sharpie. Takes night classes at Youngstown State on the GI Bill when the notion comes over him. Come 'round one day askin' us fool questions about trees falling in the woods with no one there's to hear."

"Betsy?" Three beds over, Hawkeye held up *The Last of the Mohicans*. "You think you might have some time to pick up where you left off?"

\* \* \*

"*Swing looow, sweet chariooot.*" Filbert was hymning in his baritone voice as he pushed up the hallway a four-wheeled bucket with a mop handle sticking out of its dirty water when Betsy stepped out of the ward at noon. He saw her and smiled.

"And a good afternoon to you, Missy."

"What do you know about a patient in the room upstairs?"

Filbert dropped his eyes to the dirty water. "Which room you be talkin' about?"

She pointed her index finger at the ceiling.

"The room up *there*."

"Don't knows nothing."

He pushed his bucket all the faster, water splashing over its sides, as a black stream snaked behind him.

"You what?"

"Can't tells you nothing either."

"Why . . . ."

"Now if you'll excuse me, I's gots some puke to be mopping up before Nurse Baker come back and give me more of her bitchin' grieve."

She stood looking after him, her hands at rest on her hips, surrendering her interrogation for now.

\* \* \*

She went down to Ward 4 where she for once found Randy Brindle. He sat cross-legged on his bed, a chessboard on the blanket before him.

"What do you know about the secret patient upstairs?"

"Only that Hannahole's gotta be in on it."

"How do you know?"

Randy claimed a black bishop with a white knight and rotated the board. He studied the pieces a minute before he looked up.

"That summer job Nate had for the *Journal* a few years back, when he was in Washington for a week on that special assignment for them?"

"Yeah."

"On his last day he followed Hannahole around. Started with breakfast in the congressional cafeteria and from there he dogged him to the subcommittee Hannahole chairs for Veterans Affairs and then on to Ways and Means and then to a couple of more. Made sure Nate got front row seats. Hannahole toured him around after the committee meetings wrapped up, and Nate got to meet the guys he saw every night on Walter Cronkite. Wright Patman. Wilbur Mills. William Fulbright. A bottle found its way out of a drawer in every office. Told Nate he was looking forward to a really good write-up with a full page spread to help him out come the election."

"Took up almost the whole Sunday paper."

"It were nearly midnight before they returned to Hannahole's office. Because he'd been in Congress since like even before the Declaration of Independence got inked, he had this to-kill-for view of the Washington Monument all lit up outside his windows. Hannahole turns on only a desk lamp. A bit snookered. Trouble not swaying. Nathan told him he didn't understand how he'd the energy to be on the go as he was. Asked him why so many committees. Hannahole said he made it a point to be on as many as he could get on having anything to do with veterans because he'd taken a special interest in them. Especially in this hospital here. Ever since it was built. One patient out here in particular."

"The secret patient do you think?"

"That'd be my guess, Sweat Pea."

"Why him in particular?"

"Haven't cracked that nut yet." Randy checked the white king with his black queen. "But you can bet your bottom dollar it ain't out of the goodness of his vote-stealing heart."

## CHAPTER 9

The week passed. Bartholomew hitchhiked out once and begged her to let him drive around the parking lot so he could practice for his driver's test.

"You're only fourteen, dufus. You've got two years of pedaling your bike to go yet."

"It's never too early to start. Besides, I did wash it for you yesterday."

"I wondered what you were up to." She fished the keys out of her purse. "Don't run all the gas out of it."

"Should I drive down to Pete's to put some more in?"

"You take *my* car out of the parking lot, you'll be sitting in Durkin's dungeon so quick it'll make your head spin."

"It's only *your* car until I turn sixteen. Then it'll be our car."

"Not if you're serving time in the kiddie slammer swinging a shovel it won't."

\* \* \*

She arrived at the hospital the next Saturday an hour before the start of her shift. Because today was her turn, she mopped the lower three floors, starting on the first and working her way up. Nurse Baker looked up from the patient chart she was notating behind the nurses' station when Betsy asked if she should mop down the fourth floor as well. Her eyes narrowed.

"Unless escorted by me, young lady, under no circumstances are you ever to go up to the fourth floor. Is that crystal clear? Never. Not so much as step one."

"Yes, ma'am."

Betsy put away her mop and bucket in Filbert's closet when she finished near noon and went into Ward 7 where she parked herself in a chair beside Hawkeye's bed and read to him. Two more thick books lay on the floor beside her. The warm afternoon was much like the Saturday before, and her patients napped to the far-off drone of Mennonite tractors after having tooted up as she mopped.

Such was their custom. Following lunch they wandered in twos and threes down to the duck pond where they rolled their numbers in slices of brown paper scissored from liquor bottle bags. Their special time of day. Better therapy for them than any provided by the psychiatrist who spoke with such a heavy Mandarin accent he was of no use and who they hated anyway as they hated all gooks and all who resembled gooks. They sucked in deep, exhaled the blue smoke, and gave no thought to a pilfered future they once took for their birthright. The nurses debated the patients' pot smoking, but in the end Nurse Baker voiced her approval, which was the only approval of consequence.

"How can we deny them this — this little bit of comfort — after we took everything else they once had? Everything they were ever going to have. It don't mean nothing."

Betsy read aloud for an hour until Hawkeye started to snore.

"Guess it's just not a summertime book. Maybe it's more of a curl-up-by-the-fireplace book."

She rose and stretched before walking into the corridor and down to the empty nurses' station. Water flushed. The door to the men's room swung open, and Filbert came out pushing a wheelchair patient.

"Oh, it's you."
"Sure 'nough be."
"Have you seen Nurse Baker?"
"She had to go home to get herself cleaned up."
"Why? What happened?"
"Tubby went and threw up all over her."
"What's wrong with him now?"
"Got hisself worked up into a fit. Say he be tired of that old rectal thermometer. Tale her he wasn't gonna be takin' it

thataway no more, and he'd just get it in the mouf like every other body here 'bouts."

"I wonder why she makes him take it that way."

"Well, since you ax." Filbert winked. "I thinks Nurse Baker possesses a general hankerin' to peeks at men's asses ever now and again. See what all she ain't been getting none of late."

"Maybe I should warn you then."

"Warns me 'bout what?"

"The other day I caught her peeking at yours."

"No, sir."

Betsy grinned.

"You did not."

"Did so."

"When?"

"Wednesday when you were bent over sweeping up the broken water bottle Nurse Fender dropped."

"You all be funning me, Missy?"

"What do you think?"

Filbert shook his head. He pushed his patient toward the elevator.

"Will she be back soon?"

"Expect not right soon. That Oliver called to tell her Congressman Hanna be coming out early this evening, which is the reason why she don't want to be smelling like no puke"

The elevator doors opened.

"We's all going down to the duck pond to enjoys this fine Ohio sunshine whiles we can. Snow'll be flyin' around here again 'fore you can say jackrobbins. Why don't you all come along? Get some roses blushing in them pretty cheeks of yours."

Betsy didn't answer. Atop a stack of patient charts lay Nurse Baker's key ring.

"Missy?"

"No." She turned to them. "You two go on. Maybe I'll be along in a bit."

Filbert pushed the wheelchair into the elevator. "Well, don't be long, hear?"

She looked in on Ward 7. All of her patients still slept. She returned to the nurses' station, pocketed the key ring, and hurried up the stairs. She inserted the long-necked silver key into the lock and glanced back. No one, the stairwell empty of sound, and all she heard was her own breathing, the thumping of her heart.

*Not so much as step one.*

She slipped inside and closed the door behind her. No windows illuminated the room. A single florescent bulb flickered when she flipped the light switch while the other only fluttered, filling the room with a staccatoed sallow light. Stained sheets and torn blankets rose in stacks from the floor of the anteroom to its ceiling. Beyond seemed similar to any patient room. Dresser, night table, two chairs, and a bed. Similar except that in a wheelchair beside the bed sat what looked like in the oscillating half-light to be a reject from Gulardi's Creature Feature that she and the Gang used to watch at midnight. A freeze-dried man. Old and scrawny with a tube from a near empty IV running under the blanket that covered him.

She circled the wheelchair. Strands of white hair combed its head. Eyeless sockets just ghostly accusing hollows; his pocked skin aged to the color of Egyptian parchment. A silly putty nose and its mouth a withered hole. It had but one arm, which stuck out from under the blanket, and its hand had only a single finger. No rise and fall of the chest. Graveyard stone still. Until the IV dripped. She watched. After a moment it dripped again.

She walked around to the front of the wheelchair and leaned forward, palms resting on her knees while she studied the bag. The IV dripped once more. Her eyes followed the drop as it traveled down the plastic tube and disappeared under the blanket. She reached to take hold of the blanket where it covered the arm, her fingers grazing over the unraveled threads, then drew back.

She hurried back down to the ward for her purse and returned. As she held her compact beneath the silly putty nose, two gray ovals fogged across the mirror. She snatched her hand away before they reached her fingertips and ran down the three flights of steps and out of the hospital.

\* \* \*

Hanna rolled up its sidewalks at five o'clock, and though her father forbade her to ever risk it by herself, Betsy drove the twenty miles north to Youngstown. She turned off Market Street after she crossed the Mahoning River Bridge and onto Lincoln Avenue.

"Holy shit."

Boarded up stores edged up against burned out shells of houses. Strip clubs and liquor stores lined sidewalks worked by scarecrow-thin women wearing high-cut shorts and thigh-length patent-leather boots who looked out upon their blighted world with hollow heroin eyes. Winos sporting spittle-thickened beards slept in doorways, many with Army fatigue jackets draped over their shoulders. One slouching against a light pole at an intersection looked like he might be a former Ward 4 patient discharged in February. Two teenage boys bojangling in the crosswalk eyed the rumbling Barracuda when she stopped for a red light, and they continued to eye it from the corner even after the light turned.

She circled the streets until she found a pawnshop advertising that it also cut duplicate keys. A misty drizzle had begun after she left the hospital, and the light from the gaudy red and green neon sign she stepped into bled across the damp sidewalk. The young man at the counter had never ground a long-necked key. He called his father down from their upstairs apartment, but as he too had never ground such a key he had to ask his father to come down. The old man held it up to the light.

"Haven't cut one of these in years."

He walked to the far end of the sales counter where he flicked on the grinder switch. "What's it to?"

"Sir?"

"What kind of a door does it open?"

"Oh. My grandpa's old attic. He keeps losing it, and then it takes us hours to help him find it. This way we'll always have an extra."

"Yeah, you lose a lot when you get old. Surprising how much you once had."

"Yes, sir."

The grinder wheel whirled. Sparks lighted on the old man's chambray shirt and in his hair.

"I miss these old fashioned keys. Gives me the feeling whenever I use one that I'm opening up not just a door, but a part of someone's past. A secret past. You know what I mean?"

"I think so."

"No you don't. Not yet. Maybe someday."

He again held the key to the light, appraising his work. He puffed out the steel shavings and dropped both keys — warm, almost burning — into her palm.

"That'll be six bits, young lady."

"Six bits?"

"Seventy-five cents. I like saying six bits 'cause it sounds less expensive than seventy-five cents. Shopkeeper's trick my old man taught me when I was a kid younger'n you."

She paid and thanked him and drove back to the hospital where she slid the key ring across the floor of the women's third-floor restroom to beneath the row of sinks. She listened for a moment in the doorway. All quiet save for murmurs in Nurse Baker's office. She hurried past Ward 7, a hand raised to her face.

* * *

The kitchen clock glowed eleven twenty something by the time she got pulled into the driveway. Her parents had been in bed for hours, but the door to Bartholomew's room stood open. He was bent over his desk, his back to her and Nathan's psychedelic sunglasses propped above his forehead.

"What's up, Barto?"

"Not much."

She watched him tinker. "What're you doing?"

"Trying to get everything hooked up on my radio."

On the day before Nathan left on leave two summers before, he walked over to the company PX where he bought a Foxfire-6 ham radio. He took it out of the box after he came home and let Bartholomew fiddle with the dials and switches, his kid brother's eyes as wide as any twelve-year-old's.

"Thanks, Nate. You're the best!"

Then he boxed up the radio and handed Bartholomew the stack of books he needed to study for his FCC license. Their father would have the closet key. The radio could come out the day the postman delivered his license.

"I thought you had to wait for your license to come?"

"Got delivered this afternoon."

"Congratulations."

"Thanks. Glad I finally passed that stupid exam. Was running out of books to read."

"You've gone through *all* of Nate's?"

"Almost. You done with *The Odyssey*?"

"Not yet."

"Don't forget I've called first dibs."

"A little old for you, don't you think?"

"Sounded pretty neat from what Nate was telling me. Way cooler than the creature feature."

He traced the schematic with his finger.

"Well, goodnight."

"Night." He did not look up.

\* \* \*

That night she dreamed she again sat in the dewy grass, the tombstones gleaming gray in the misty moonlight. Fog eddied through the trees, and from within the fog the shadows of thousands of boy-soldiers walking in mile-long lines passed her in silence. Some smiled. One pointed behind him. In the last line walked Nathan between two others, his arms falling from their shoulders as she stumbled to her feet. He again mouthed something to her before the three continued on out of the cemetery. He turned back after they crossed the tracks, his hand raised. She took a step toward him, but he shook his head. Then he too disappeared into the dark of the woods.

## CHAPTER 10

Nathan experienced his own premonitions before he shipped out from his last leave home. Maybe not dead kid-soldiers tramping through cemeteries, but shaken he definitely was and doing two packs a day, maybe three even. Too bad he wasn't shaken before he dropped out of college three years before to enlist. He was so out-and-out cocky then that Betsy threatened to club him over the head with Barto's bat. He wouldn't listen to anyone, not even their father. It was on his first evening home at the end of spring term that he told them he had enlisted. Betsy and her father were sitting out in the family room watching Walter Cronkite as was their custom, her father cursing the idiocy of the world and the idiots running it as was also his custom when Nathan came downstairs from unpacking.

"I went over to see the dean after finishing exams. Told him I wasn't coming back. Not for four years anyway. Maybe never."

Betsy had giggled, certain he was joking. He had like a 3.88 GPA, double majored in math and music. Her father closed his eyes as Nathan went on. Betsy stopped giggling.

"Your *reasons* for enlisting are nothing more than excuses. Excuses to run off so you can ride home a hero, but there's not a girl breathing on planet earth worth it no matter into how many pieces she's hammered his heart."

"What do you mean excuses?"

"Same damn lies I told myself. Same ones. What in the name of sweet Jesus do you think you're goin' to do for those dumb sonsofbitches anyways?"

"Maybe — "

"Other than come home packaged as hamburger yourself."

"Maybe you're right. Maybe I can't do anything. Then again, maybe I could."

"How?"

"It's like if your neighbor's house catches fire. Even though you think him a damn fool for smoking in bed, you still help him save it. It's no different with the kids."

"The hell it's not."

"It's not their fault they're young and so naïve they believe the babble flowing out of Washington. Find themselves betrayed and butchered on nameless hills known to the Army only as numbers. Maybe I can get some of them home who otherwise won't make it."

Their father's hands clenched the armrests of his La-Z-Boy, their knuckles white.

"Why in the name of sweet heaven do you think they force you to recite the Pledge of Allegiance to the wall for rather than teaching you to think for yourself?"

"So we'll be patriotic citizens."

"So they'll have an endless supply of patriotic hamburger is why. You won't be fighting communism, son. You won't even be fighting for freedom. You'll be fighting to get re-elected a chicken-little-flock of politicians who don't want to be on the inside of the coop of cards they stacked when it finally collapses in on them and then have to listen to the squawking that'll be croaking from the other chicken-little-flock of politicians who'll be pointing their beaks at them and cackling it was their fault they lost it." Dad's voice shook. "You can't lose something you never had."

Nathan's eyes searched the floor.

"Just because our clowns in Washington think it's one humdinger of an idea for them to send somebody else's child off to die a death a dog shouldn't have to suffer so they can keep getting re-elected while they and their families stay home — fat, dumb, happy, and safe — doesn't mean it's your patriotic duty to go. It doesn't mean . . ."

His voice broke. For a minute he sat looking down into the glass well of his now unclenched hands, one grasping the other. How often when she was a little girl had Betsy sought out those hands, calloused as bone from growing up on a farm followed by his years in the Army and then as a machinist at National Rubber working with steel all day, their nails jagged and grease filled. The only times she saw them clean was when they came home at the end of their summer vacation from up on Lake Erie. Hands that had comforted her all her life; hands holding within them a lifetime's worth of lessons.

"Sometimes your patriotic duty is not to stand up but to scream No! at the top of your lungs." The tall case clock out in the hallway tolled the half hour. "That's the great grim reaper of youth. No sense yet of mortality, and supposed heroism is his twin brother."

Betsy watched Nathan's face. For the slightest of seconds the ghost of doubt clouded his eyes. Please, God. Please. Then it vanished. The toes of his Keds tapped the carpet. He looked at the door leading into the kitchen where their mother was setting the table.

"There's something in a young man that makes him want to go off into the world to prove himself. To quest and be tested. I know because I suffered from the same disease, but if you live long enough to grow some gray hairs, you'll see it's a sucker's game. You'll see that the one constant in history is greed and foolhardiness and a lust for blood that even God's powerless to purge from man's soul."

The television set blared, See the USA in a Chevrolet.

An image of President Johnson flickered onto the screen as Dad crossed the room.

My fellow Americans.

When he hit the on-off knob with the heel of his fisted hand, he smacked it so hard he knocked over Nathan's cap-and-gown photograph, face down.

"Goddamnit."

Nathan and Betsy glanced at one another. Their father's curse filled the room even after its sound ceased. He righted the picture frame, rapping his knuckles three times on the wood cabinet. Their mother stepped into the doorway.

"Five more minutes. Come get washed up."

Nathan stood.

"Isn't that all the more reason for someone like me to go? Not for the glory of it all but to bring home some of our kids. Someone with good intentions."

"Do you remember what that Irish playwright had to say about good intentions and the road to Hell?"

"Yeah. Sort of."

"You'd remember it more than 'sort of' if you had. I've been to war. You think you know what it's like but you don't."

"Well, what it's like?"

"It's not like nothing excepting maybe it's a lot like Hell, and you ain't been there yet, though you seem to be fixin' to step out onto the road that'll get you on your way lickity-split."

"How is it like Hell?"

"What'll happen to you is bad enough but what you'll do will live with your forever. Not just the boys not much different from yourself you'll be sending home in boxes. It's the heartbreak you'll cause their families. The heartbreak you'll cause your own if you're sent home in one yourself. Suffering that'll last the rest of folks' lives, and you'll pay for it. We all will. I've been paying for mine, and I've some more paying to do before I'm done with it. Should I end up in Hell for what I done, my just punishment should be to stand by and watch the heartbreak I've caused. The heartbreak caused by others of my kind. Helpless to give comfort if there's even any comfort to give."

A refrigerator door opened and closed. A spoon chinked on a china plate. "Stop your politicking out there. Supper's on the table and getting cold."

"You better break it to your mother."

\* \* \*

Nathan left for boot camp on July 5th. He served a twelve-month tour in Viet Nam, and when he came home he trained for Special Forces before he volunteered to serve another tour. On his last evening before he shipped out, he and his father sat up out on the front porch, Betsy eavesdropping from the bay window. When their father asked if he wasn't a little nervy, Nathan lighted another cigarette with the butt of the one between his fingers. Gray smoke eddied out over the yard. He said during his last week before he went on leave he'd been out at the rifle range, popping away at a black target that could have been a silhouette of himself, its solar plexus square in the sights of his M-16. As the bell at the base chapel tolled, a shiver ran from his trigger finger straight to his heart. He clicked his rifle on safety and walked away. He wished he had kept on walking.

Their father leaned forward, searching his son's face obscured within the haze of smoke. Searched for what he hoped he would not see. He rode in the first wave to hit the beach at Iwo Jima where in their landing craft he must have looked into the eyes of a dozen boys that early morning as they bounced toward shore, bullets pinging its sides. Waited in the minutes before the lives of almost all of those with him ended. He had learned by then to see in the faces of boy soldiers if death was coming for them, and because he had seen it before, knew the hues it journeyed under. Knew what death looked like. Recognized the stench of its breath when come it did.

When he saw what he wanted to see — or what he could not bear to see — he walked to the far end of the porch, the watch-spring swirling nebula of the Milky Way unwinding above him, his hands at rest on the porch rail, one atop the other. He had been a praying man all his life but dropped the habit after the Casualty Assistance Officers knocked at their door, even at the supper table. Not so much as a God bless. The closest he came to prayer were those evenings he contemplated the empty chair from which Nathan once bragged to them about his victories that day at school and out on the playground. Shared with them dreams of his glory days to come that they drank in and made their own.

# CHAPTER 11

Sundays were Betsy's own following early Mass except for her chores. She and her father cleaned the downstairs after she started the week's laundry with him vacuuming and her going room to room with a dust rag and the can of Pledge. Together they cooked Sunday dinner. She found in an antique tea box the recipes for Irish stew and soda bread her mother once served every Sunday. Other meals her father stabbed at whatever lay before him, staring out the window for a minute before he started cleaning off the table, but on Sundays he ate as much as he did during the rest of the week, and he made an effort to leave nothing on his plate.

"Besides being as pretty as your mom, you're getting to be darn near as good a cook."

While Bartholomew accompanied her to Mass, he shared Sunday dinner with the family of a friend, leaving Betsy and her father to eat alone in the kitchen. Her father took a tray of Shredded Wheat and a glass of milk upstairs after they cleaned off the dinner dishes, and she went out to the driveway to wash and wax the Barracuda. Sometimes when he came down he would go out to watch.

"Not only is this your first car, but with the way you're taking care of her, she may be your last."

Betsy stopped rubbing and stepped back. She shook her head at her distorted self reflected in the polished metal.

"It'll never be my car. Not now. Not ever."

\* \* \*

At lunch on Monday, Betsy set her tray on the cafeteria table where Filbert sat squeezing mustard over the three hotdogs lined up along his plate.

"I went into his room."

Filbert raised the first of his hotdogs. "What room you be talkin' about?"

"The one across from the attic."

Yellow zigzags streaked Filbert's white shirt when his hotdog thumped on his plate. "I said you's ain't suppose to be a going in there."

"No. You told me you didn't know anything about him."

"Ain't nobody supposin' to be a going in there but me and Nurse Baker."

"Why not?"

Filbert raised himself from his chair, his eyes canvassing the cafeteria. "Keep your voice down, will ya?"

"Why?"

"'Cause I ain't suppose to be talkin' about him to nobody."

"How come?"

"'Cause I ain't is how come."

"Why not?"

"'Cause he be a secret."

"But you know who he is."

"I don't knows nothin' about who he be."

"Oh, come on, Filbert. We're friends."

"Nobody — neither friend nor foe — knows nothin' about who he be."

"Nobody?"

"As in *no*body."

"I don't believe it."

"*Well, that be what Nurse Baker told me, and for a woman she be as honest a person as I ever chanced upon.*"

"How long's he been here?"

"Nobody know that neither."

"Somebody must."

"Nope."

"How can that be?"

"Missy, you's young and pretty and white."

"What's that got to do with the patient upstairs?"

79

"Me, I be just a colored cotton picker who drifted thisaway after gettin' hisself honorably discharged from the Army all in one piece, helpin' out a poor old mama raise my younger brothers and sisters."

"So?"

"So I's seen how ugly peoples can be."

"What do you mean?"

"This here's a veterans hospital."

"So?"

"So nobody works here for long even if they's sufferin' from the giantest Jesus complex there ever was. They stays just long 'nough 'til they's can go somewheres else."

"What about Nurse Baker?"

"Ain't nobody white or colored with a better heart beatin' inside 'em, but even she's been here for less'n three year and ain't nobody been around longer 'ceptin' the Congressman hisself."

"Didn't anyone say something to her about him when she first came here?"

"Head nurse she was replacing' did."

"What'd she say?"

"Told her to take care of 'im. Whatever he needed, but not to breathe a word about him to nobody if she fancied stayin' here."

"Didn't she say something about who he was?"

"She didn't know nothin' neither."

"She didn't?"

"That's what I'm tryin' to tale you. Lord knows how many head nurses must of passed through our doors since he first come. Ten. Twenty even."

"Who was working the hospital when he first got here?"

"Don't nobody know."

"Why don't they?"

"'Cause they don't know when he first come."

"Where's his chart?"

"Ain't got none from back then."

"Every patient has one."

"Not him."

"What happened to it?"

Filbert smiled. "Don't never forgets we's workin' for the VA."

"So?"

"VA is worser than the Army. If they's a means to inclement somethin' all the way to Hell and back, they finds it, and if they cain't finds it, they's invents it."

"Couldn't his be here somewhere?"

Filbert scratched the underside of his chin. He chuckled. "It *could* be."

"What do you mean, could be?"

"They keeps them old ones up in the attic."

"Well, couldn't his be up there?"

"Could be but it'd take you a mess of Sundays to find it if'n it was and ain't nobody gonna let you in to look to begin with."

"Maybe I should talk to Nurse Baker."

"Don't."

"Why not?"

"They'd fires me for starters."

"Why?"

"Because he'd be one red-faced embarrassment to them if'n word ever got out."

"Why would they fire you? It's not your fault they lost him?"

"'Cause if'n I be talkin' to you, they'd be a wonderin' what other John Henry I be talkin' to. Like maybe that Matt McLain who always be snoopin' around looking for stories he can get written up. This one would be a grand slam doozy for him, sister. He'd be proppin' his shined shoes up on a desk at the *New York Times* inside of a week."

"Why would the patient be such an embarrassment?"

"'Cause he's been here for half of forever. Has hisself a family they must of told long time back that he be dead. On top of that they lost him."

"They wouldn't have told his family that he's dead."

"You think they's going to admit they's lost him?"

"No, I guess not."

"Heads would roll, Missy. Somebody or somebodies would end up losing they's jobs over our patient for sure."

Betsy sat back in her chair. "Yeah, I guess you're right."

"Glad we's got that settled."

"Hasn't someone seen you or Nurse Baker going up there?"

"Once in a blue-dog moon. Usually nobody does cause we goes up real early or real late or in the afternoon when the boys be napping. Mr. Randy's seen us one time but he's a Section Eight. Ain't nobody goin' to be payin' him much mind."

"Nobody knows about him?"

"Nobody." Filbert dabbed a napkin at the mustard streaking his shirt. "Not that it's going to matter much."

"Why won't it?"

"Ain't suppose to be with us all that much longer."

"They're moving him? To another hospital?"

"No, Missy." Filbert laid the crumbled napkin beside his plate. "Our patient be dying'."

"Dying?"

"Ever time we goes in he's lookin' worser and worser. Usin' less and less of his IV. Cain't be lasting much longer. Doc Barnes says a month at best, but who knows."

Betsy fingered the long-necked key beneath her blouse she wore on the same chain as Nathan's watch.

"A shame really. Waitin' all these years to get home and never gettin' there."

Betsy picked up her tray.

"Where's you hurrying off to? You just parked yourself."

"Something I need to do. I'll see you around."

"Hopes you do." Filbert reached for a hotdog. "Surely hopes you do."

## CHAPTER 12

Betsy took the stairs two at a time after she left the cafeteria to the third floor where she found Nurse Baker at the nurses' station, frowning behind a two-foot stack of patient charts. So far she had assigned her the hospital's must-do jobs. She assisted the Ward-7 patients as needed, mopped down the lower three floors when it came her turn, and lent a hand in the kitchen when a worker called in sick or showed up drunk. Nothing yet, however, that pertained to administration.

"Might be something I can study when I go off to college in a couple of years. So if you ever need help with anything, like maybe patient records, let me know."

Nurse Baker did not look up from the chart she was notating. "Let me give it some thought, sweetie."

\* \* \*

It was Friday night before Betsy could again sneak up to the fourth-floor. She played her poker hands that evening with unusual abandon. Twice she drew to an inside straight. Quick Draw shook his head.

"My girl's got guts. I'll grant her that."

She surrendered her chair to a late-arriving intern when she was down to the seven dollars and change she needed to fill her gas tank for the coming week and wished them a good night.

This time he was not sitting in a wheelchair but lay in bed. Filbert had replaced the flickering fluorescent bulb, and the IV bag looked fuller, heavier. She scooted one of the chairs to the side of his bed next to the IV. No twitch of muscle. Only the slightest rise and fall of his chest. The no-eyed man with one arm and without legs seemed as still as a roadside-mangled dog. She sucked in her breath, reaching out a knuckle, and touched the blanket where it outlined his one arm.

His index finger jumped alive, and Betsy snatched back her hand. She leaped more than stood. For the better part of ten minutes his finger twitched. She stepped forward once it stopped and again reached out a knuckle but drew back her hand and hurried out of the room. Out in the corridor she leaned against the wall, her heart slamming into her ribcage. How man boys had died in that very room? Boys who now lay in the overgrown cemetery hidden behind the hospital.

When she returned to the third floor, she stood a moment in the doorway to the lounge. Cigarette smoke rose from the poker table and carouseled about the ceiling lights. No one looked up, the eyes of her patients divining what luck or unluck they held in the cards before them. She reached beneath her blouse for her brother's watch. Her shift was over, and she had given up her seat at the table. She took the stairs and left the hospital.

*   *   *

On her drive home, she tuned in her rock station.

*Here we cooome, . . . walkin' down the streeet. . .*

She turned off the radio and from the glove box took the last pack of cigarettes Nathan bought before he left. Their mother had asked him to pick Betsy up from cheerleading practice at the gym, and on their way home he had stopped at Reash's. When he returned she was staring out at the rain. He lighted one before handing her the pack to put away.

"You seem to be smoking an awful lot since you've been home. Like old age isn't something you need get in a sweat over. Didn't you buy a pack yesterday?"

He grinned at her. "You don't let up for a minute do you?"

"Let up on what?"

"Like the AAA map you left on my bed with the route to Canada marked in black hi-lighter. Surprised you didn't stuff gas money in an envelope."

"If I did, would you go? I have money in the bank."

"That's your college money, Squirt."

The rear tires fishtailed on the slick pavement when he pulled out onto Court Street.

"Now on top of that, you're keeping count on me. I pity the poor bastard who ends up married to you."

She watched him a moment more, an unasked question pausing on her pursed lips, before she turned to look out again at the quicksilver drizzle of autumn rain.

\* \* \*

The house was dark when Betsy pulled into the driveway except for a light coming from Bartholomew's window. She rapped a knuckle on his door.

"You decent?"

"No, and I'm making whoopee in here with two Leetonia floozies."

"Are there any other kind?"

She pushed open his door. He sat at the radio with a book in hand and Nathan's psychedelic sunglasses propped above his forehead. He didn't look up.

"What would you've done if I really was buck naked?"

"Gagged. What're you doing?"

"Studying."

"For what?"

"My license."

"You told me it came in the mail."

"My beginners." He turned a page. "Now I need to go for my intermediate."

"How come?"

"More bands. More hams to talk to. Besides, my beginners is only good for twelve months."

"Twelve months? What a gyp after you studied for two years and flunked it your first time up."

"Yeah, tell me about it."

She looked about the room, more disheveled than when she had come out of the bathroom that morning. She picked up a shirt from the floor and folded it. "You had supper?"

"Yeah. Macaroni and cheese."

"That's not much."

"I sliced in some hot dogs. Only ate half of it. You want me to warm up what's left? It's pretty good with ketchup and mustard."

"That's okay." She laid her brother's shirt on his bed. "Thanks all the same."

"Okay if I ride out to the hospital with you tomorrow?"

"What for?"

"Practice in the parking lot some more."

"I guess. Goodnight."

"Night, Sis."

## CHAPTER 13

Betsy switched off the engine and handed Bartholomew her keys.

"I've only got a quarter-tank left so leave me enough to get home."

"Sure."

"Congressman Hanna's supposed to be out today — he's had Nurse Baker busy calling families — so try not to run him or them over."

"I won't."

"How are you getting home?"

Bartholomew thumbed the air.

"Drive carefully and don't you dare go out on the road."

"All right already."

\* \* \*

At the nurses' station, Nurse Baker handed her a chart. "Will you run this downstairs to Nurse Fender for me before you go into the ward,?"

"Yes, ma'am."

As Betsy searched the second floor rooms, Matt McLain came out of Ward 4, his head down and his notepad flipped open as he wrote. She had not seen him since the funeral. When she caught herself gaping, she stepped back into the doorway. He walked by her as he wrote without looking up. She leaned against the doorjamb, fanning herself with the chart and staring down the corridor after him.

"Damn, Sam."

Dr. Barnes came out of the room across the hall. "Do you feel faint, Betsy?"

She blushed, her eyes not letting go of the young man receding down the corridor.

"You need to up your water intake for these hot ones."

"Hot ones?"

Dr. Barnes followed her gaze.

"Oh, just the young man I need to speak with about Sunday. Matthew, wait up."

* * *

Congressman Hanna began taking a special interest in the hospital even before he became the district's representative in 1922 when he was but an aide to then Congressman Brown. It never failed to deliver good publicity for him even in Democratic newspapers, and he was up for re-election in November. His opponent, Judge Thomson, Kennedy handsome and much in demand as a cemetery speaker on Memorial Day, had in elections past proved to be quite the vote getter in his own right. Notwithstanding who his opponent might be, Hanna knew no way to run for office other than to go for broke, and for this visit to the hospital he brought along with him a one-star general he bullied the Pentagon into flying out. The two paraded in lockstep from floor to floor as they presented medals and commendations while Oliver passed around to their families facsimile-signed photographs of the congressman looking ten years younger and twenty pounds lighter. When Hanna spotted McLain, he raised his hand.

"How goes the muckraking business, Mike."

McLain studied the photograph Oliver had handed him. "Mucked."

He kept to the opposite side of wherever in the room Hanna politicked. As the congressman hustled votes, McLain talked to the boy-soldiers about where they were from and how their lives had changed since they left home. The families there today had received invitations printed on expensive congressional stationary. Those who could came to watch their sons receive from their government some trinket of gratitude for their sacrifice. While many of the boys were local, a number were not, and their families had risen early or driven all night over from their Indiana farms and up from West Virginia coal hamlets. All asked about the girl who wrote the letters they read or gave voice to their sons on the telephone. Listened if no one else would. Hawkeye's mother started to cry when Betsy hugged her, and she had to help the woman outside to her car. Hawkeye allowed Stud to lead him by the arm to his bed.

"That's one of the advantages of having your eyeballs burned out for you by willie peter, Hawkeye."

Matt, standing at the foot of Hawkeye's bed with notepad in hand, stopped writing.

"Which one's that?"

"Cain't cry no more."

"I hear you, brother. Now I need not be worrying' no more about catching a dose from any promiscuous woman I might have the pleasure of meeting up with."

"There you go."

"Yes, sir. My mama'll be real happy if I ever get home 'bout not having to wash the sheets ever morning. Nighttime omissions no more will be my motto."

"You had sheets in your house?"

"Sure 'nough did."

"Well, now don't that make me feel a whole lot better about our situation we got goin' here."

"Why's that?"

"Here I thought the only white folks they was sendin' over there were us rednecks but here all along they was sending off some of you rich fellers too."

"Guess they was at that."

"Goddamn if this ain't a hell of a fine country."

"Ain't it though?"

Matt pocketed his notebook. He walked out into the corridor as Betsy was coming up the stairs. He cocked his head into the ward.

"Quite a spectacle."

"It breaks up the monotony. Makes them feel special for a day."

"What'll they do tomorrow?"

"The secret for them is not to think about tomorrow. Here you learn the true meaning of one day at a time."

The ancient elevator rattled in its shaft. The floor numbers lighted up above its door. "B," "1," "2," "3". "4."

"What's up on four, Betsy?"

"Mostly an old attic."

"Mostly?"

"An old attic."

"You said mostly. They don't have patients up there, do they?"

"Hey, don't ask me. I'm just a striper paroling her way back into high school."

"Who would know?"

"I better tell Hawkeye that his mom's okay."

She crossed to where Hawkeye and Stud debated the idiosyncratic advantages of their individual wounds.

"Yes, sir, Hawkeye, my motto is that when life hands you a fist full of lemons, reach for the salt shaker and a bottle of tequila."

Matt rapped his notebook against his fingertips.

"You may be pretty, sweetheart, but stupid you're not. You know more than what you're letting on, and there's almost always a story when someone's got something they don't care to share." Betsy leaned her ear to a wheelchaired patient. "Think I need to be taking lunch in the cafeteria someday real soon."

He stepped out into the corridor when Betsy turned her back and climbed the steps up to the attic.

* * *

The next morning when Betsy reported to the nurses' station, Nurse Baker told her she was taking the girl up on her offer to help out with administration.

"Sort of."

"Really?"

"Really." She held up a stack of charts. "I'm already drowning in trash, and I just got loaded with a dumpster more."

"I'm sorry."

"A Democrat on one of the committees that Congressman Hanna sits on has introduced legislation to abolish all VA hospitals."

"That must not've sat well."

"It didn't. Come with me."

At the door to the attic, Nurse Baker inserted a tarnished brass key into its lock. Betsy glanced across the corridor.

"What's in there?"

"Nothing you need be concerned with."

"Yes, ma'am."

A long finger of sallow light pointed across the floor from a brown window at the far end of the attic. Between the window and door rose stack upon stack of bankers' boxes.

"Your job is to organize the old patient charts."

"These are *all* charts?"

"Oh, yes. Going all the way back to when the hospital opened in nineteen-seventeen."

"Man."

"Hanna's instructed his bureaucrats to initiate a study comparing their quality of care against other hospitals. Your job is to organize the charts by year and within each year in alphabetical order before they're shipped off to Washington. The Congressman spoke to me when he was here yesterday. He's expecting a favorable outcome."

"Will any of our patients have charts in here?"

"No. Only our discharges." She pointed to the window. "The older ones are way at the back. Start there. I don't know how much progress you'll make before you return to classes, but accomplish as much as you can. You're to work up here in the mornings before it gets too hot." She put a hand on Betsy's shoulder. "I need to be running up to our regional office in Cleveland. You going to be okay in here by yourself?"

"Sure. What are a few more ghosts?"

The attic ran the length of the hospital. Betsy walked back to the window through a canyon of Telarian-webbed boxes stacked from floor to ceiling. Families of rats claimed tenancy in the bottom boxes, adding to the air their own tongue-curling flavor.

*What have I gone and gotten myself into?*

She found Filbert downstairs who led her to the closet where he kept a broom and stepladder and handed her a rag and a bottle of Windex.

"Better take two rags."

"Good idea."

He reached again into his ragbag. "Maybe even three."

"All right."

"You just don't know when to say uncle, do you?"

"Say uncle to what?"

"Good luck, but don't be wastin' no time up there. His clock's ticking with the minute hand on the upswing."

The light in the attic improved somewhat after she cleaned the glass panes. She set up the stepladder alongside a stack of boxes and swept away the cobwebs. As she opened each box she carried down the charts until she had five smaller stacks. These boxes did indeed hold the charts of patients admitted to the hospital beginning in June 1917. She found she had to handle the pages with care because the brittle paper crumbled to dust in her fingers. Though she had no idea what she was looking for, as she organized the charts, she searched for some clue about the patient across the hall. All of these first patients, however, had been admitted with a diagnosis of influenza. An Evelyn Wolf notated many of the pages, H.N. following her signature.

*Head Nurse maybe?*

By one o'clock, perspiration dripped from the tip of her nose and sweat-runneled dust streaked her face. She hadn't eaten since breakfast, and when her stomach began to gurgle, she stood, slapping the acrid dust from her hands.

The corridor was quiet. Her patients downstairs slept their post-cannabis naps. She reached a hand under her blouse and entered his room where he once more sat in his wheelchair, this time with no IV setup. His one-fingered arm snaked out from under the blanket. She touched what remained of the hand, and again his index finger jumped alive, twitching for a good fifteen minutes before it stopped. She touched his hand again, and again his finger came alive. She tried holding his hand, but his finger continued to twitch with a stubborn insistence, and it still twitched when she locked the door behind her.

\* \* \*

That night she dreamed of the patient's twitching finger. She tried to will it to slow, but it would not. She passed into another dream, and when she woke she remembered neither the second dream nor how she passed to it from the first because little anymore was of any consequence to her. She remembered only the blur of his finger.

## CHAPTER 14

The next morning Betsy pulled into the hospital parking lot an hour before her shift started. When Nurse Baker came up before noon, she showed her Evelyn Wolf's signature.

"She's on almost all of them."

"That's interesting, sweetie, but I've never heard of her."

"You wouldn't think someone would up and disappear. Look at all the lives she touched. Someone must remember her."

"Not so surprising when you consider our staff turnover. Besides, those someones are for the most part dead. It'd be a real stroke of luck if anyone remembered her."

Betsy's progress with the charts was steady, slow, and disappointing. Because Nurse Baker came up to the attic at least twice each morning to check on her, she did not chance entering the patient's room all that week. Twice a day, though, she heard the door across the hall open and close.

Who was he?

\* \* \*

Bartholomew was washing the family Rambler out in the driveway when she went home Saturday evening. The stack of boxes she worked on that day had been particularly dusty.

"They got you digging ditches out there now, Sis?

She explained her attic assignment. Without mentioning the patient, she told him about the frequency of Evelyn Wolf's signature written in so many of the charts. "I've never even heard of an Evelyn Wolf living in Hanna. Have you?"

"Nope." Bartholomew hosed off the soapsuds. "Is she listed in the phone book maybe?"

She went inside and came back, running her finger down a back page of the directory. She shook her head. "Can you believe it? Not a single Wolf listed in here let alone an Evelyn Wolf. Could she have married, do you think?"

"Search me, but do you know who would if anyone does?"

"Who?"

"Mrs. Hanna. She knows everyone who ever was and everything that's ever happened around here since Creation."

"A lot of good that does me. She must still be in Chicago because I've not seen her at Mass or outside in her yard."

"Maybe she'll be coming home soon. She's been gone since like before Thanksgiving." He twisted off the water. "Why does it matter?"

"It doesn't. I'm just curious. Village history and stuff."

"Well, maybe she'll be at Mass tomorrow."

\* \* \*

Mrs. Hanna did not attend Mass the next day. As Betsy stood at the top of the church steps following early services with her purse open and fingers searching for her cigarettes, Father Kaplan called to her as he came up the sidewalk. She pulled out a tissue and pretended to sneeze.

"Catching cold?"

"A little hay fever's all."

He smiled. "Amy's been giving me glowing reports about you."

"Really?"

"Outstanding, in fact. Keep it up and we'll welcome you back as a junior this fall."

"I will, Father. Thank you." She glanced over her shoulder at the massive twin oak doors. "Have you heard anything about when Mrs. Hanna is coming back?"

"No. Not a word. Why?"

"Oh, just wondering how she's doing. She was my first piano teacher."

"I'll ask around."

"Thank you. I'd really appreciate it."

\* \* \*

After another Sunday dinner during which her mother stayed in her room, she read the paper with her father.

"Looks like for certain Nixon's going to manage to get himself impeached." Her father ruffled the *Plain Dealer* to the next page. "I guess the only question now is whether Hanna will make a run for it in seventy-six."

"Wouldn't that be good?"

"Maybe. He's done a lot for folks around here. Lots he never took credit for, but he voted in favor of every troop increase Johnson asked for. Backed Nixon when he bombed the bejesus out of Cambodia. Guess that's the difference between having sweated it out in a foxhole and swatting flies while seated behind a desk in the Pentagon where the only blood you draw are from self-inflicted paper cuts."

When she finished reading the paper, she began to work the crossword puzzle, and her father opened the Book-of-the-Month-Club selection that had come the day before, an account of World War II in the Pacific. Fifteen minutes later it thudded to the floor.

"Think I'll take a walk."

"All right, Pops."

His Sunday walks always took him up Cemetery Hill. He did not invite her to join him. He never had and never did he return that his eyes were not red-rimmed and puffed.

Her mother stayed in her room. Despite sleeping twelve hours a night, she needed her afternoon naps. This afternoon at least she was not screaming. A month before, Sandy Jackson stopped by after Sunday dinner.

"We never see you anymore."

"Well, you know. Work at the hospital and all."

From upstairs came a long, banshee wail.

*Nooo.*

Sandy's eyes widened. "What in the world?"

*Please, God, no.*

Betsy now kept the one or two friends who on occasion stopped by out on the front porch, if not in the driveway near the street, the front door closed.

After she solved the puzzle, she went upstairs. Bartholomew's door stood open he at his desk with his back to her. His hand clicked at something.

"What're you doing?"

"Practicing."

"Practicing what?"

"My Morse Code."

"Whatever for?"

"It's on the test for my intermediate."

"Why would they want you to Morse when you can talk instead?"

"You've got me. Maybe they're trying to weed some of us out."

She raised her hand and yawned. "Think I'll lie down."

Okay, Sis. You won't hear a thing from me."

Yet so still was the house that even in her sleep she heard his clicking down the hall as she dreamed of her patient's twitching finger.

\* \* \*

The regional office had asked Nurse Baker to again drive up to Cleveland the next afternoon for an all-hands conference, and before going down for lunch Betsy took the longneck silver key out from under her blouse. He lay in bed, facing the ceiling with what little face remained, his skin pallid, his wasted torso outlined beneath the wool blankets. A few strands of filament-thin hair combed his head. Who was he?

The door behind her creaked.

"Good God almighty!"

She twirled in a semicircle. She had forgotten to shut the door and Bartholomew, wearing Nathan's psychedelic sunglasses with their concentric rainbow circles spinning about the lenses, stood gaping at the bed.

"What are you doing up here?"

"Came out to drive the 'Cuda around the parking lot."

"How'd you find me?"

"You said they had you busting butt up in the attic." His eyes had not left the bed. "You didn't say anything about that."

"He's a he, not a that."

"He looks like a dead ringer for a that."

"He's not. What he is, is a mystery. No one knows who he is. He can't talk, and he can't write. All he can do is twitch his one finger."

"It's not twitching now. Is he dead?"

"No, he's not dead."

"He looks dead."

"Watch." When she touched the patient's arm, his finger jumped alive. Bartholomew watched. His face clouded.

"I don't think that's twitching."

"What do you mean? Of course it is. Just look at it."

"It looks like longs and shorts. Looks like Morse Code to me."

Betsy studied the patient's finger. She looked at her brother.

"Do you know what's he saying?"

Bartholomew watched. He shook his head. "No, not really. This guy's gotta be a pro. I can recognize maybe a couple of words."

"What words?"

"'Who.' Maybe a 'where'."

The patient tapped on.

"Come stand beside me."

"Why?"

"Just come stand here, dufus."

"What're you going to do?"

"I want you to tap on his arm that he's got to slow down."

"Are you crazy? I'm not touching him."

"Come over here now."

"No way!"

Betsy rolled her eyes at the ceiling. "Don't be such a baby. He's not going to bite you. He doesn't have any teeth. He hardly has a mouth. He's not going to gum you to death."

Bartholomew stared at the eyeless face.

"It'll only be for a couple of seconds."

Bartholomew shook his head.

"I want you to tell him you're only a beginner and he's going too fast for you to follow."

"No way."

"Do you want the car keys or not because I've no problem with keeping them in my purse for the rest of the summer and beyond."

"Damn."

"Damn indeed. Now come here."

He crossed to the bed, standing shoulder to shoulder with his sister.

"Now tell him."

Bartholomew reached out his hand. He tapped just below the elbow. The patient's finger did not slow.

"Are you sure you told him he's going too fast?"

"Sure I'm sure."

"Well, tell him again but tap harder."

Bartholomew tapped once more. The patient's finger slowed then lay still. Betsy started to go out of the room.

"Where're you off to?"

She did not answer. The sound of her footfalls disappeared down the stairwell. Bartholomew stared at the bed. He took a step back. Then another. He was two steps from the door when she returned, holding a pen and the tablet she used to write letters for her patients. She shoved him back toward the bed, closing the door behind them, and pulled up two chairs to the near side of the patient. She pointed her pen to the chair beside her.

"Sit."

"I'm not a dog."

"Sit, I said."

He sat, scooting his chair back a little. He looked at the one-fingered hand.

"Ready?"

"As ready as I'm going to get."

He touched the patient's forearm. The finger began again to tap.

# ACT II
# CHAPTER 15

It was while serving in northeastern France with his Majesty's Royal Canadian Expeditionary Force that the patient was wounded. He had just crawled back into their trench and was about to share a cigarette with Private Johnson. The two were the last members of his squad to come in under the wire from their night patrol. The men he led were not Canadian but, like him, American, part of a newly arrived company assigned to the trench sector south of his. Their captain had asked for the Canadians' assistance in seasoning the Americans before their first battle, and his sergeant detached him to teach his countrymen the ropes of trench life, telling him they would be more willing to listen to one of their own than to some Canuk foreigner.

They crawled over the trench parapets at a little past midnight as a bloody-eyed moon rose out of the fog to the east. Their mission he planned to be routine, repairing the larger of the artillery-blasted wire gaps, which he thought to use to teach them the tricks of navigating No Man's Land in the dark without getting them too far from their own trenches in case something went wrong. Though nothing should have gone wrong, Johnson got himself separated when he dropped behind to evacuate his bowels in a shell hole and been too embarrassed to ask the others to wait. By the time he got himself buttoned up again he'd lost sight of them.

He crawled for hours, trying first to find the patrol and then just to find his way back. He must have become disoriented in the foggy night because when the patient found him, the boy was crawling toward the German trenches, not a hundred yards away. Even then he spotted him only because the fog had begun to lift, and one of the German star-flares fired off every quarter hour caught Johnson making his way on hands and knees. Since he was not lying belly flat as the flare dropped, he might just as well have been walking on stilts waving the Stars and Stripes whistling "Over There" because not only did he spot him, so did a half dozen enemy observers.

    For the rest of the night the Germans shot off one flare after another. The two lay flat as they crawled, or when they could, squeezed into any carrion and feces filled depression they chanced upon. Machinegun fire searched for them, their halfpenny lives, a zipping over their heads with a whip of air, a whisper out of the beyond. Midway to their trenches, a machine gunner let up to change belts and Johnson bolted. He scrambled after the boy, tackling him, and he lay on top of the whimpering soldier, softly talking to him as he would a thunder-terrified puppy while pinning his wrists into the life-sucking mud.

    Once the boy's panic passed they inched forward during breaks in the flare drops, praying the aimless fire would not find them and they made it back before it grew light enough for the German spotters to call in their artillery without fear of obliterating their own patrols still out. For three hours they crawled the five hundred yards, and the two came in under the spiraled razor wire as a drizzling dawn broke with barely enough light for an enemy spotter to have skylighted them.

    Johnson sobbed as they tumbled into their trench. The boy stood again and again, exposing his head, and he had to kick Johnson's knees out from under him. Twice he backhanded him across the face so hard that blood streamed from his nose. He fished a cigarette from the pocket of his blouse, all the while his hand gripping Johnson's knee. He pulled a long drag, but when he handed the cigarette across, Johnson's eyes pointed heavenward. He cocked his ear, and he too heard its singing. He let go the cigarette and knocked

Johnson flat, blanketing the boy's body with his own so he not run again. The singing crescendoed to an angel wail that fell upon them like a judgment. A burst of scarlet melted his eyes, and they slid down his cheeks like cracked eggs over a greased skillet. The earth rolled beneath them followed by a rush of skin-scalding-breath-of-God wind. He had seen enough of others to guess what he looked like. Skin pocked and broiled, scorched black as obsidian. Far luckier to be one of the dead. But no. There would have been no justice in his death. He had a penance yet to pay.

## CHAPTER 16

The patient's finger's stopped then tapped again. Bartholomew looked at his sister.

"He wants to know if I'm death."

"Why would he think that?"

Bartholomew tapped.

"A hand different from mine sometimes taps to him. He hoped his time had come."

"Taps to him? You mean like Morse code?"

"Let me ask."

The patient tapped two longs. Two shorts. Then his finger laid dead-snake still on the bed sheet. The withered muscles in his stick-thin arm relaxed, and his already shallow respiration slowed to nothing.

"We killed him!"

"Don't be such a dufus, Dufus." She placed two fingers to his wrist. "Sleeping. He's got something resembling a pulse."

"This guy's gonna give me a heart attack for sure."

"You'll get over it."

"So what do we do now?"

She sat back and read over her notes. She shook her head. "He didn't tell us where he's from. Didn't so much as give us a name."

"I wonder who else has been Morsing to him."

"The only ones who come in here are Nurse Baker and Filbert."

"Do they know Morse Code?"

"Can't imagine they do. I mean how many people know telegraphy anymore? If they did, I doubt if he'd be here."

A shadow darkened over the patient.

"What are you two doing in here?"

Betsy twirled around. In the doorway, her face red and eyes afire, stood Nurse Baker.

"You," she pointed at Bartholomew, get out of here. Now. You, young lady come down to my office."

* * *

The walls of her office shuttered when Nurse Baker slammed the door behind them, and she stood before it with her hands gripping her hips.

"I am as furious with you, Betsy, as I've been with anyone in my life."

"With me?"

"Who was that with you upstairs?"

"My brother."

"It's a good thing I had to come back for a report I'd forgotten. I know I locked his door before I left."

Betsy put a hand to her throat.

"How did you get into his room?"

"I borrowed your keys. Had a duplicate made."

"So you could show him to your brother. Your little friends."

"No, I just happened to be in his room when he found me. He's been coming out to practice his driving in the parking lot."

"What were the two of you doing upstairs?"

"Morsing."

"You were what?"

"You know how his finger sometimes looks like it's twitching."

"Nerve damage."

"It's not really twitching. He's using Morse Code. Bartholomew's learning it for his ham license, getting pretty good at it too, and the patient started tapping when we were in his room."

Nurse Baker's arms fell to her sides.

"Are you sure about this, Betsy? Truly sure?"

"Yes, ma'am." She reached into her apron pocket. "I took notes as my brother dictated what he told us. Listen."

Nurse Baker paced her office as Betsy read, her eyes cast downward. She walked to the window where a plum-colored sky darkened over the cemetery. When Betsy finished, she looked up.

"Did he tell you his name?"

"No, ma'am."

"What about where he's from?"

"Not word one."

"What else did he tell you?"

"Only what I read just now. That he was in the Canadian Army, but he's really an American."

"Yes." Nurse Baker nodded. "The Canadian Army would explain much. Explain why we have no name."

"Ma'am?"

She went behind her desk where for a moment she studied a framed photograph that hung on the wall. She and another woman along with a dozen unshaved men with weary eyes grinned into the camera, their fatigues showing beneath bloodstained surgical aprons and their arms slung over each other's shoulders. Behind them stood an olive-green tent with a large red cross within a white circle on either side of the roof. A stack of body bags in the bottom corner the photographer had not quite succeeded in clipping out.

"I asked the Army to send me. Told them I could be of some use. I suppose I was. Just not always enough. Wasn't uncommon for us to lose ten boys a day. Some days more. After a while I too told myself it didn't mean anything. I lasted at it for almost two years. Dr. Morris found me after midnight, talking to a body bag holding one of the boys we'd lost that afternoon. I'd left his bedside for only a minute. Not even a minute. He had a solid chance of making it home too. Shrink said I was sleepwalking, but I can't remember. Don't want to remember. I vowed then I would never again not get a patient home. A stupid promise for me to make, really. If you're going to save lives, you're going to lose lives too. Still, since coming home — since coming here — I've not not gotten a patient home. I don't intend to begin now."

She pulled out her chair.

"Tell your brother — what's his name?"

"Bartholomew."

"Tell Bartholomew I'm truly sorry. I didn't know, but this is the patient I care most about. Perhaps because he has endured the most."

"Yes, ma'am. He has."

"Can you get him to come back? To find out his name? Where he's from?"

"Sure."

"We've got to get him home."

"Yes, ma'am. We do."

"It may not be easy. You know how reluctant the boys here are at first to tell you anything about themselves. Sometimes it takes us months. We wouldn't know names for half of them if they weren't written in their charts. Who knows how reluctant he'll be after half a century. You may need to listen — listen for some time — to what he has to say until he's ready to tell you."

"Yes, ma'am."

"We don't have much time, Betsy."

"Because he's dying."

"Because he's dying and because if Congressman Hanna hears what we're up to our patient will get moved." She snapped her fingers. "In the blink of an eye."

"Why?"

"I don't know why. He's probably been a patient here since Hanna's been a congressman. He asks about him whenever he calls. Goes up to see him every time he comes out. I think just to be certain he's still here, that I'm not lying to him. He trusts no one, you know. Sits in his room all alone with him. Always alone. Won't even let Oliver come in with him. Something's wrong. I don't know what but something."

"Yes, ma'am."

"You've got to discover our patient's past."

"Congressman Hanna may know something about Evelyn Wolf."

"Who?"

"Evelyn Wolf. I showed you her name in the chart. She was the head nurse back then."

"I'm certain he would. He knows the name of every patient we've got. Where they're from and all about their progress, but he'll want to know why I'm asking questions about Evelyn Wolf, and then I'll be gone as quick as the patient. This job is all I have. All I have."

"Yes, ma'am."

Spider webbed skeins of lightning above the cemetery reached up, piercing the clouds as though into some other sky. Some other world. From a long way off a peel of thunder rolled.

"You better go check in on the ward."

Betsy started for the door.

"When do you think your brother can come back?"

"I'll talk to him tonight. Maybe tomorrow."

"Good. Tomorrow would be good. Every day counts. He doesn't have many left."

\* \* \*

Betsy went downstairs to the cafeteria at noon where she got a Cobb salad and a bowl of tomato soup. She sat at a vacant table and from her apron pocket took out the copy of *The Odyssey* the Army had sent home with Nathan's effects.

"Some light poolside reading, I see."

She looked up. Matt McLain stood beside her table, holding his tray and smiling.

"Mind if I sit with you?"

She nodded, a soupspoon protruding from her mouth. She had not flirted with a boy since before her brother's death.

"I'll take that as a yes."

He unwound the napkin from his utensils and was about to stab at his French fries. He grinned. With a fork he tapped the edge of his mouth. When Betsy looked cross-eyed at the still protruding spoon, her face reddened to scarlet, and in her panic she socked herself in the jaw with The Odyssey, which fell in the bowl, splashing soup and crunched crackers over her face and staining her white apron.

"I'm so sorry." Matt stood. "Let me get some paper towels."

She was gone when he returned, The Odyssey soaking in her soup bowl. He walked out into the empty corridor. He looked down to the restroom, waiting a good five minutes before he returned to their table. He picked up the soggy book by the corner of its cover and let it slide back into the soup. After he finished eating, he carried their trays to the trash bin where he slid the remains of their lunches into the garbage along with the only book Nathan never finished.

\* \* \*

"No and hell no."

Betsy had waited until after supper when her brother was alone in his room to ask him.

"But Nurse Baker says she's sorry."

"Cool but the answer's still no."

She pleaded.

"No way, Sis."

"How come?"

"Why should I spend what little summer I have left cooped up in a hospital room with no windows that smells like diapers with some hundred-year-old-codger with no face, one arm, and a non-stop finger that'll have the kids laughing at me next month for turning cross eyed over the summer?"

"Come on, Barto."

"I'm a businessman. Before school starts, I've lawns to mow and money to make. Girls to neck with at the movies."

Betsy walked over to his desk where she ran a finger along top of his radio. "Too bad."

Bartholomew shrugged. He stooped to one knee and began lacing up a sneaker. "That's life."

"Too bad for you, I mean."

"Why for me?"

"I could hardly follow his finger he's so fast. After a while it hurt my head to watch."

"Yeah, but you're not a ham."

"I'll bet if you Morsed with him for only a few hours, it'd be a cinch for you to pass the test for your dumb old intermediate."

Bartholomew tapped the toe of his sneaker. He looked up. "You think so?"

"Absolutely. Be a shame for it to go back in the closet because your license expired and you couldn't get your intermediate."

Bartholomew stood, shaking his head. "I pity the guy who marries you. Poor sap won't stand a snowball's chance."

\* \* \*

The next morning at the echo of footsteps from the stairwell, Nurse Baker raised her eyes from the invoices she was checking off behind the nurses' station. When Betsy pointed to the floor above, she held up both hands, their middle and index fingers crossed.

Betsy scooted two chairs to beside the patient's bed and took from her apron pocket the pen and thick stenographer's tablet.

"Guess it was good thing Mom made me take shorthand."

"What do you need those for?"

"In case we don't remember everything he tells us."

"What's there to remember? We ask the coot for his name and where he's from. Him and me chitchat for an hour or so and then I'm out of here, practicing for my intermediate."

"You think so, huh?"

"Sure. What else is there?"

"Ask him then. Then maybe some day from my notes I'll write a novel with us in it. Me as the heroine, of course, and you can be the dufus kid brother. Of course."

Bartholomew raised his eyes to the ceiling. "You ready, Nancy Drew?"

"You know how I love a mystery."

Bartholomew tapped. The patient took a long minute to raise his finger. Bartholomew looked at his sister. "How can he not remember?"

"Half the guys downstairs told that one when they got here, and the other half made one up."

"So what'll we do?"

"Find out how he got here."

"Ask him flat out?"

"Too direct."

"What then?"

"He was lucky he learned to Morse, so see if they taught him in Canada."

# CHAPTER 17

Betsy had always been addicted to the guesswork of mysteries, their inferences and deductions. The summer she turned twelve she would be standing outside the library before they opened their doors to return the Nancy Drew she had read the day before and checking out the next. If somebody was a day past due with the one she wanted, she demanded that Mrs. Urbschat track her down and read her the riot act, Betsy standing by her desk. There was then something like forty books in the series. After she read them all, she started all over again, but Nancy was nothing like the mystery lying on that hospital bed before her. Reading his life was like peeling an onion, tears not excluded.

He had not learned telegraphy in the Canadian Army but before he enlisted when he was but a hayseed farm boy. As to his luck, he said it remained too early for him to say if his learning telegraphy was fortunate for him. The Greeks of Homer believed no man could claim to have lived a good life until he expired his last breath and so could not know if his life had indeed been blessed. They believed luck to be as a coin spinning through the air. What we see as our providence today may turn to our sorrow tomorrow. Had he not learned telegraphy he knew now the girl he would have married. The girl who would have born his children and raised them on the farm he had learned telegraphy in order to escape from. It was too early to say if such a fate might have been a spot of luck too not now to be despised. They would have to make up our own minds if they had the time to hear him out, and if he had the time left to him to tell them. He would like someone to know. Someone to hear his story.

Before enlisting he worked as a telegrapher for the Pennsylvania, Fort Wayne & Chicago Railroad at a whistle-stop depot three miles up the tracks from his family's farm, bountiful only in producing stones dropped by the melting of the last ice-age glacier. By their late thirties when he came along, his father and mother had already withered worn-out old. He was their youngest child, the only one to make it to his second year, the other four succumbing to cholera and typhoid and one of the influenza pandemics. His father dug the graves for each in a back corner of the farm where a rock-filled dais good for nothing else cropped its grasping fingers up out of the earth.

Farming their one hundred-eighty acres came back-breaking, heartbreaking hard. Too much or too little rain falling too soon or too late or if blessed with just the right amount you could lay riverboat-gamblers' odds on a miles-long cloud of locust to cast over them its hand-of-God shadow. His sole salvation lay in the start of the fall term at the convent school where the sisters taught him composition and Greek, postulates and theorems, and he worked late into the night by the flickering light of a coal-oil lamp to keep his grades perfect. On the last day of his sophomore year as he and his classmates filed out following their final exam his geometry teacher asked to speak to him. Sister Roberts said if he did as well for the next two years there was no reason why he could not win a scholarship. Would he please come see her at the end of next year's term if he were interested?

If he were interested? If he were interested? As Molly trotted them home, he hooked his boot heels fast in the stirrups less he twirl off his mule into the clouds. God himself held his salvation out before him as a carrot on a string. He found his mother stooped in their acre strawberry patch over a broken-handled hoe, her body crooked in a lifelong question mark as his father walked the back pasture fence behind her. When he raised his arm to him, his father didn't wave back, but in his excitement he took no note.

He uncinched Molly, setting the surplus Union cavalry saddle on the top fence plank to dry, and went into the kitchen where he pumped a mason jar full of iron-tinged water and walked it out to his mother. She drank in long greedy swallows as she listened. When he finished she laid a hand on his shoulder, telling him they were very proud of his accomplishments, and they could talk over Sister Robert's suggestion at supper, which she had better get started, and handed him the hoe. Taking hold of the hoe, he watched her enter the kitchen. What was there to talk over?

When he came in to wash up, he could now see they had been talking. He should have waited. After they said grace, he repeated what Sister Roberts said, his father shaking his head as he listened and taking so long to butter his bread he tore a hole in its center. His father told him that after the boy left for school that morning, he had walked the fence line, finding where one of their heifers broke through the barbed wire and gotten twisted, nearly amputating her leg, and he had to crack her skull with the blunt edge of an ax. Only two heifers got born the spring before, and the loss of the one was not inconsequential. This Sister Roberts was filling his head with bales of blarney. They needed him here. He could not even go back in the fall let alone think of leaving. They were too old to work the farm alone. Without him there full time they would lose it to the bank for sure. They would be destitute, living at the county home, and they would as soon hang themselves from the barn rafters as be living at the goddamn county home. He looked to his mother, she forking her food in little circles around her plate, looking down but nodding.

Hanging themselves from the barn rafters was no figure of speech, not some idle threat. So upward toward its apogee his coin began its spin.

## CHAPTER 18

His finger ceased to tap. Bartholomew turned to his sister. "Sleeping again?"

Betsy looked up from her stenographer's pad. She nodded.

"For how long do you think?"

"Your guess is as good as mine. Let's leave him be and come back."

"What'll I do until he wakes up?" Bartholomew rubbed his hands together. "Maybe drive the old 'Cuda around the back roads some?"

"We'll see about you driving *my* car around the parking lot, but first you're helping me in the attic."

"Doing what?"

"If he can't, or won't, tell us his name, maybe we can find the chart he had when he first got here."

"*If* he had one and how are we going to find it if we don't know his name?"

"At the end of a chart, it says what happened, whether they were discharged or something."

"Meaning like they died something."

"Well, he wasn't discharged and he didn't die so his should just stop."

"I *am* getting behind the wheel before we go home."

"Yeah, yeah, yeah."

An hour after they crossed the hall, Bartholomew dropped the chart he held on the stack before them.

"I see what you mean. Evelyn Wolf is almost the only one signing these things." He picked up another. "Not in the phonebook. I wonder what happened to her."

"You know how I love a mystery."

"Maybe she was a German spy who got caught and they hanged her. Have you checked out the cemetery for her?"

"Keep reading."

"Well, it's possible." He flipped to the end of the chart. "Holly sh . . ."

"What?"

He turned the chart to her. His finger pointed to the last entry. "Look."

No signature appeared at the end but Evelyn Wolf's chilling calligraphic script was unmistakable.

*Deceased and good riddance. Goddamn his soul already roasting in hell eternally.*

\* \* \*

Betsy went down to the cafeteria near noon and brought back their ham sandwiches and cartons of milk. After they ate, they crossed the hall. The patient still slept.

"I should go down to the ward." She put a hand on her brother's shoulder. "Can you keep searching the charts?"

"Should've known you were scheming to stick me with the worst of the grunt work."

"Isn't your Morsing better?"

He wiggled an index finger at his nose.

"Yeah, I guess."

"Then stop being such a baby, and don't forget who has the car keys."

"Damn."

"Wonder what Dad would say if he knew you were hitching out here to drive. Even in the parking lot, it's not like you're insured."

"Double damn."

"I'll come get you at the end of my shift."

\* \* \*

Nurse Baker stepped into the ward doorway mid-afternoon as Betsy wrote a letter for Hawkeye to his mother and waved her out into the hall.

"Yes, ma'am?"

"Matt McLain cornered me in the cafeteria."

"What about?"

"Randy Brindle's got him interested in our patient upstairs."

"What's he want?"

"A story. One that'll get him off the *Journal* and let him maybe move up to the *Plain Dealer*."

"Well, isn't that good? Wouldn't an article maybe help us find his family?"

"They *could* still be local. The VA makes an effort however ineptly to keep patients close to their homes. After all these years, though, they're likely long gone. Or maybe he was an orphan when he enlisted. Lots do. Or maybe the VA didn't know any more about him than we do and warehoused him here when we were new and less crowded."

"What's there to lose?"

"Besides my job, our patient. If his family doesn't step forward, like immediately, the Congressman will be embarrassed over his pet project. His government paid for publicity machine. Blame us for losing a patient for fifty years and me for doing nothing to find his family."

"We've no time to lose."

"How'd it go today? Did he tell you his name?"

"Still says he doesn't remember. I'm not certain if I believe him."

"Why not?"

"He has no trouble remembering everything else."

"Keep at it. Gain his trust. The more he tells you, the more likely he is to let something slip."

"All right."

"You must do it quickly, though."

* * *

A little past six o'clock, Betsy went upstairs where her dust covered and sweaty brother sat flipping pages, the attic air summertime still even with the window open.

"You about ready to go home?"

"I was ready before you blackmailed me into staying."

"Let's check on him before we leave."

The eyeless patient lay facing the door when they entered. Betsy set her purse on the nightstand and put an ear to what mouth remained.

"Still asleep?"

She nodded.

"He sure does sleep a lot."

"We probably exhausted him."

"You want to try waking him?"

"No. We'll start fresh in the morning. Let's go home."

Bartholomew stood studying the patient.

"Do you think he even knows we're in his room now?"

"I don't know." Betsy shook her head. "Who can say? It's horrible to think that anyone could be so alone."

\* \* \*

Betsy was reaching to her side as they walked up to the Barracuda. "Oh, goddamnit!"

"What is it?"

"I left my stupid purse up on the nightstand."

"Get it tomorrow. It's not like your boyfriend's going to run off with it."

"The car keys are in it."

Bartholomew groaned.

"Wait here. You look like one petered out dude."

He sat on the front bumper, propping his elbows behind him on the hood. "I ain't goin' nowhere."

When she came out of the patient's room, Matt McLain stood waiting, his thumbs hooked in his trouser pockets and smiling his sweetest college-bar-pick-up smile.

"Thought I saw you running up the steps." He chucked his chin at the door. "So this is where they warehouse your mystery patient?"

She tried walking around him, but he stepped in front of her.

"A story might help find his family, Betsy. Have you thought of that?"

"Might not too."

"Why wouldn't it?"

She head-faked around him and started down the stairs. "Sorry I haven't time to chit chat."

"Maybe I'll see you at lunch again?"

Betsy stopped. She rapped her knuckles on the mahogany banister. "No talking about patients?"

"No talking about patients. He raised the middle three fingers of his right hand. "Scouts honor."

"Let me think about it."

Betsy's footfalls echoed up the empty stairwell. Matt smiled. *Maybe get the story and the girl. Now, Grandma McLain, wouldn't that be the cat's pajamas? But first the story.*

He took the steps down to the third floor and went into Ward 7.

\* \* \*

The next morning the patient still slept so they set to reading charts. When she went down at noon, she found Filbert by the nurses' station mopping up a pool of vomit.

"Watch where you all be stepping, Missy."

She walked around and stood next to his bucket, leaning over so her face was level with his. "Can I just-suppose you a question?"

"Yes, ma'am, you may."

"Suppose a girl kind of liked you sort of but made a fool of herself the first time you tried to talk to her. Would you let her try to talk to you again? Just suppose."

Filbert stopped mopping. He rested his hands on the mop handle, rocking his head as he judged the question. "All depends I reckon."

"Depends on what?"

"On whether she be as pretty a girl as you."

Betsy grinned. "You're the best."

"So's many a sweet lady's told me so. You goin' to lunch now?"

"I think I might."

Filbert winked. "Happy hunting."

"Besides, I want Nathan's book back."

She headed down the corridor. Filbert's grin fell away. He leaned to his mopping.

"Missy, you needs to be allowing the dead to bury the dead. They's understands. Ain't no shame on you. They knows the livin' needs to be trudging along this trail of tears as best they can."

After she walked through the lunch line, she sat at an empty table in the middle of the cafeteria where she could watch without seeming to watch and pulled from her apron a paperback copy of *Rosemary's Baby*. Matt followed her into the cafeteria a minute later, and she pretended to be reading. Twice while he stood in line he glanced over his shoulder to look her way. When he came up behind her, he reached over her shoulder, lifting the book from her hands. He smiled, his teeth Pepsodent commercial white and straight as Grandma Addison's string of fitted pearls, and she saw in the pupils of those gray eyes her reflected self looking back.

"Two accidents in two weeks would be two too many, don't you think?" He nodded at the empty chair opposite her. "May I?"

"No patient talk."

"No patient talk."

He looked at the book. "You seen the movie yet?"

"Not yet."

Matt again smiled. A young man weighing the possibilities. He set down his tray and began to unfold the napkin holding his silverware. "So you must be a reader like Nathan?"

Betsy blinked. She lowered her sandwich. "What?"

"You seem like you must be a reader like Nathan."

"What makes you think he was a reader?"

"He'd written his name on the inside of the book you dropped in the soup the other day."

"I want it back."

"You want what back?"

"Nathan's book."

"I tossed it in the trash."

"You what!"

Betsy stood.

"Please sit down. You'll give me a complex if you run off again."

"You had no right. It was my . . . it was Nathan's. It was . . ."

"It was ruined."

"I don't care if it was."

"It was so soaked through the print was running and the pages were coming out of the binding."

"That has nothing to do with anything."

"It what?"

"Goddamn you." Betsy's voice shook. "Goddamn you to hell anyway!"

Her words thundered off the tall cafeteria walls. The servers behind the counter fell silent. Patrons twisted around in their chairs. Betsy covered her mouth with cupped hands and ran out of the cafeteria.

* * *

She was supposed to have gotten lunch for Bartholomew. She didn't want to return to the cafeteria and she needed time to calm her breathing, so she drove to the Dairy Queen in town. After Bartholomew ate, they went into the patient's room.

"Do you want me to ask him his name this time?"

"No. If he doesn't remember, the question may frustrate him. If he does he may get suspicious and clam up. I think he does, though. He remembers way too much."

"Why would he not tell us?"

"That's our key." Betsy touched the chain about her throat. "When we understand the why, we'll know the who."

"What should I ask him?"

"Ask him what happened after he quit school."

## CHAPTER 19

He said the summer of 1913 was the misery of his life. Up to then anyway. All summers on the farm were an endurance, but in summers past he had the school term to hold onto. Now his sole respite fell on the first Saturday of the month when his mother sent him into town for their mail and whatever they couldn't grow or make or make do without. Thread. Needles. Buckwheat flour and maybe sugar if they ran short of blackstrap molasses. She had always driven the buckboard in herself, and it seemed to him to be her own respite. In June, though, she asked him to go instead. She was busy with the strawberry jam preserving, and she claimed she didn't have the time let alone the gumption to make the trip.

On those Saturdays he left after dinner, his mother handing him on his way out the door a red bandana full of greasy coins and told him he could take a dime to spend on himself. After picking up any mail at the Post Office and their supplies at the general store, he went into the tobacco shop to purchase the Cleveland and Pittsburgh papers and maybe a bag of lemon drops before he crossed to the village square where he sat on a bench beneath a sycamore across the street from the courthouse where he read until the horizon reddened.

It was there on his September trip that a former classmate spotted him on his way into work. Mark had taken an evening job the winter before as a messenger at the telegraph office down at the depot. To pass the time on slow evenings, the chief telegrapher taught him Morse Code. Late one night the depot manager slipped in by the side door, standing in back where he listened for less than a minute before he promoted the boy to assistant telegrapher. When he asked Mark if telegraphy was difficult to pick up, his friend told him anyone with a head for postulates and theorems could learn it easy peasy because Morse Code was nothing more than hearing the patterns. So on Sundays following Mass, he rode Molly over to Mark's house. His own father did not protest, not caring what his son did with his bit of spare time so long as it did not interfere with the farm.

His friend proved right. It did not take him long to learn telegraphy, and once he did, when Mark wanted a Saturday evening off to court Sally Anne, he covered his shift. No wonder to him that his friend took the time to teach him. She was the prettiest girl in the county. Mark's father, however, was its wealthiest robber baron, and that January he made Mark quit the telegraph office. The stench of war already fouled the air, if not 1913, the next year for sure. England and Germany and France consumed all the steel they could smelt and still they required more. The smokestacks twenty miles north at Republic and Sheet & Tube glowed a fiery red even at midnight, and the mills needed all the coal they could buy or hijack from the railroad foremen they bribed. When its price hit a dollar a ton, the mines south of town, abandoned since Lee's surrender at Appomattox, opened. Mark's father owned an entire six sections of fertile bottomland. He ran the village and county politics, and no one got elected without his financial backing, not even their congressman. During the depression of the 1890s he bought up for a song hundreds of acres of coal leases he intended now to mine. He needed his son, though, to help with the farm after school. When Mark gave notice, the depot manager drove out to ask his father if he could fill in until he found someone permanent. His father did not see why not, but come spring he would need his son back.

So that winter he helped his father with what farm chores there were until he rode into town to work the three to nine o'clock shift. Some afternoons Sister Roberts stopped by after classes to give him encouragement and lend him a book. When traffic grew slow, he read, plotted his escape, though how to escape without sending his folks to the county home?

By spring the depot manager hired a replacement telegrapher out of Canton, and he returned to the farm. He helped his father with the planting but still rode into town on Saturdays to work the afternoon shift where he seemed always to receive more telegrams than he sent. The birth of a baby girl in Cincinnati. The death of a great-grandfather in Toledo. The slippage of life somewhere else.

Another summer passed with him withering a little more each day. Up before dawn. Milking followed by breakfast followed by hours stooped over a hoe in the shadeless cornrows stretching two furlongs from backwoods to road followed by the afternoon milking. Except for Saturdays, in bed before the sun set. Something had to happen. He could not go on dying bit by bit, day after day.

He learned of the start of the Great War on a Saturday afternoon in August when he stopped at the Post Office. A gaggle of village wise men were gathered around the sidewalk bench beneath a hundred-year-old oak, jawing over what it all meant. Higher crop prices for sure, said Mr. Cutler, because there was never a war yet that was not the farmer's best friend. He stopped and listened. When Isaac Rohrer asked him what he thought of it all, he told the men he needed to be getting on into work. First, though, he crossed to the tobacco shop where he purchased his papers. So spun his coin.

The village laid graveyard quiet in the smothering heat. No telegram came or went, and he studied his papers. While President Wilson pledged America's steadfast neutrality, the Commonwealth countries immediately answered the call of their King. Australia and South Africa enlisted volunteers. Gurkhas would soon disembark out of Mangalore. The paper ran a feature story on its back page about a recruiting office the Canadians set up in their Cleveland consulate where they offered an enlistment bonus to any American willing to throw in his kit with them. He read the article over once more before cutting it out with a penknife and folding it away in his billfold. Perhaps with higher crop prices and the enlistment bonus the Canadians promised his folks could get by without him.

He held out until the Saturday before Thanksgiving. He worked his usual shift until he heard the whistle of the 8:47 where it crossed the trestle two miles east of town. He took off his eyeshade and walked to a side window where far down the tracks a knifepoint of light slit open the fabric of night through which he would slip. In the glass stared back his reflection, and he and his mirrored self nodded one to the other as might two buccaneers going off in search of their common reckoning. He crossed the office and lay on the counter an envelope addressed to his folks that held his saved-up pay except for the dollar in his billfold.

The Pullman was almost empty: A snoring salesman embracing an oversized suitcase that stood upright in the next seat and advertised women's undergarments, the top of a corkless bourbon bottle and something frilly sticking out of the man's coat pocket. A mother not much older than he comforted her child. No one looked like they might take an interest in talking to an excited hayseed farm boy. He walked to the end car after the conductor punched his ticket where he stood shivering on the platform as he watched the night swallow up the countryside.

There was a layover in Akron. Debs had led the regulars out on a wildcat strike, and their scabs took so long to change the locomotive that dawn reddened his window shade before the train pulled into Cleveland. He ate a dime breakfast at an all-night diner catering to scabbing Negroes and with his ear so untrained to their dialect he had to ask the waitress to repeat everything she said. After she left, he swiveled around with coffee cup in hand and listened to the ragtime voices of more Negroes in one place than he had ever seen before. Because the village he left had a contingent of Klansmen forever in search of amusement, it was rare for him to see even a single colored man. Those occasions when he did it was a tramp trotting the tracks at dawn or in the failing light of evening in a hurry to be somewhere else and quickly.

He wandered the city streets after he ate, his face skyward as he marveled at the twelve story buildings and not watching where he went. He stumbled into a mounted policeman who pointed him in the direction of the Canadian consulate and asked after him in his Irish brogue what was wrong with the lad that he would want to fight alongside a bunch of stinking kipper eaters.

The Canadians kept their enlistment office open even on Sundays for any fool who the night before had wenched away his week's pay and this morning lacked adequate funds to settle up with his landlady. The marionette heads of a hung-over sergeant and corporal snapped up from their folded arms when he pushed open the door. Their florid faces beamed one to the other. The sergeant raised a finger to his lips, winking their stroke of luck at the corporal. With Thanksgiving upon them, the recruiters were more than a little light in meeting their quota, and they had no wish to be replaced and shipped off to France where they would be separated from their American sweethearts.

The sergeant said they could dispense with their annoying questions, except for his name and address. He gave them an alias — one he claimed to have long forgotten — and the address of the depot. Then he raised his hand to swear allegiance to a King never to be his, to a country he would not see for the first time until evening, and in the name of a God soon to reveal to him His salvation for the trick it truly was. The recruiters slapped him on the back and poured him a whiskey neat to seal his oath and themselves a double each so he would not drink alone. As they handed him a one-way train ticket for Ottawa, another boy walked through the consulate door with hat in hand and corn-silk hair falling into his eyes. Tom Stanton hailed from a crossroads village south of his own and like him could not bear the thought of living from daybreak to backbreak for a God-given dollar. The sergeant again winked their stroke of luck at the corporal.

With a four-hour stopover at Buffalo, he and Stanton hopped a streetcar to Niagara Falls where they watched the plunge of water, the ghost fingers of mist dancing above the river, the roar of water deafening. A young couple at the far end of the lookout were grasping hard to the iron rail. When they opened their eyes, the couple signed each to the other and kissed. Stanton asked if he could imagine life without sound. He could not. Such a world would drive him mad in a day if not an hour.

Once aboard the connecting train, a boy with a lumpy, bag-of-potatoes face walked over to their seats. The day before he too had enlisted after running off from a farm outside of Erie. The Canadians kept the three together through their too short training, a suffocating troopship to Liverpool, and the ferry that carried them across the Channel to Calais. For two weeks the boys called themselves the American Brigade until a Mauser bullet threw the boy with the bag-of-potatoes face back against the trench wall, a crimson fountain spurting from his eye while his other still held in awe whatever it had last seen across No Man's Land.

The boys arrived in northeastern France between Christmas and New Year's. Because the ground was frozen, they missed what the veterans referred to as the Great Mud. Cahill told them of his corporal stepping off the duckboards to piss and seeing him swallowed up whole. A fine way to be saying howdy-do to Saint Peter, holding onto your pecker, but least down there the rats would not be getting at him.

He hailed from Cape Breton Island and was twenty-eight years old though he looked forty-eight. His great misfortune in life, he bemoaned, was that unlike four-fifths of all coal miners he still held claim to all ten fingers. Only a couple of teeth but all of his fingers. If he had but lost his trigger finger, he would be safe at home, laying siege only to the district milkmaids on their Sunday afternoon walks. He was short and permanently stooped from tunneling the mineshafts that ran out beneath the Atlantic for more than a mile, which made him prime fodder for trench life among the rats.

When the boys asked why they had done nothing about the rats, Cahill told how a month before he and his bunkmates had purchased from a local peasant a cat the size of a pit bull and twice as vicious. They starved the big tom for a week before they threw it into their dugout, sealing him inside for three days. When they went back in, only the cat was gone. They could not find so much as a bone of the big tom. Only a few tuffs of bloody hair feathered by the door where it had tried to scratch its way out.

## CHAPTER 20

Nurse Baker waved them to the nurses' station the next morning when brother and sister came up the hospital steps.

"Can't go in today, guys."

Betsy's eyebrows arched.

"What's up?"

"He likely suffered one of his little strokes during the night. When I went in this morning to change his IV, his finger never twitched. It always twitches when I touch him."

"Morsed." Bartholomew wiggled his index finger at her. "His finger doesn't twitch, he Morses."

"Yes. Morsed. Sorry."

"Will he be all right?" Betsy said.

"I hope so. He may only be exhausted from his Morsing, his remembering from yesterday, but I've been up to his room twice more this morning and nothing. His hand's so still."

"What do you want us to do?"

"Let him rest to Monday, and we'll see how he is. Until then the two of you can search the attic for his chart."

"Yes, ma'am."

They started for the steps. Bartholomew shook his head.

"The old man's always telling me the truth sometimes hurts. Nobody ever said it could kill you too."

"I guess then what he's telling us must be the truth."

"Or at least what he thinks it is. How would we know if it wasn't?"

\* \* \*

By the time they left the hospital on Saturday evening, though they had made good progress in their search of boxes, they had not found the patient's chart. Bartholomew slouched back in his seat as they drove home, his eyes closed.

"The heat in that attic was a real killer this afternoon."

"No kidding."

"I'm going to sleep for a million years tomorrow. Maybe a billion."

"After Mass."

"Yeah, yeah, yeah. After Mass."

* * *

Betsy halted in mid-step as she cut across their front yard on her way back from Mass and looked down. Her patent-leather flats were soaked through and her ankle socks wet. The grass had grown so long it remained dewy even at that late hour. For the second Saturday in a row her father had forgotten to mow the lawn. She looked up to the darkening sky.

"Might get it cut before it rains. Might."

She changed into her faded cutoffs and T-shirt and went down to the garage where she filled the lawnmower gas tank. After she coaxed Mr. Simms out of his hammock where he lay reading the Sunday comics to pull the start rope for her, she mowed the back and two side yards and had started in on the front when a dusty-windowed Volkswagen beeped its horn as it slowed and hung a U-turn before parking at the curb. She stopped mowing but failed to disengage the engine. When Matt stepped out, waving to her from the street with a bag in his fist, she dropped her hands from the mower handles. So lock-eyed were the two of them that neither noticed the path of the mower until it collided into the passenger door. The engine sputtered and the wheels spun gashes in the grass before the mower stalled out. Matt ran a finger over a half-dozen dings and scratches. He shrugged.

"Nothing I can't fix in five minutes with a little sandpaper and a touch of spray paint."

When he turned to Betsy, she was sitting in the grass with her face buried in her pulled-up knees.

"It's only a car, Betsy."

She sobbed.

"In fact it's only a Volkswagen. Barely an official car even. That's why it's called a Bug. Some days I have to almost peddle it to get the goshdarn junk up a hill. The thing leaks when it rains and refuses to start in the winter."

"I'm so sorry," Betsy moaned into her kneecaps.

"It's okay. Really."

Betsy shook her head.

"Now if you'd rammed my Rolls, I'd be a tad urinary over it."

She turned her head, one eye squinted open. "You don't have no goddamn Rolls Royce."

"Maybe not today," he held up the bag, "but I do have this."

"What?"

"*The Odyssey*, minus the soup course, and annotated by some Harvard professor." He took the book out of its bag and handed it to her. "You're lucky. Last one they had in stock. I guess Greek classics aren't high up on most people's list for summer reading."

Betsy flipped through the pages. "Thank you."

"My pleasure."

He mowed the front yard while she watched from the porch steps, and when he finished he put the mower away in the shed out back.

"Well, I need to be going."

"You can't sit with me for a minute or two? Or three maybe."

"Relatives coming over for a reunion picnic. You know how that goes."

"Yeah, we have those all the time."

"Just wanted to replace the book."

Betsy nodded. She tried to smile.

"See you around."

She walked out to the curb where she stood watching down the street until the Volkswagen disappeared around the corner onto Court Street. She raised Homer's *Odyssey*. "See you." A rain drop darkened the sidewalk. Then another.

* * *

The telephone rang and Betsy went in. When Bartholomew came home from his baseball game soaking wet from the rain, she told him as he stripped out of his clothes in the garage that he might as well stay home tomorrow.

'Nurse Baker called. Congressman Hanna's coming out to the hospital to pass out some more medals."

"Again?"

"She says he's like this every election. Not that Judge Thomson has a snowball's chance."

* * *

Betsy was standing between the Quick Draw's and Johnny Handsome's beds as Congressman Hanna made his way down those that lined the wall opposite, Matt following behind as he wrote in his notepad, when Randy Brindle appeared in the doorway.

"Well if it ain't our asshole congressman come to pay us another visit."

The ward fell still as a held breath. All eyes shifted to the doorway.

"Now that Garfield's got his thieving' butt slung in the hoosegow, you must be worried more than a little you won't be able to so easily steal this next election like you did all them others."

Hanna, dressed in a vested dark suit the close heat notwithstanding, stepped out from within a circle of patient families. He pointed his cigar. "You sound like a young man with much on your mind."

"You're not as dumb as you look, Hannahole. Just dumb enough to think you've got everyone here snookered."

"On the contrary, I consider my constituents to be the most intelligent in the country, which is the reason they return me to the halls of our great and majestic capital year after year."

If the families guffawed their approval at the congressman's retort, the patients did not.

"Let it go, boy," Quick Draw whispered under his breath. "Let it go."

"What about your constituent upstairs?"

Hanna's ochre-stained smile fell away.

"Upstairs?"

"You know who I mean, and you know why he's upstairs."

"I haven't the faintest idea of what you're babbling about."

"Where's the first place you go when you get here?"

"You're hallucinating, son."

"It ain't the wards, is it?" He cocked his chin at Dr. Barnes who was whispering to the congressman's aide. "It ain't to see your idjit you've got running this nuthouse."

The staff and patients and the patient's families all looked to the congressman as Oliver crossed the ward and leaned to his ear. Hanna smiled.

"Friends, you must forgive Sergeant Binder. He suffers as do all men who must wrestle with a guilty conscious."

"I ain't got no guilt to be wrestling with my conscious about."

"Ever since he ran out on what remained of his men after losing most of them in an ambush — an ambush he lead them into I might add — it has weighed on his conscious grievously. Most grievously. As well it should. It must be impossible for him to live with himself. I'm surprised he does. That he can. Maybe that's the reason he can't sleep at night."

Oliver again whispered into the congressman's ear.

"Ran like a scared jack rabbit, I understand. The only one to make it out of the jungle."

"You're a liar. That was all put to rest at the inquiry. We had us a squad a hundred yards back I was running to for help."

"Running?" Hanna smiled. "Did you say running, young man?"

"You sonofabitch. If there's any truth to what you're saying I wouldn't of been where I was when we got napalmed by our own goddamn planes."

Hanna shook his head. He turned his back on the soldier with a melted Tupperware face.

"Friends, please forgive this outburst. I know some of you aren't from around here. That you drove all night just to be with your sons. The ones who stood tall for their country. Stood fast."

Doctor Barnes took Randy by the elbow. "Come on, son. This isn't doing anyone any good."

"I didn't run. That's one of his goddamn Washington smoke screens. He knows who's upstairs, and he knows why."

"Come on, son. Let's go back down to your ward."

"He knows, goddamnit!"

"Come on, son."

Randy lowered his head, and when he spoke again his voice broke. "He knows."

"I know. Come on."

Randy allowed Doctor Barnes to lead him away, his emaciated and pale buttocks flashing between the split in his hospital shift.

"He knows," came Randy's cracking voice from the stairwell. "Goddamnit, he knows and you know he does."

Betsy walked to the doorway and looked down the hall toward the stairwell. When she looked back into the ward, Hanna stood chuckling within a semicircle of family

members, one father patting him on the shoulder. Matt rapped a pen on his notepad. He looked to Betsy.
*Bastard*, he mouthed.

# CHAPTER 21

They were sitting at the breakfast table the next morning when Bartholomew sneezed. Betsy looked up from Matt's *Journal* account of Hanna's visit to the hospital the day before.

"Are you coming down with something?"

"No."

"Yes, you are."

Bartholomew wiped his nose with a sleeve.

"It's from Sunday when you came home soaking wet from your baseball game."

"Maybe a cold is all."

"Then you better stay home."

"It's only a summer cold. I'll be okay."

"You may be okay, but if he catches it it'll kill him."

"I hate to lose the time, Sis. His tapping's weaker than it was even a week ago."

"All the more reason for you to stay away. If we're going to get him home, we need his story, and we can't get it with him dead."

"Yeah, yeah, yeah. Lay it on me, but you know who might know something more?"

"Who?"

"Randy Brindle."

"What makes you say that?"

"From what you said last night at supper. How long's he been out there? Two years maybe?"

"I already did speak to him."

"Well, try talking to him again."

"Good luck on finding him. I've seen him like twice, maybe three times out there and — "

"And what?"

"Once was yesterday. When Congressman Hanna came out."

* * *

Betsy parked where she always parked. Matt's Volkswagen would not be there this early, but before getting out she fumbled in her purse for her compact anyway and dabbed at her nose. When she went to flip the visor mirror back up, her hand froze.

"No," she whispered. "Please no."

Though the roof Randy Brindle squatted on was four stories up, there was no mistaking his napalmed face, his rotted-grape eyes sagging from their sockets. She lifted the door handle and inched sideways out of her seat. Randy gave her a little wave, grinning like a jack-o-lantern prankster.

"Hey there, Sweet Pea." He nodded at the Barracuda. "Heard you comin' up the drive. You've got 'er purring like a Siamese kitten. Nathan'd be right proud of you."

"Hey there yourself. What're you doing up there?"

"Takin' in God's good morning. Attending' to some business."

"Strange place to be saying your prayers."

"Wasn't saying 'em."

Betsy's mouth dried to ash. She glanced across the parking lot into the overgrown cemetery. No one. The sun lay long across a meadow beyond the cemetery that rolled and dipped into pockets of darkness. Dew on the grass, resplendent as angel spit, glittered. In the upper limbs of a half-barren tree at the far edge of the meadow a perched crow silhouetted against the sunrise watched them.

"I've a few minutes before I've got to clock in. Why don't you come take me for a walk around the pond. There's some new-born ducklings we need to get named."

"'Fraid not, Sweet Pea." He stood. "I've other plans to attend to this morning."

"Randy, you come down from there right now!"

He kicked off his laceless sneakers, sailing them over the roof, his thin hospital shift parting to expose his wasted buttocks, hips of Christ, so pale and white.

"Bet you didn't know I was captain of the diving team?"

"Sure I did. You were our star. Our hero."

He arched up on his toes.

"Randy, please come down. We'll get some apple pancakes in the cafeteria. My treat."

"Made it all the way to the state semis."

He bent his knees as he swung back his arms.

"One last time to get it right. One last time."

*Randy — !*

But his body already sliced the early-morning air, his legs straight, toes pointed, arms extended from his sides in a dive so perfect he would have easily made it to the state finals, falling to earth like a returning Christ-on-the-cross, his destroyed face with which he looked upon a destroyed world pushed out before him, smiling.

\* \* \*

Betsy screamed without sound into her cupped hands. Seeing and not wanting to see and never not to see. Filbert burst through a side door out into the parking lot, yelling back inside.

*Get one of those worthless sonsofbitchin' doctors off his goddamn ass and get 'im out here!*

She crossed to the iron-wrought fence that bordered the cemetery where she could not see and sat in the uncut grass, her knees pulled to her chest and staring across the gravel parking lot. The hospital had no emergency room and it took some minutes before Sealy's Ambulance Service, siren screaming and lights flashing, bumped up the rutted drive. Nathan's watch ticked against her heart. In a minute the flash of the ambulance lights ceased. Nurse Baker stepped from around the corner and sat beside her. She wrapped an arm around Betsy's shoulders.

"You hanging in there, sweetie?"

The ambulance appeared from behind the hospital and started down the hospital drive, taking its time now to avoid the deep ruts. Betsy stared after it, her eyes caged, looking at nothing, her face slipping off the face of the world and off of it onto still another. Nurse Baker fingered a strand of chestnut hair from Betsy's forehead and kissed her on the temple.

"How are my patients doing?"

"We heard someone screaming. Was it you?"

"I don't remember."

"Then Filbert shouting. We all ran to the windows. I came down as soon as I saw. When I looked back up, no one was there."

"Didn't they come down?"

"No, sweetie. They went back to their poker game or whatever it was they were doing."

"I thought they liked Randy. That they understood."

"They do understand. As did Randy, but that's how they've learned to deal with the death. They ignore it. They tell themselves death means as little to them as life. They have a saying. It don't mean nothin'."

"I've heard it. I've even heard you say it. I'm not certain I understand."

"It means life means nothing. It means death is a part of life, in the end resolving nothing. It's the way they keep themselves off the roof."

"That's me. Climbing up that ladder to the roof, one day, one rung, at a time."

Nurse Baker took Betsy's shoulders in both hands and shook her.

"Don't you dare crawl inside there on me, Betsy. Do you hear me? Don't you dare. It's too easy to trap yourself inside your heart. So easy. So hard to fight your way out again. I know. Every day I fight to get out. I want to feel, to feel something, anything, and I can't, not the way I did once. Don't let it happen to you. You can't. Not to Betsy."

Betsy said nothing. A hay-scented summer breeze blew. The church bell at Saint Paul's tolled in from the village.

"I need to go. Someone should call Mrs. Brindle."

After she left, Betsy lay in the grass, their leaves scissoring at her ears. Death is nothing. Bequeath yourself to us. Death is nothing.

# CHAPTER 22

When Henry returned to the offices of the *Hanna Morning Journal,* he spotted through its plate-glass window the congressman sitting behind his editor's desk as he cored an apple with a watch-chain knife.

"Not today, goddamnit." He took a step back on the sidewalk. "Of all days not today."

Hanna smiled, shaking his head, and with the knife waved him in.

"Damn."

The brass bell jingled when Henry pushed open the pebbled-glass door but Hanna continued to core his apple without looking up. He lowered himself into the chair before his own desk, and it took a minute before he hazarded to address Hanna.

"Didn't I hear you say you were heading back to Washington this afternoon?"

"You did unless you've turned stone-cold deaf. Was until I walked out on my front porch this morning for my paper and heard the siren. Dead reckoned its direction."

"You know about the Brindle boy then."

Hanna flipped an apple peel at the wastebasket, missed, and continued to core his apple.

"Doc Barnes was croaking about it in my ear before Brindle made his first dead-cat bounce."

"Sorry piece of business for the village to have to go through again. What with Nathan getting boxed home not six months ago."

The pungent odor of melted lead steamed up through the floorboards as an ancient Rheingold typesetter began to clank in the basement.

"I was just out at the boy's house to get the story for his obituary."

Hanna stopped coring his apple. He looked up, his eyes narrowed.

"We'll run it in tomorrow's edition. Don't think his mama said two words to me the entire time I was out there. Not much of a place. A tar-papered shack really. Just stared at a photograph setting beside the radio of him in uniform before his face got burned off. What facts I got came from his kid sister, but I've enough to give him a real nice write up. Something that'll help the family muddle through this mess. Like what McLain did for Nathan. I didn't know him much. Forgot he was on the basketball and diving teams. Seems like he was a real nice boy. A boy we'll all miss."

"Not quite all." Hanna fixed Henry with his kerosened-coal eyes. "We're not running any goddamn obit for a stinking coward who couldn't face himself in the mirror."

"Sir?"

"Nor do I want to see any stories in my paper about Brindle dishing himself up as cat pizza."

"But Carl's typesetting tomorrow's edition right now. We just have to add the obit."

"Well, have Carl unset it right now without the obit. Write something up about the awards I handed out there yesterday."

"We did that in this morning's edition."

"Yes, but your piece wasn't nearly long enough. Have you forgotten I've an election to win in November? Get McLain to write up a human interest story about one of the other boys out there. One who the village can be proud of."

Henry sat open mouthed.

"I believe you really have gone stone-cold deaf on me."

Henry stared for several moments at Hanna, but finally took the steps down into the basement. The clickety-clack of typesetter gears clanked silent. A diminutive man dressed in grease-stained overhauls and cleaning his hands on an oily rag came up the stairs followed by Henry. Hanna ate his apple as he read the paper, the heels of his spit-shine wingtips propped on an editorial Henry had been writing before he left for the Brindle house. Henry put a hand on his printer's shoulder.

"Why don't you go on home, Karl. Have the missus give you dinner. I'll call you in about an hour once I have the replacement piece written."

"Yessir."

Henry returned to the chair before his desk.

"So why kill the story, Mr. Hanna? Folks in the village already know about Randy's leaping off the hospital roof."

"Because they'll have forgotten about Brindle taking a flying fucking leap by tomorrow unless we go reminding them of it all over again. Because this is an election year, and we don't need to be feeding fodder to Thomson for him to be asking fool questions about the goings on out at my hospital. So just kill it and stop asking me your ignoramus questions."

"But . . ."

Hanna pointed the watch-chain knife at his editor's throat. "Just kill it."

"Yes, sir. If you say so."

"I do say so."

Hanna stood.

"I need to be stopping by the Legion and VFW posts to speak to their commanders. There won't be any marching an honor detail up Cemetery Hill tomorrow. No sense risking one of those over-aged and over-weight boy scouts keeling over in this heat from a heart attack for a stinking coward."

"Don't you think that's . . ."

Hanna's lips curled at their edges. Then he smiled. He appraised his editor up and down. "That's a dapper suit you're decked out in today, Henry."

"Yes, sir. I wanted to wear something respectable for when I called on — for when I went out. This is the best suit

I've got hanging in my closet. You gave it to me five years ago after you almost threw it out."

"I'm glad you remembered who gave it to you."

"Yes, sir. I do. I'm grateful."

"You just keep on being grateful."

Henry nodded.

"Good day, Henry. Run my paper down this evening. I'm leaving early for Washington, and it'll give me something to read on the plane."

"Yes, sir. I will. Good day."

Hanna stood on the curb outside the plate-glass window with thumbs hooked in his vest pockets as might a turn-of-the-century robber baron appraising his company town. He inclined his head each time a passing driver lifted a hand from his steering wheel. When he had seen what he wanted, or perhaps only allowed himself to be seen, he started down the sidewalk, his slender umbral self trailing behind. Henry walked to the plate-glass window that ran the length of the newspaper office.

"You son of a bitch. You son of a whoring bitch."

\* \* \*

Betsy entered the third-floor restroom at a little past noon where she changed into the navy blue dress she wore to her brother's funeral. She left the hospital and crossed its gravel parking lot to where she had parked far away from where Randy had jumped. When she turned her key, the engine failed to turn over.

"Not today. Please not today."

She tried again. The engine did not so much as click. She slumped back in the seat. "Why today?"

"Sounds like you've got yourself one dead battery." Matt stood thumbing his chin behind her. "You off to the funeral?"

"Was."

"Lucky I've got my jumper cables."

He pulled his Volkswagen up adjacent and hooked his cables to the four battery terminals and got back in and revved his engine. "Try it now," he shouted.

Nothing.

"Why can't you start it?"

"Damn."

He climbed out and rechecked his cables.

"We've got a good connection."

"Well, can you fix it or not?"

He walked around to her window.

"When an engine won't turn over and when you can't jump start it, a fair guess is your alternator's gone kaput. Did you notice a light flashing on your dash?"

"I meant to ask my dad last night. Why today, God?"

"What time's the funeral?"

"One-thirty."

Matt checked his watch.

"Come on. We can still make it."

\* \* \*

Randy had been a village boy with local people, and village opinion and gossip notwithstanding his mother would not consent to his being buried in the overgrown graveyard behind the hospital among the orphans and nameless ones. Yet Betsy and Matt had to search for the mourners up one footpath of Cemetery Hill and down another, past rectangular granite tombstones of recent years and limestone tablets that dated back to the founding of the village weathered almost smooth before Matt spotted the tops of five heads in a remote corner. Circling about the open earth other than the Unitarian minister found by Father Kaplan, stood only Randy's mother, Darlene, Nurse Baker, and Father Kaplan who gestured to them.

"Are we these the only ones attending?"

"I'm afraid we are, Betsy."

Nurse Baker stood on the other side of the open grave beside the mound of darkening earth with her veiled face bowed. The minister in front of her flipped through the pages of his Protestant Bible as though he had yet to find his text. Next to him on a retractable gurney rested a government-issued aluminum casket with a talon-grasping eagle embossed on its lid. Betsy mouthed *I'm sorry* across to Darlene. The girl nodded, gripping her mother's arm a little tighter.

The minister glanced at his watch and turned to Mrs. Brindle. "Do you want me to wait a little longer, Dorothy?"

The stout woman neither answered nor raised her eyes out of the hole that gaped before her. He looked at Darlene who leaned to her mother's ear. "Mama?"

Mrs. Brindle shook her head.

The minister rushed his words, snapping the scriptures closed at the end of the seven-minute service and slid them under his underarm-stained coat. He looked at his watch once more before he and Darlene led Mrs. Brindle down the grassy knoll to a dusty limousine where the head of its driver bounced from side to side as a caterwauling Mick Jagger whined on about his dearth of satisfaction. No sooner had the minister closed the door than the limousine tires screeched, the back of the car falling with a thud as it passed over a speed bump. A grinning cemetery worker standing by the garage shook his head after it. He flicked a cigarette into the ankle-high grass he could not be troubled to mow the day before and climbed aboard a backhoe. Father Kaplan laid a hand on Betsy's shoulder.

"I've not visited Nathan's since December. Will you walk with me?"

"Thank you. That would make it easier."

She looked across the grave.

"I think Amy requires this time to be alone with her thoughts."

The three started down the rise, but halfway Betsy stopped and looked back.

"I thought there would be more people."

"Like at Nathan's?"

"It seemed as if all of Hanna was here. It doesn't seem fair. The war killed Randy too, didn't it?"

"Indeed."

Father Kaplan stooped when they reached the mud-splattered gravestone and pulled a handkerchief from his trouser pocket.

> BORN JANUARY 28, 1949
> DIED DECEMBER 13, 1973
> Failing to fetch me at first keep encouraged,
> Missing me one place search another,
> I stop somewhere waiting for you.

It was a minute before Betsy found her voice. "Why did he, Father?"

"Randy learned all too well the most heartbreaking lesson life has to teach us. That you cannot resurrect those you love more than life itself. The ones Randy left behind haunted him. Then you heard about him and the girl he was engaged to. The one with whom he hoped he could begin anew. I can't blame her. How many of us at her age have within us that kind of strength? I'm not certain I do now."

"He and Nate played basketball together."

"Randy was Mr. Popularity. Often I heard the girls giggle about his eyes as they walked the halls between classes. Dark as violets, like deep water, but shiny. A smile that dazzled. The kind that told you he was a young man bound to go far in life."

The cemetery worker had brought his backhoe down the hill and began to dig nearby, the black smoke belching. Father Kaplan shook his head.

"It'll be years before they'll bury anyone near him. By then the villagers will have forgotten how he died. Forgotten that he never truly came home."

The breeze blowing down the knoll smelled of turned earth.

"I need to be looking in on the Brindles. It was a pleasure seeing you again, son."

"Mine too."

"Have Betsy drag you to Mass some time."

"I will."

The priest, however, did not leave, but stood clutching and unclutching his trouser leg. "My failure to bring Randy home will be keeping me awake for some nights to come."

"You're too hard on yourself, Father."

"I am — all of us are — charged with being our brother's keeper. Yet it is the vainest, most heartbreaking of the Commandments imposed upon us." He smiled. His face reddened. "I guess I've been giving you my confession. Good afternoon, children."

"Father."

The two watched as he walked down the hill, the sun behind him, God's shadow on earth. Matt started for where they had parked.

"Come on, we need to be getting back."

Betsy looked once more up the rise to where Nurse Baker still stood beside the grave.

"Coming?"

The two walked toward where they had parked, their hands so close they almost touched.

"I am getting him home."

Matt nodded. She stepped out of her shoes and ran through the grass the rest of the way down the hill like the little girl she had once been.

* * *

Bartholomew drove out to the hospital with her the following Monday.

"The geezer wasn't making much in the way of what I could call progress when we left him. Hadn't told us his name. Not even where he's from."

"He's mentioned Cleveland. Pittsburgh. I'll bet you anything he's from close by here. He could be from one of these farms along this very road."

"Yeah, he could be. Could also be within a hundred miles close by. Maybe two hundred."

"I don't think so."

"He left us off in France. Somewhere. We don't know where exactly, and it's winter. A hundred years ago. Where's that leave us?"

Sister and brother drove on, the radio off.

"Ask him what he remembers from after their friend died."

"Why?"

"He's already told us a lot without meaning to. The more he tells us the better chance is he will let something else slip."

## CHAPTER 23

They endured no skirmishes that winter of 1915. Boredom proved a more imminent enemy, so he undertook to teach Stanton telegraphy. With little else to occupy their time, Stanton picked up the basics in days. On nights when they stood guard duty at opposite ends of their trench sector, they telegraphed back and forth with spoons their life stories and jokes and tales of promiscuous women known to them only by rumor. Anything to stay awake so they would not be shot for sleeping while on guard duty, anything to take their minds off the frost-biting cold.

The troops speculated all winter long about how soon their generals would order them over the top, but after the man-swallowing bogs of mud dried it was the Germans who came over first on a fine morning on the fifteenth of May, a wine-red sunrise at their backs bleeding out across a gray and Godless sky. As wave upon wave of Germans approached, his sergeant ran along the trench behind them ordering his boys to hold their fire, and he watched from his peephole as the spike-helmeted soldiers crossed, bent low and trotting, more and more of them dropping as their mile-long waves drew closer. He remembered from home the line of Amish hay-reapers who worked farm to farm, the great sweep of their scythes swishing back and forth as the men mowed, cutting six-foot-wide swaths, the reapers spread across a field and the blade of none ever nicking the shoulder of another, but at the end of the day he had to look hard to find even a single hay reed standing. Three days later at dusk the Germans took their turn to scythe the Canadians.

To cross No Man's Land was a nightmare from which there was no waking, a madhouse without doors and one exit. They ran toward blazing rifles and withering machinegun fire while artillery shells sang down all around in a wailing death fugue from the heights above the Aisne Valley, past fallen soldiers who pleaded for his help as they reached out with half arms, some calling out to him by name. Soldiers lying in pools of blood, their neck-cleaved heads looking back with disbelieving eyes at lives that once had been but a moment before. A mule that stumbled ahead of its wagon with oozing intestines trailing through the mud behind it like some feeding snake conjured up out of Teutonic myth. Everywhere he saw faces screwed up and writhed in dead belly laughter and upon their retreat finding in the trenches huddled men expended of the last of their courage. Some driven mad and crying. Others shouting, swearing, and even laughing like the lunatics they now were at the great God-joke just played upon them. At stand-to the next morning half the faces he'd seen the day before lay in the mud behind them, and the Canadian had not made it to within a hundred yards of the German trenches.

That afternoon the lieutenant rewarded them for the failed crossing with their first bath since his arrival, and he laughed when he pictured his mother's scowl if she knew how long it had been. They marched two miles behind the lines where they turned in their uniforms to fat-armed peasant women. Much bellyaching accompanied their undressing because hair had grown through their underwear sometimes causing cloth and skin to peel away like thinly sliced bacon. Cahill poked his finger at a long, hairy strip from his crotch and asked him and Stanton if they did not suppose there to be at least one nut in there somewhere.

The peasant woman had bucket filled a half dozen wooden tubs once used by their village to foot press grapes before artillery fire ravaged their vineyards and large enough to hold ten or more soldiers. In them they soaked so long their skin wrinkled like octogenarians, and they refused to exit until their lieutenant ordered them out. They sat around in their new underwear, laughing and smoking as they waited for the return of their uniforms. The lieutenant — they no longer bothered to remember their names since they had lost four during the winter and spring to sharpshooters — carried in a case of dusty wine bottles, and they drank in long, brain-anesthetizing swallows. By the time they received back their uniforms, he and Stanton could barely stand to dress let alone walk any distance, and they curled up on a mound of mice infested hay where they slept until dark, throwing up on their freshly laundered uniforms only a little.

Stanton woke first and shook him awake. After they rinsed out their mouths at the water pump in front of the barn, the two walked into the village. They found a bistro and sat outside where they drank coffee and smiled at the arm-in-arm girls who strolled by eying the Canadian soldiers rumored to carry silk stockings in their pockets they would exchange in return for a favor. He and Stanton in truth each carried in their pockets two condoms and a packet of stationery the lieutenant had passed out, and when all the girls had gone home they sat writing letters to their families.

He told them where he was and how he'd gotten there. He asked how the planting went that spring and wondered if the prices they got had gone up. He did not say he was sorry. In the envelope he folded a twenty-franc note. They gave him no real money. They didn't even give him any Canadian money, only this funny looking French stuff, but he asked her if she would buy him as many pairs of wool socks as she could and send them so they came before winter. Frostbitten toes, while painful, were not sufficiently debilitating for an honorable discharge, just the firing squad if thought to be intentional. He gave her his *nom de guerre* she should use if she wrote back.

He and Stanton wandered about the village after they finished their letters. On a side street they came upon a half-dozen French officers whom stood sipping glasses of wine as they waited their turn in front of a house set aside by the army for their entertainment. A girl younger than they sat laughing inside the front window on an officer's lap. She wore only her underwear, which was the same color of red as the girl's fire-hydrant hair that flamed out from under the officer's *kepi* turned backwards on her head. One of the officers standing out front turned away from his conversation. He studied the uniforms of the two boys gaping into the window from across the street before he shook his head, waving an index finger. Calling them lads, he informed them that the entertainment for the enlisted men was three blocks down, two over.

The girls set aside for the troops seemed to them not so pretty and not so young as the one they saw in the window even after their second glass of wine. As he worked on enhancing their comeliness with a third glass, he heard behind him a laugh sounding so much like a girl he knew from home that he almost dropped it, his stomach a hundred bits of knotted string loosed from their kite. What was she was doing in France? Especially what was she doing here in France? The woman smiled at him with plum painted eyes, and when she tossed her head her shiny crow-black hair flowed about her shoulders. She frowned a pout and asked him to buy her a glass of champagne. Though she had a laugh reminding him of the girl from home, she looked nothing like her, but she was very sweet to him all the same. She had picked up some English in her profession, and he remembered some French the sisters had taught him. He liked her. Liked it when she laughed and whispered ooo-la-la to him in the dark, and he liked lying beneath her, her dark hair whisking his chest, and he liked listening before he fell asleep to the going-coming-humming-heel-clatter up and down the stairs of chattering women.

The bloody summer passed. To hang on to what remained of their sanity, he and Stanton adopted a dozen ragamuffins. They took them gifts of Hershey kisses or

Spearmint gum on their trips into the village. When an Army photographer passed through, they bribed him into taking pictures of them alongside the ragamuffins and then making duplicates they handed out to the children. Stanton even sent one to his parents, who since had sold their land and bought a Nebraska hog operation after they wagered the prices of Ohio hill-farms had nowhere to go but down after the war. He considered sending one to his parents as well but never did.

The winter rains did not blow in off the North Atlantic until the week before Christmas, and those on both sides of No Man's Land sent up prayers of thanksgiving when fall they did, a respite however brief from their crazed generals. He agreed with Stanton who claimed it was the best Christmas present he ever had or ever would. They thought their second best would be a delousing and bath followed by a night of monetary romance. When they got to the barn holding the grape press tub, however, their lieutenant told them that some sentimental French bureaucrat, undoubtedly married, had closed the houses for the holidays in order to give the girls a chance to return to the countryside to visit with their families. So following their bath he and Stanton walked into the village and ate. Each bought two bottles of too recently bottled Chianti, which they drank as they sat at a sidewalk bench. On a dare from Stanton, each chugged their second before they set out, stumbling up one street and down another. Near the village outskirts they retched up their dinners, which a contingent of wasted war mongrels trotting behind them lapped up with relish, and the two staggered into an alley.

When he woke he lay for a long time watching his gray breath plume and dissipate in the moonlight. A slobber-mouthed one-legged dog hobbled into the alley and began to lick his lips. He rolled over onto his stomach, pushing himself up, and leaned against an alley wall. The cathedral bell tolled one o'clock. He looked up and down the alley.

No Stanton. He walked out to the street empty save for a white cat, her milk-swollen teats almost touching the cobblestones, and her belly low and heavy with the kittens she would deliver before dawn. When he whispered to her, she arched her back and hissed back at him before waddling to the other side of the street where she disappeared into the shadows.

The other end of the alley led to a sheep-cropped pasture and across the pasture stood a cherry orchard with black fruit rotting in limbs long unpruned. He followed a frozen mud path through the trees for half-a-mile until he came to a log lying along a rutted road. He sat and smoked while he watched to see if Stanton might stumble along. He held his breath as he listened for the sound of vomiting but heard nothing but the emptiness of a winter's night, the quiet thumping of his heart. Odd he could not hear the war. He might have dozed. After a while he heard from far up the road the plaintive singing of women's voices. They might have recently lost a loved one because their song sounded reminiscent of the Gaelic dirges his mother sang as she went about her labors, though it must have been in some dialect for it did not sound French. Three gray-haired hags, one completely bald on the left side of her head like a half dead tree, rounded the bend, the three walking abreast, and when they strolled opposite him all three pointed and cackled as at a carnival spectacle. They turned in unison and continued on with the dirge, their serpentine arms laced behind one another as they disappeared into the misty dark. He told himself in the nights to follow the three hags were but an ill dream of women brought on by too much cheap wine on a cold night. Sometimes, though, when he woke in the pitch black of the dugout, his heart slamming against his ribcage like some incubus trying to quit him, he was not so certain, not so certain. When he returned to the alley he found a sleeping Stanton. He lay on the stone pavement, drawing his great coat around him, and after a while he drifted asleep but not before the cathedral bell tolled one o'clock for a second time that night.

His mother's box of three pairs of hand-knitted socks awaited him upon his return. He unwrapped the butcher-paper package as he sat at a table with Stanton and Cahill inside an earthen dugout that stunk of sweat and urine, their gray faces hanging like shrouds in the dim light cast by the coal-oil lantern. Pinned to the outside of one sock was a letter written in pencil on a page torn from one of his school tablets. He wondered at first whom it was from for it was not his mother's calligraphic script that sang across paper like notes dance on hymnal pages but in the spidery handwriting of an old woman. An old and broken woman.

She prayed he remained well and whole. They were getting by. The spring planting had been difficult, their harvest more so. With corn prices doubled from the year before, his father as well as every other farmer in the county planted every inch of soil he guessed might germinate a seed. Fencepost to fencepost. Mark's family had carted down from Youngstown a dozen new-landed Hungarian immigrants to lay over five thousand feet of clay tiles in order to drain the two hundred acres of swamp bottomland below theirs where he once trapped muskrats in winter and they intended to sow come spring. Their harvest had not gone bad until the night his father stayed out too late, working by lantern light. When the kitchen clock struck ten o'clock and he still not in, she took their one other lantern and went out searching.

With so many acres under till, there were no spare hands to be had without upfront cash. Farmers who prided themselves on never working their womenfolk as common field laborers now did so. They claimed in the village that classes seemed more like girls' finishing schools because the farmers with cash in hand paid a dollar a day to every strong back, his, and near the end of the harvest even her if she were big boned, age notwithstanding. His father had to bring in the harvest alone.

He had unhitched the mules to let them blow while he loaded corn shucks into the wagon. For the prior two weeks he had worked from sunup until well into the evening. Some days when he came in for his dinner at noon he fell asleep in his chair. Before he unhitched Molly and Martha, most likely he'd not set the brake, and the wagon rolled over him as he worked with his back to it, crushing three ribs, one of which punctured a lung. When she found him, he lay face down in the dirt. Blood bubbled out of his mouth. He was a big man, and she lacked the strength to lift him into the wagon. She caught up Martha and fastened the harness under his shoulders and dragged him across the rocky field to the barn, cutting the back of his head only a little.

She forked hay down from the loft and rolled him over onto the mound. She considered riding to a neighbor's for help, but twice when he came to he was delirious, talking crazy, and she feared if he woke while she was gone he might stumble down the steps into the barn cellar. She wrapped him in feedbags, giving him her warmth in the frosted autumn night until first light when Isaac Rohrer saw Molly trampling their harvest. She brought in the rest with help from Isaac and some children Father Michael drove out from town. His father still lay in bed. Their luck had not been all bad. With the higher prices, they managed to almost break even. Managed to keep their farm out of the hands of the goddamn bank owned by Mark's family for one more year. One more year to see if come home to them he would.

When he finished his mother's letter, he took his billfold from his pack and except for a five-franc bill mailed all of his money to her. He wrote that if she sent it to a bank in Cleveland they might exchange it for American. He would see the company purser when he next came around about sending her an allotment of his paycheck.

Still, so fierce went the fighting come spring he considered his father and mother lucky. Considered himself and Stanton luckier. Save for the two of them and Cahill, every member of their company with whom they had shared their first bath was dead or gone, as was every member with whom they shared their second a month later, and there were not all that many remaining from their third.

He looked forward to the baths. He and Stanton afterwards returned to the house with the entertainment for the enlisted men. The woman with the laugh like the girl from home, though, had gone away. The matron seemed to have no clear idea of where she might be, but Cahill told him that likely she didn't want another homesick boy falling in love with one of her working girls. When he woke early one morning in April, the rose-lipped woman beside him still slept. He began to dress, first pulling on his hand-knitted socks. Where had his mother found the time? He put his feet on the floor and looked down at them. When he lowered his face to his hands, the woman half opened her eyes before rolling over on her side and turning her back to him. They almost always wept before they left her bed.

## CHAPTER 24

The patient's head slumped toward them, the hollow eye sockets not looking yet somehow looking. Longing to look. Bartholomew shook his head.

"One second he's with us, the next he's gone."

"We've been here for better than an hour." Betsy massaged her right hand. "The speed of his Morsing. I don't think I'll ever get my fingers uncramped."

"Still don't know his name."

"Not yet but we definitely know he's from Ohio. Know he had to have been transferred to a hospital near his home. There aren't that many Ohio hospitals they could transfer him to now let alone back then. There's a good chance his chart's across the hall."

"So what do you want to do?"

"Get your dufus butt out of that chair and let's get to work."

\* \* \*

They read in the attic until an hour past her shift when Bartholomew tossed a chart on the pile before him. "I'm going blind, Sis. There's not enough light anymore to read by."

Betsy flipped a page.

"We can't make up for time lost last week in one lousy day."

"We can try."

"We can also miss something trying."

Betsy read on.

"Something important. Like this guy's name."

"Yeah, yeah, yeah." She lowered the chart she held and looked across to her brother. "How do you feel about maybe coming in an hour early tomorrow?"

Bartholomew stood, swiping with his hand the back of his shorts. "Let's just blow this pop stand, can we?"

\* \* \*

He was singing along to the Beach Boys' *Barbara Ann* on their way home when Betsy reached from the steering wheel and turned off the radio. Bartholomew stopped bongo drumming his knees in the middle of his rendition of *Ba-Ba-Ba*.

"Hey!"

"Hey yourself. Know what I think."

"Haven't a clue and turn my song back on, will you?"

"I'll buy you the record."

"You told me last night you didn't have any money."

"Not so you can neck with your girlfriend in the back of the movies."

"Lucy's not my girlfriend. She's just uninhibited."

"You want to hear what I think?"

"The song's over by now so you might as well."

"The reason he ran away is because that girl from home he mentioned with the laugh like his French girl broke his heart. That's what I think."

"You're just boy crazy like the rest of your goofy girly friends."

"Why then, all of a sudden and right before Thanksgiving, did he decide to run off?"

Bartholomew looked out his window. A mile off on the other side of a just-cropped hayfield to the east the tar-brown crosses of telephone poles ran along a road parallel to theirs.

"Don't you suppose that's the reason he ran away?"

"You mean like Sarah broke Nate's?"

"No, I didn't mean . . ."

"The bastard got what was coming to him if he did."

"Barto!"

"Ran off so he could get a uniform and come home a hero to win her back after shooting somebody's brother who never did nothin' to nobody."

"You don't know . . ." but Betsy's defense whispered off.

The two drove on. Neither spoke. When they pulled into the driveway, both got out. Betsy walked up to the garage and opened the door, but Bartholomew was not behind her.

"Oh, for the love of Pat and Mike."

She walked down the driveway to the sidewalk. Bartholomew was almost to the cross street, his head lowered, the psychedelic sunglasses raised above his brow, his shoulders rising and falling beneath a two-sizes-too-large shirt that had been his brother's favorite.

"Barto!"

He started to run, disappearing into a neighbor's backyard.

"Damn."

She got back in the Barracuda. Maybe he was right about the patient, maybe he wasn't, but she needed to find her brother and bring him home.

\* \* \*

She stopped to the turn into the park and waited for the light to change. What sounded at first like shouts originating from a baseball game turned out to be coming up ahead from a car full of teenage boys catcalling to a stout woman seated on the cemetery steps. The woman did not so much as flinch when a beer bottle arcing out of a car window shattered at her feet, the car driving off and veering back and forth over the center divider.

"Snotnosed assholes."

Betsy switched off her turn signal and drove up another block where she parked on a side street and walked up the sidewalk along a brick wall to where the woman sat. Glass crunched beneath her shoes. "Are you all right, Mrs. Brindle?"

The woman stared out at the park across the street with depthless eyes the color of lead.

"Have you been . . ." The rusted hinges of the cemetery gate creaked. "Are you going home now?"

Mrs. Brindle wiped her nose with the elbow of a yellow housedress washed so thin her Goodwill undergarments showed beneath.

"Or if you're going inside, I'll walk with you."

She shook her head, and when she spoke it was in a thick Ozark voice as corrupted by grief as a Negro spiritual.

"My boy's done tired of walking."

"Ma'am?"

"That's all he done out there."

"What was it he did?"

"Walked. Oh, maybe he'd lie down awhile, but he never slept. Sometimes I'd go out and be settin' in a chair next to him so he would, he all the while watching the winder, the door, then the winder again. Them nights I weren't settin' in his room Nurse Baker tale me he'd be up all night walking about the hospital. Checking his perimeter he called it."

Betsy sat on the step.

"He'd walk the sun up. Sleep for an hour, never more. Then he'd be up and walking them woods round the hospital until nightfall. Walking. Always walking."

"He was very nice to me."

"Last time I be out there he said he didn't have all that long left. Said some of them boys in his unit had taken to visitin' him at night. Standing at the side of his bed with the blood just a flowing out their noses and mouths. Seeping from their eyes if they had 'em."

She wiped at the knee prints muddying her dress.

"A few days before he . . . he said they'd been calling him from the graveyard they got out there. Telling him 'come on, Sarge, time for you to be crossing on over Jordan too. You've done paid your dues.'"

She leaned and spat. "My son never done nothing to pay nobody no dues for. Not nothing, and I don't care how them papers write it up."

"He was a good person. A sweet boy."

"Then he said there be something funny going on out there. Said he wanted to fix it up if God'd give him the time but wouldn't tell me what it was."

They sat. A flaxen moon rose into the bruise colored sky before them.

"Never did come home. Not for so much as a hour. A minute even."

Betsy wrapped her arm around the mother's shoulders. "Maybe he's home now."

Her face clouded. She looked at Betsy.

"Really? You think so, honey? Really?"

"I'm sure of it."

Mrs. Brindle grasped the iron-pipe railing and pulled herself up. "Well, he'll be hungry then."

"Ma'am?"

"My boy's a big eater. Always has been. Why, I've seen him tuck away four burgers in as many minutes alongside a plate of fries and a quart of milk."

"Mrs. Brindle, I . . .", but she had already set off down the sidewalk and was soon swallowed up within the falling night.

Teenage summer traffic passed up and down Park Avenue: Brief bars of rock-and-roll blared from car radios. Kids sang off-key lyrics and laughed. Girls sat beside their summertime boyfriends, wind from rolled-down windows whipping their hair they all wore shoulder-length now.

The courthouse clock struck nine. Betsy looked at the open cemetery gate, the slender tombstones just inside clawing from the earth.

"What was it, Randy? What was it you were going to fix?"

\* \* \*

She drove past the sign that announced she was entering Mark Hanna Park. By the light of a streetlamp she spotted Bartholomew's friend from the parish hitting flies into the dark of the outfield. She got out and asked Robbie if he'd seen him, but he said he had not since the Sunday before.

"On what world has he been hanging out on this summer?"

Behind the closed door to Bartholomew's room she heard the singsong voice of a woman who sounded like maybe she could be Chinese, and Betsy continued on down to her room. She pulled on one of her summer nighties and sat in the rocker by her window. From a bed table drawer she took out a collection of Wilfred Owens' war poems she had checked out from the library the weekend before, and she read for an hour before laying the book on her lap.

Her closet door she'd left open, and on the top shelf was the Christmas card box where she kept her Kodaks. She got the box down and carried it to her bed and began to shuffle through them. One of her and Billy Hufnagel when she had asked him to the Sadie Hawkins dance two Februaries before. She smiled as Billy's face grimaced back at her with the teenage-boy-terror of girls leaking from his eyes, Betsy's orchid corsage only beginning to wilt at its edges. Another of her and the Gang on a slumber party in Sandy's basement, a two-sizes-too-big fedora slouched over Betsy's forehead and she bogarting an unlit cigarette out of the side of her mouth. A picture of Nathan standing with his squad, their faces painted for war with eyes looking out at her bearing a wary and haunted cast.

The television set in the family room fell silent followed by her father's step on the stairs and the metal click of the door to their room. She returned the Christmas card box to its shelve and crawled under the single bed sheet. A sweet and irrefragable moonlight fell through the window, resting upon her the way a kitten in search of comfort would curl up on her tummy, and she fell asleep to the hush of Dutch elms and sugar maples outside her window, that Ohio susurrus of late summer.

\* \* \*

Bartholomew came into the kitchen the next morning as she stood at the sink washing off her breakfast dishes.

"So you quitting on me?"

"Let's see how it goes today." Outside the kitchen window the leaves of the sugar maples had started to yellow along their veins. "Summer's about butt-shot anyway."

"I heard a woman on your radio last night. She sounded oriental."

"Vietnamese."

"They have hams over there?"

"Only a couple. Guess it's a good way to get shot."

"What'd you talk about?"

"Stuff." He took an unopened quart of milk from the refrigerator, dropping it in the wastebasket after he emptied the carton. "Let's go."

"You drank *all* of it!"

"I wasn't all that hungry when I got home last night."

\* \* \*

When they were halfway up the hospital drive, Bartholomew leaned forward. "Stop!"

Betsy hit the brakes.

"What is it?"

He pointed to where Matt McLain sat next to Stud on the duck pond bench with his notepad resting on a knee.

"Do you think he's doing a story about Randy?"

"That was last week's news."

"You think he suspects something about our geezer?"

"I know he does, and if he fits all the pieces together, Hanna will ship him to where we'll never get him home."

"Would they even run the story?"

"Somebody might. Matt told me he wants off the *Journal* in the worst way."

"So what do you want to do?"

She raised her foot from the clutch.

"That woman I was talking to last night."

"Yeah?"

"Her son's in the Army. Says it's been three years since she's heard from him."

Betsy sat tapping her key fob after they parked. She looked at her brother. "We'd better find out where he belongs."

# CHAPTER 25

When McLain returned from the hospital, he sat swiveling in his office chair flipping back and forth through the pages of his notes taken that morning during his duck pond reconnaissance dressed in what he considered his reporter's uniform: Hiking boots never once hiked in and tatty jeans into which he had tucked a faded chambray shirt with a midnight blue knitted tie left loose at the neck. With his wire-framed glasses he possessed the sartorial air of a teaching assistant, which he had in fact been before he took a year's sabbatical to gain some real-world experience in journalism. He read with the vacuum-tube radio tuned low to WKBN in order to catch the staticky news reports at the top of the hour. The ceiling fan above him churned the humid-heavy air but provided little by way of relief, and the yoke of the back of his shirt darkened as the day advanced.

A car horn honked. Then another. He looked up. A line of vehicles headed by the Hearse from Warrick's Funeral Home jammed Court Street. Congressman Hanna cut across the traffic from the other side, walking between the Hearse and a limousine filled with mourners behind it. He stepped up to the plate-glass window that ran the length of the paper's front wall, its backward spelled name stenciled in the same Baskerville Old Face font as appeared at the top of its front page, and raised a hand to each temple, his cigar scissored between two fingers. McLain pretended to read his notes. The brass bell above the front door jingled followed by footsteps crossing to the front counter.

"Anybody here inhabiting this godforsaken firetrap of a rat hole?"

McLain looked up at the office window above him. Maybe were he still a skinny high-school kid but not now. Too high and too small and definitely not enough time.

"Back here."

Hanna came into the doorway. "My cousin anywhere about?"

"Just missed him. That's Sarge Hunt's funeral procession you cut through. Henry's up covering it. You might've heard. The village's last World War I vet."

"Hunt was a horse's ass if I ever met one and in Washington my opportunities aboundeth."

"Still, our last veteran of the war to end all wars."

"He was a goddamn cook who never left San Diego except to maggot the whore houses in Tijuana."

"Yes, sir."

"You've heard of Typhoid Mary."

"I have."

"Well Hunt was Syphilis Sammy."

"No kidding?"

"No kidding. Had us a real epidemic here once he was discharged. More than a few marriages got ruined." Hanna studied the traffic out the plate-glass window. "I'll catch Henry up at the cemetery then. Wanted to check in. Hear what's been sliming about my mill pond this week."

"You can't be worried about November."

"I was born worried, son. That's the secret of how I've held onto office since nineteen and twenty-two. Always looking over my shoulder for the faggot coming up to gnaw off my backside."

"You really think Thomson's up to giving you a horserace?"

"Those Thomsons always do. First his granddaddy when I won my seat the first go round. Barely won by all of fifty-two ballots. Had to have us three recounts before we got her squared away. Thomson claimed for years after, up until the day some slut's husband shot him, that I stole the election out from under him just because our Vote Commissioner ended up on my staff in Washington. Then Thomson's daddy tried twenty-six years later to requite his granddaddy. Made me sweat more than I'd grown accustomed to." He pointed his cigar at McLain's notepad. "That a re-election story you're working on?"

"No and not really one for the *Journal*, but if you're worried about Thomson, might have a duzzy of a story brewing out at the hospital that Thomson might like getting a hold of. Don't know how much you might've heard about it."

Hanna's eyebrows arched.

"Story you need to get out in front of before Thomson can harvest hay using your wagon."

"You know that hospital's my baby."

"Yes, sir, so you've told me. More than once."

"Best source of legalized vote buying Washington ever concocted. A bridge over Mill Creek or another monument to General Burnside is good for one election, maybe, but my hospital is Washington's gift that just keeps on giving."

"County needs all the jobs it can muster."

"It's more than jobs, son. It's the contracts we hand out to local businesses. Businesses of my supporters and when we have a war raging it gives me a chance to meet the boys who've sacrificed so much. Caucus some with their families who talk me up to their neighbors when they go home. At church socials and American Legion posts and such. Tell about what a regular guy this Congressman Hanna is. I figure for every medal I pin on some boy's shot-to-hell chest is good for at least twenty votes. Not just in the next election but on into perpetuity." Hanna pulled on his cigar. "The longer we keep dragging out this war, the safer my seat gets. Who knows where it could lead to."

"What I'm saying is it might be less safe if Thomson gets ahead of you on this one."

"What in hellfire are you jabbering about, McLain?"

"There's some sort of secret patient out at your hospital."

Hanna's cigar slipped from his fingers. His eyes narrowed to thin slits.

"What kind of secret patient?"

"Don't know yet. I'm still digging."

"You're digging yourself a dry hole, son. You can't be putting stock in anything Binder said. Besides being an out and out coward he was delusional. A Section Eight."

"May have been on to something too."

"Well, where are they hiding him? This mystery patient you've confabulated?"

"Fourth floor. Room across from the attic."

The circling shadows cast by the ceiling-fan blades cleaving the heavy August air staccatoed the congressman's now clouded face.

"What's he look like?"

"Haven't seen him yet."

"So you don't know if he really exists or if he's but a bit of an undigested McDonald's fry you slept on one night?"

"I might not know for certain yet, but I have a strong suspicion. Once I saw a staff member go up to the fourth floor. I'd never been up there, so I followed her. She unlocked a door, went in, and locked it behind her. Then a few days later . . ."

"You call that investigative reporting? Why, that could be anything, son. Simply anything."

"Could be, but a secret patient seems a possibility worth ruling out."

"Nonsense."

"I saw them loading a crash cart into the elevator and taking it up to the fourth floor but before that . . ."

Hanna fixed the boy with his kerosened-coal eyes, and when he spoke he enunciated each word with singular clarity. "I'm telling you you're sniffing up the wrong dog-pissed tree."

"Wouldn't be the first time."

"No, boy, if you're looking for a story, look for one we can actually publish. One that'll help us out come November. You should be looking at Thomson."

"I have. So far nothing."

"Look harder. His granddaddy had an eye for the ladies as did his daddy. Not just the ladies either. Both enjoyed harvesting the saplings. I'll wager you my ten dollars to your one the apple didn't fall far from the tree in that orchard. Start there."

"I've learned taking the opposite side of too many of your bets is an expensive ticket on the express train to the poorhouse."

"Smart boy." Hanna pulled on the gold chain draping his vest and clicked open his watch. "Well, I expect I need to be making my appearance up at Hunt's funeral."

"Yes, sir."

"Mind what I told you. Start digging up dirt on Thomson after he leaves the courthouse. See how long it takes him to get home. Where he goes along the way."

"Yes, sir."

"Good boy. You know, you've the makings of a crackerjack press secretary. Who knows? I may bring you to Washington after November."

"You told me a press secretary isn't worth a bucket of warm piss."

"A politician's prerogative is to change his opinion from time to time."

"Yes, sir."

The brass bell above the office door jingled. McLain rose and stood watching the congressman through the front window.

"To hell with Washington. I need to get out of this firetrap of a rat hole."

Hanna turned at the corner

*Think I'll stop by Seth's Liquor. See if I can catch some of the boys down by the duck pond after lunch.*

\* \* \*

Sweat shined Nurse Baker's upper lip when she found them reading charts in the attic. "Anything?"

"Still no name." Betsy shook her head. "No town where he grew up, but a good chance he's from around here."

"McLain's in my office. Says he has enough for an exposé. Some other paper if not the *Journal*."

"He can't. He'll get moved if his family doesn't step forward. What if they aren't around any more? He'll die all alone."

"Maybe you two should come downstairs."

\* \* \*

Her office lay in shadows with only an antique brass lamp setting on a desk corner lighting the room. McLain stood before the window looking down to the duck pond where Hawkeye and Stud and Johnny Handsome passed among them his pint bottle of Seagrams wrapped in a brown paper bag. Nurse Baker walked behind her desk. She held a hand out to the two chairs before it. Betsy shook her head. McLain turned from the window. "Someone needs to pay for what we do to them."

"He has paid." Betsy pointed at the door. "Over and over and over. Now he needs to come home."

"I agree, Betsy. Tell me where's home?"

"I'm not certain yet, but we're so close. We're getting clues every day."

"Clues? What kind of clues?"

"We know he served with the Canadians," Nurse Baker said. "Not the Americans."

"Do you know his company? His regiment? Something we can tract down."

"No," Bartholomew said, "but this morning he told us he was stationed next to the Twelfth Canadian Infantry below the Aisne Valley."

McLain looked out the window. He nodded at the cemetery.

"Before I took my sabbatical, I was — still am I guess — in ROTC. Last summer they stuck me in the Graves Registration Service outside of Washington."

"I met some Graves Regs during my spell in the Army," Nurse Baker said. "Never quite understood what they did besides ship dead soldiers home."

"They do more. Much more. They manage and care for the remains from the time a soldier dies until the Casualty Assistance Officer delivers him to his family. Part of what they do is an inventory of personal effects. Wallets, rings, letters. For those effects they can't match to a soldier, they put into storage until they're claimed. I'm told they had boxes in their warehouse going back to nineteen-seventeen. Too bad he served in the Canadian Army and not the American."

"He told us that when he got wounded he was with some Americans who'd just arrived," Betsy said. "Maybe they thought he was an American."

"May have been nineteen-seventeen or more likely nineteen-eighteen." McLain took his notepad from his breast pocket. "An American serving with the Canadians on loan back to the Americans stationed in France. Near the Twelfth Canadian Infantry. That does narrow it down."

"What's on your mind?" Nurse Baker said.

"You're right. Without a happy ending, it's too soon to run this, and it'll be a better story with a name. Maybe a long-lost family."

"Thank you," Betsy said.

"While I may be on sabbatical, I'm still in ROTC, at least until I can figure how to weasel out of it. I should be able to talk Graves Reg into letting me into their warehouse."

"What'll you be looking for?" Nurse Baker said.

"Anything. Everything. Do you have any information on him, Amy? Anything at all?"

"Very little." She unlocked a drawer and held out a chart. "See for yourself."

McLain leafed the pages. When he reached the end, he turned the chart to her.

"What's this?"

He had folded back the pages to a photograph of a half-dozen peasant children, the youngest grasping onto a soldier's John Brown belt as though he was all that held her fast to this world, the black edge of the photograph where the rest of the soldier should have been charred.

"It was in his chart when I started here. No explanation to go with it."

McLain studied the photograph, shaking his head. "Who was this guy?"

Whispered voices passed in the corridor.

"I've got some vacation time due me."

"When are you leaving?"

He laid the chart on her desk and started for the door.

"I'm already gone."

\* \* \*

Forty-eight hours later, he stepped off the bottom rung and scooted his ladder over another two arms-lengths and climbed to the top shelf forty feet up. Sweat dripping off his face stippled the dust-layered floor. His second day searching the warehouse maintained by Graves Registration at the end of a Dulles Airport runway and he had moved his ladder but thirty feet from where he started.

His first day on the post he wore a pressed ROTC uniform and tried with negligible success to hide his collar-length hair beneath an officer's cap. Showing a military I.D. to Corporal Coogan in turn led to a series of telephone calls that took her an hour to make before she walked him out back and unlocked the door. Forty steel shelves ran the length of the three-hundred-foot long warehouse with corrugated cartons the size of a shoebox jammed into every foot of shelve from floor to ceiling. McLain shook his head.

"Where do I even begin?"

"Got me, ROTC boy. This here's been my post of duty for going on a year now, and this be only my second time in here. First time ever anybody's even been wanting to be in here I've heard tell of." She twirled her key ring around her finger as she turned to go. "Let me know when you've had enough so I can lock up."

\* \* \*

When he walked into her office at the end of the day, he found her squatting before the open drawer of a file cabinet. She shook her head as she inspected him from head to foot.

"I can't spot a square inch of dry fabric about your person no place, ROTC boy. Hope you ain't considering comin' back tomorrow."

"Coming back until I find what I want or I run out of warehouse."

"Then you might want to consider dressing some to accommodate our Washington weather. I won't snitch on you. Besides I don't want to be giving you no mouth-to-mouth on account of you passing out from heat prostration. Mama promised me if she ever heard tell of me putting lips to a white dude she'd slice 'em off. You ever tried supping soup with no lips?"

\* \* \*

The next morning he came in wearing his pair of hiking boots, a T-shirt, and the ragged pair of fatigue shorts he had sliced the legs off with a pocketknife the night before in his room at the Holliday Inn. Still he swore he sweated buckets and through the day his thighs reddened with heat rash.

His search soldiered on Bataan-Death-March slow. Some of the boxes he opened were crammed full. Some held only a single item. A rotting wallet or tarnished wedding band. Brown letters with their writing long lost. A typewritten five-by-seven card Scotch-taped on the inside of the lid of each box stated where the effects were found and when and sometimes Graves Registration's best guess as to the unit. He started at the top shelf along the west wall and worked his way down the ladder, opening each box within arm's reach on either side and examining its contents until he reached the bottom shelf. Then he pushed the ladder over another six feet and began anew. He had no clue what clue he was searching for. Near noon on his third day he was almost to the bottom of the ladder when the steel door creaked open.

"You plannin' on joining us for Christmas this year, ROTC boy?"

"If I'm not still here for the Christmas after this Christmas, I'd consider it the Lord's own blessing." He nodded at the rows of boxes stacked on shelves along the wall opposite. "Even that might be too optimistic."

"Well, maybe this'll get you out of my hair before then." She held up what looked like an old-fashioned deed registry still found in country courthouses, two feet by three feet and four inches thick, bound in black leather. "Got me a catalog of what all we've got in here."

McLain hopped off the ladder. "Why didn't you tell me about when I first walked into your office?"

"Don't go snappin' at me like you's a big bellied bad-assed turtle, ROTC boy. You ain't my superior officer just yet."

"Sorry."

"Didn't tell you on account of I only found out about it this morning after having some beers with my buds last night. Got to laughing ourselves wet-pants silly over my deluded white dude I'd been babysitting this week. My friend Melissa come from a family been in the Army goin' back to the Civil War. Turns out she's got herself a retired uncle who did what I'm doing. Called him this morning, and he asked her if we still kept a catalog hereabouts."

"Why isn't it kept in here?"

"Take a deep breath, ROTC boy."

McLain inhaled.

"You sniff that?"

"What is it I'm sniffing?"

"Sure can tell where you wasn't raised. Thems rats, which is why this here's in charge of our chaplain."

"Well, let's see what it says."

"First let's get us some decent light and where I can keeps you downwind."

They found a patch of grass in the shade of the warehouse.

"Melissa's uncle say the Army organized the shelves by geography and where the effects was found, then within each section in chronological order of when they was found."

McLain flipped open the cover.

"So do you know when and where?"

"About."

"Then praise the Lord you's almost out of here."

"The soldier I'm searching for was wounded in Northern France in nineteen-seventeen or more likely nineteen-eighteen while serving in the Canadian Army. Don't know his unit, but it was close to the Twelfth Canadian Infantry. When he got wounded he was on loan to an American unit."

"That's what you be calling 'about?'"

"Checked with the Canadian embassy." McLain pulled a map from his hip pocket and unfolded it on the grass. "Their military liaison put me in contact with the Twelfth's historian."

"Now you's cooking with gas."

"My guy was here." He tapped the map. "Below the heights of the Aisne Valley."

Coogan flipped the catalog to the end and ran her finger down the table of contents almost to its end. She tapped the page. "You needs to be looking over here."

"Where's here?"

"Just about cattycorner from where you was looking." Coogan grinned. "At the rate you was hustling booty, you might of clambered yourself over there by Christmas."

\* \* \*

Late next morning he stood at Cogan's desk, brown corrugated box in hand.

"What you got there, ROTC boy?"

"My man, I think." He set the box on her desk and lifted its lid. "No name on it, but . . ."

He unwrapped a sheaf of yellowing newspaper and held out a sepia photograph of a row of farm children, a young girl holding onto the Sam Brown belt of a soldier missing from the picture. "This is my man. The guy not in the photograph."

"How'd you know?"

"There's an exact copy of it in a hospital drawer back in Ohio. My man was probably carrying it on him when he got wounded, which would explain its burned condition if he was hit by an artillery shell. Somebody along the way must've made a copy to go in the box, and the original stayed with my guy's chart in case his family went looking for him."

Coogan wiped the dust from the inside of the lid with a tissue she had taken from her purse and copied down the numbers from the index card taped to it.

"Those numbers mean something?"

"No, I just likes staying in practice so I don't turns into a college illiterate. Of course they means something."

She crossed to a table and opened the catalog.

"What're you doing?"

"Melissa's uncle say that after the war, folks of soldiers who was what we now call MIA would come here to see if they could finds something that belonged to their boy. If they did, it got noted in the catalog."

"See anything?"

"Give me a minute, will you. She ran her finger down the column. She turned the page. Then another. "Here."

"What's here?"

"Family by the name of Stanton from out in Nebraska identified the photo."

"When?"

"Nineteen twenty-five."

"There an address?"

"Yeah, there is, if you'll stop halitosising down my neck and give me a second." She tore the sheet from the pad and handed it to him. "So what're you going to do now that you've got what you come here for?"

McLain stuffed the page in his hip pocket and headed for the door.

"Driving to Nebraska. Got me maybe a new newspaper job that isn't in the Army."

"New job not in the Army?" Coogan closed the catalog. "And white folks claim coloreds is plumb crazy. They needs to meet up with this loony tunes."

\* \* \*

Betsy and Bartholomew faced one another seated on the floor crevassed within a canyon of rat-gnawed boxes when Nurse Baker came up mid-afternoon.

"McLain called."

Two heads snapped up in unison.

"He's certain he's found the patient's family."

"All right!" Bartholomew slumped against the stack of boxes behind him. "Paroled out of this pop stand at last."

"Really?" Betsy beamed. "Where?"

"Nebraska of all places."

Betsy's face fell. Sister and brother looked at one another, and when they spoke it was with one voice. "Nebraska?"

"I'm needed downstairs." Nurse Baker turned to go. "Oliver called. The congressman's coming out this evening. I just wanted you to know."

"Nebraska?" they again repeated.

Betsy crossed the floor to the ambered window where she looked down into a cemetery consecrated to soldiers who never made it home. Soldiers with no home to go to.

"He never talked nothin' about Nebraska, Sis. Some about Cleveland and Youngstown. Pittsburgh maybe once, but the only time he's mentioned Nebraska is when Stanton's family moved there."

"I know."

"Should we go in and find out?"

"I'm not certain he'd tell us."

"Got any thoughts at all?"

"A couple of times he's talked about a girl."

"Should I ask him?"

"Not about her. Not directly. Ask him why he enlisted."

## CHAPTER 26

He and his father worked their farm during that last summer before the start of the war. On Saturday afternoons he rode one of the mules into the telegraph office. Nothing memorable that summer about the farm; nothing memorable about his riding into the depot. Nothing memorable until the last Saturday in July.

All afternoon the tin roof crackled like fireplace popcorn in wintertime, and by the time he locked up that evening the yoke of his sweat-stained shirt his mother had stove-ironed the night before clung to his back. He crossed the alley to the village livery and led Molly out to the street. If he had mounted up behind the depot, she would have taken off for home at a dead gallop. She liked home. He wore out his birch switch driving her into town, but by the time they reached the barn on their return trip, his arms ached from pulling her in. Tonight he needed to think, so he led her down the street. Walking beside her seemed to confuse the mule as to their true destination. Mules might be God's most stubborn beast but they were not His brightest.

No light shined from the windows they passed and only the orange glow of the village gas lamps lighted their way as the clop of mule hooves on baked clay echoed down the deserted street. The village musicians out in the park struck up *And the Band Played On*, popular since the sinking of the Titanic, and he hummed along. Near the crossroads he stopped to pass a bridle rein over Molly's ear, asking her if she was ready to bust a gut getting them home. His voice must have carried in the quiet night air because as he swung his leg up a voice called to him from out of the dark, demanding to know if he had grown so pathetic he now held conversations in the public street with dumb animals. Molly, her eyes all white and big as goose eggs, shied, catching him off balance. He landed flat on his back when he hit the street and let go the reins. As he rolled over onto his stomach he saw only the shine of moon on the mule's flanks as she turned west. The girl who had called out to him was leaning over a porch rail as she looked toward the crossroads, and when she looked at him she shook her head, opining that for a farm boy he sure didn't have much to recommend him as much of a muleskinner.

Sally Anne and he had been classmates. She had always excelled in her subjects until their last year when she confided to him she could not for the life of her get a handle on geometry, what with its stupid theorems and idiot postulates and unfathomable whathaveyous, though she seemed able enough to answer Sister Robert's questions when called upon. So during their lunch hour he took it upon himself to tutor her, her mother letting them study at the dining room table as they ate and making the doctor sit with her out in the kitchen with the door closed. Sally Anne told him at the end of the year that she had managed something north of a C, but quickly hid her report card inside her blouse when he tried to snatch it from her to see how far north his pupil had traversed.

He pushed open the gate and half-walked-half-staggered up the slate walk toward the porch. She tossed her snow-blond hair about her shoulders and looked down the street once more. She told him his mule was for certain home by now, but not to worry because the doctor would give him a ride when he and her mother returned from the concert, and he might as well come up on the porch to rest his busted head. She smiled at him with her hazel, double-sized almond eyes and sat on the swing, running her hands along the sides of her gingham frock accentuating her breasts. He looked for a moment at the seat beside her before sitting on the top step. While her mouth pouted, she did not surrender her suit.

He asked her how school had gone, and when she finished telling him about all the fun he had missed, the football games and parties he had not attended, the lavishness of the spring prom, he said nothing. The band played on. Crickets choired. A basket of poppies hanging from the porch eaves twisted in the breeze, its moonshadow vacilitating over the floorboards between them. After a while the music ceased and soon a carriage clacked down the street on its iron-rimmed wheels.

When he told her he heard Mark took her to the spring prom, she claimed it was the most fun she'd ever had in all her life. He'd taken a fancy he had to walking her home after school when the weather was nice or even sprinting over to his daddy's general store where he kept his office for their Flivver if it turned inclement, which, in case he didn't know, meant nasty. Foul. When he suggested to her that Inclement sounded like an appropriate name for their mean old rooster, she aimed a pillow at his head and told him he could stop being such a smarty-pants just about any time.

After her parents got home, the doctor held a lighted match to his eyes. He diagnosed no sign of concussion or, glancing at Sally Anne, any other symptom of bustedness, and they drove him home in their crimson Pierce-Arrow. They stopped halfway down the lane where Molly grazed along the fence posts. She let him take up the reins, and when he waved goodbye, Sally Anne gave him a smile as sweet as a remembered kiss. He stood watching the carbide headlights recede until they disappeared around a grove of locust trees. For some weeks he surrendered his plans of escape.

What should have been his senior year started on the Tuesday after Labor Day. The following Saturday evening as he again walked Molly down the street, he heard her laugh gambol out into the night, his stomach a hundred bits of knotted string loosed from their kite. Her head rested against Mark's shoulder as she looked down the street, but she may not have seen him, may not have known he always walked past her house at this hour on Saturday. Mark said nothing but raised an index finger from her shoulder, partly in greeting, partly in claim of ownership. From hand to hand he passed the bridle reins behind him before he pulled at his mule to follow, and they cut across to the alleyway that lead to the road home.

On the morning of the next to last Saturday in October, he repaired breaks along their north fence in the rain. He looked up when he heard the chug of an engine approaching from town to see a crimson blur roll out of the gray mist. He raised his hand, but the car, its windshield wipers flailing, failed to slow, raising a wave of mud as it passed by that slopped down over him. Then in the afternoon when he stopped at the Post Office, Sally Anne's stepsister, Maude, home on an early Thanksgiving break from boarding school, stood inside as she shuffled through the family mail. Mark's father had gotten him admitted to college a year early after finding an overseer to manage his farms. She asked him if he didn't think it all horribly exciting about her father driving Sally Anne over to Mark's college for homecoming and the pigskin prom tonight. Who knew? She might even come home engaged. Did he not see it would all be too perfect? Her father would be right there for Mark to ask his permission. Stranger things had happened, but wasn't it all horribly exciting?

Yes, it all sounded horribly exciting to him too, and he went out and down to the depot, the wind-driven rain harrying over the street and pecking his face shrouded under his father's slicker as a crow feeding at carrion.

## CHAPTER 27

Hanna stood in the plate-glass window studying him as Henry returned the telephone receiver to its cradle. He pushed himself up from his chair, hand raised, and Hanna in turn raised his cigar and came in. The scent of cigar smoke and Jade East cologne filled the office.

"What's up, Congressman?"

Hanna ignored his editor's question but studied the merchant notices thumb tacked to a corkboard. After a minute, he cocked his head at the door leading down into the basement.

"Bit early for tomorrow's edition, isn't it?"

"Special advertising supplement A & P has us running for them."

"Well, well." Hanna smiled. "Little extra business right now's good during our slow summer months."

"Might not be slow much longer. Might soon be hopping like an Old Testament infestation of rabbits around here."

"What're you jabbering about?"

"That was young McLain I just got off the phone with."

"Boy's got all the earmarks of a comer, which could be good for us. Or maybe not."

"Yes, sir."

"So which is it today?"

"Can't say yet but it has to do with the hospital."

"Then it can't be good."

"You might be right, but even if it's not we've got to get on top of this one before Thomson does. McLain says the hospital's been hiding' some sort of secret patient out there since World War I. Nobody knew his name or where he's from. Not until now leastways."

Hanna glanced into the darkened doorway leading down into the basement. The gears of the hot-lead press clacked.

"Even if we don't run it, if he finds out about it Thomson will have no problem getting Feldspar down at the Times Leader in Martin's Ferry to run it. He's had it in for you for years."

"So what's the name of this so-called secret patient?"

"Matt didn't say. He took what he had left of his vacation days to check it out. He's asking for a couple more to confirm everything up."

"He isn't going to confirm anything up about a secret patient hidden away out at my hospital. Not now. Not ever. Where's McLain at now."

"Holliday Inn in Washington."

"What in hell's fire is he doing there?"

"Following up a lead."

"Get him on the phone."

"But . . ."

"Get him on the phone. Now."

Henry handed over the telephone receiver after he dialed.

"McLain. Hanna here. Get your carcass home. Now."

There was a pause.

"We're not running that kind of a story until after the election, and if your butt isn't sitting behind your desk in your office by this time tomorrow, you're not going to be working for a paper to run your story in. Not now. Not ever. Am I making myself crystal clear?"

Hanna slammed the receiver into its cradle, his breathing short and fast. Henry stood waiting.

"Need to pay a call on that toady of a sheriff I've got squatting on my payroll."

"Yes, sir."

"Campaigns can be a nasty bit of business. I've got an uneasy feeling about this one already. Better to be prepared."

"You're the maestro. You know what's best."

"When McLain gets in, you give him a week off. Without pay."

"Why? I need him here."

"So he'll get a taste of what it's like not to have a job."

"If you say so."

"I do say so."

At the door, Hanna turned back to his editor.

"Say hello to my niece for me when you go home tonight."

"Of course."

"You might remind her of how lucky you are to have this job. A man your age would find it more than a little difficult to locate another. Perhaps even impossible."

Henry lowered his eyes to the articles spread across his desk. He nodded.

Hanna went out of the office and for a moment from the sidewalk regarded the village. The telephone rang.

"Yes, Mayor." Henry listened. "Just stepped out. Let me see if I can catch him for you."

He looked through the plate-glass window, but Hanna was gone.

\* \* \*

Betsy and her brother were sitting across from each other when the attic door creaked opened. Bartholomew kicked her shoe.

"Wasn't he busting butt out to Nebraska?"

Matt walked back, a paper bag clutched in his hand.

"Thought you two could use a little help."

"You've got that right." Bartholomew flipped a page. "In spades."

"As well as a little wholesome nourishment." He sat cross-legged between them, opening the bag, and held out two wax-papered sandwiches. "I've got one chicken salad and one tuna."

Bartholomew grabbed. "Gimme the chicken."

"Barto!"

"Please."

Matt handed him the sandwich and the tuna to Betsy. He pulled the two-foot stack toward him. "So tell me what it is I'm searching for."

He was looking at her openmouthed when she finished. "Good God almighty."

"More of a humdinger than you supposed?"

"Yeah. No kidding."

Bartholomew slapped crumbs from his hands.

"Gotta hit the head."

After the attic door closed, Matt scooted an inch closer to her.

"So how come you're not on your way to Nebraska."

"Boss pulled me off our story."

"Why?"

"I can't be one-hundred percent certain, but I've got a pretty good hunch a certain somebody doesn't want your guy across the hall known about."

"Congressman Hanna?"

"Yeah and to be certain I got his point, Henry gave me a week's vacation. Without pay."

"Ouch."

"Yeah. Very ouch."

"So what're you going to do?"

"There's gotta be a reason Hanna doesn't want me chasing down a first class story. Maybe the answer's in this room."

"Maybe."

Betsy began again to read.

"Kind of spooky up here, isn't it?"

"Kind of."

"You like spooky?"

"Yeah, I guess I do."

"I thought you did. So I was thinking. *Rosemary's Baby*'s still playing in a few places. If you'd like to go."

Betsy looked up. She blushed.

\* \* \*

She sat on her front porch steps come Friday evening with hands clasped over her knees as she looked down the street. About once a minute she pulled out from her collar Nathan's watch and looked down the street again for maybe another minute. She wore the pastel dress she bought at Fitzpatrick's that afternoon, and she smelled of the Windsong perfume that came from a sample bottle Anita had slipped into her shopping bag after Betsy told her about her first real date with a college guy.

"It drives Gus wild." Anita touched her fingers over her breasts. "Just wild."

A cream-colored 1937 S Continental Bentley rounded the corner. Mr. Sims sat up on his knees from where he was hand clipping his grass along the sidewalk. The Bentley parked at the curb, and Matt stepped out its right-side door.

"Hellfire and damnation, boy."

He started to cross the lawn only to stop midway where she had chained the reel lawnmower to a tree. He knelt and yanked on the padlock. He grinned. "Taking no chances, I see."

He sat next to her on the step and nodded out to the street. "A gem, isn't she?"

"You really do have a Rolls Royce."

"For tonight."

"What do you mean 'for tonight.' You didn't hotwire it, did you?" Betsy's eyes narrowed. "Tell me the truth."

"Me?"

"Is that a denial?"

He raked his eyebrows.

"I've heard stories about you boys from Cleveland."

"I'm from Shaker Heights."

"With an even worse reputation."

He pulled a ring of keys from the pocket of his iron-creased jeans, jangling them before her. "No need to when Uncle Wesley loaned me these guys."

"Uncle Wesley?"

"Wesley Barnes. You've seen him around."

Betsy shook her head.

"Dr. Barnes?"

"He's your uncle? But why would he give you the keys to a car as cool as this? I've never even seen it at the hospital?"

"On account of he lost a dumb bet."

"A dumb bet on what?"

"That I couldn't get you to go out."

"What would it have cost you if I didn't?"

"May have had to hotwire it."

Matt stood.

"I guess that means we should be going."

"Only if we want to catch the flick."

"I really do. Sandy says it's scary as all get out. She's still having nightmares. I hope I can watch it."

"You can hold onto my arm. I won't complain."

Betsy smiled.

"I should meet your folks before we go, don't you think? Let them know you're not going out with some slasher type."

Betsy's smile fell away. She looked behind her to the porch windows with their closed curtains pulled tight. "They turn in early. They both have to work tomorrow."

"On a Saturday?"

"Yeah. Sometimes on Sundays too. Last year they even worked on Christmas."

"Maybe another time then."

"Yes. Another time. We should be going. I really do want to see the movie."

"Then let's be on our way," and the two set off across the grass, their fingers grazing off one another's, pulling back, then grazing again. They were almost to the street when they heard Betsy's mother.

*Nooooo.*

They stopped. Matt looked up at the open second-floor window.

"What the . . ."

Betsy slumped to the grass.

"No. Please no. Not tonight."

"Are you all right?"

She shook her head.

"What's going on? It sounded like . . ."

The bedroom window thudded shut.

Matt's fingers fidgeted the legs of his jeans. No lights came on inside. Betsy held out her hand.

"Please help me up. I need to go in. Daddy will need me."

He pulled her to her feet. "Should I wait?"

Betsy shook her head. "Sorry you drove over here for nothing. I guess you lose your bet."

"I didn't lose my bet. You're giving me a rain check is all, and it wasn't for nothing. Got to see you. Your pretty dress"

She tried to smile but her face wrecked and she ran into the house. Matt returned to the porch and sat, the sounds of a summer evening dying away until even the crickets fell silent. The courthouse clock tolled ten o'clock. He turned and looked at the closed door.

*He needs to have his story told, Betsy. Told so people will see how we snuff out the lives of innocents. Twist those of their survivors into the walking dead.*

* * *

It was after midnight when Betsy half woke. A door in the hall opened and closed. Then the door to Nathan's room. She slept. In her dream she again sat in the dewy grass, tombstones gleaming gray in the misty moonlight. Fog eddied through the trees, and from within the fog the shadows of thousands of boy-soldiers walking in mile-long lines passed her in silence. Some smiled. One pointed behind him. In the last line walked Nathan between two others, his arms falling from their shoulders as she stumbled to her feet. He mouthed something to her. The three continued on out of the cemetery. He turned back after they crossed the tracks, his hand raised. She took a step toward him, but he shook his head. Then he too disappeared into the dark of the woods.

When she woke, her summer nightie clung to her clammy skin. She listened to the dead of night outside her open window for a minute before getting out of bed and descending the steps bare-footed to the light falling through the doorway of the television room where she found her mother staring bleary-eyed at the Indian chief test signal.

"Mama?"

She turned, her fast graying hair straggling into her face, and smiled. "What are you doing up, dear? A working girl needs her beauty sleep."

"I woke. Something seemed amiss."

"It is." She reached out and switched off the set. "Amiss and missing but nothing to be done about it tonight. I should go back to bed."

"Me too, I guess."

They went up the stairs, her mother's arm wrapped around Betsy's shoulders. Instead of going into her room, though, she went into Betsy's where she sat in the rocking chair. She pulled the light chain on the table lamp and slumped back, grasping the ends of the armrest, the blue-black veins of her hands spiderwebbing beneath the rice-paper-thin skin.

"Did you know I nursed you sitting in this very chair? Bartholomew too."

"And Nate?"

"Oh, yes indeed. Here I taught him his words." She nodded at the window. "He was a winter baby so the birds returning in spring caught his eye as they nested. I would say *bird*, and he smiled and gurgled. *Just you wait, Mommy, his milk bubbles seemed to say, before long you won't get me to shut up.*

"Nathan never seemed to be much of a talker."

"No. Not unless he had something to say. Yet, even as a child if he spoke his dreams, I listened. He had a way of looking at life as young as he was, yet old as the world. He was deep, as you are. As Bartholomew is turning out to be. You three are my gold mines of thought. My wells of wisdom, philosophers all."

"Nate was your favorite, though, wasn't he?"

"Yes. Until you came along. Then Bartholomew."

"And you had to split your love up among the three of us."

"Wasn't necessary to split anything, Betsy. When you came along, my love for Nathan was the same. Then overnight a whole new bouquet sprouted for you, like poppies in spring. Grew out of nowhere. Then another for Bartholomew. You don't know where the love for the next child will come, but come it always does. Love always comes, Betsy, dies only when you do. That is its blessing. Its blessing as well as its curse."

* * *

Betsy never heard the door to her mother's room open and close again that night, but when she left her room the next morning to return to the hospital, muddy footprints coming up the steps and entering her parents' room tracked the carpet. Her father knelt at the bottom of the stairs on hands and knees with a soapy bucket of water before him.

"What happened, Daddy?"

He ceased his scrubbing. His eyes followed the tracks up the steps.

"Your mother was sleepwalking."

"Sleepwalking where?"

"I followed her tracks in the dew, but after they left the yard I lost where she'd gone. Where she'd come from."

"Where do you think?"

"Last night she asked me to take her up to Nathan's. I said I would." He rinsed out his brush in the water. "Guess I should have done it then."

* * *

On their way out, she found a note from Matt scotchtaped to the mailbox telling her he was taking his week's unpaid vacation to drive out to Nebraska.

*His story needs to be heard.*

"Do you want me to ask him his name again?"

"No, but I know now the chink in his armor."

"What?"

"Ask him if he heard anything more from Sally Anne after he ran away."

## CHAPTER 28

He soon grew certain the three hags who had accosted him that Christmas had been only a cheap-Chianti dream because he saw them now every night as they strolled arm in arm across the quiet of No Man's Land, stopping from time to time to point out to one another some grotesque peculiarity of the grimace-faced dead. He pondered what his dreams meant. Pondered what the long quiet of that winter meant. Quiet until the artillery bombardment in April that killed young Robbie Foster.

Because the boy came into the trenches only the week before, he never joined them for a night of hijinks in the village. He would have, though, because he and Stanton took to him as they would a runt pup. Foster swore himself red in a cracking voice to be all of eighteen yet only patches of peach fuzz dusted his flushed cheeks. Damned bonus-grasping recruiters Stanton cursed and guessed him more near to sixteen. Who could say? Maybe even fifteen.

He and Foster had been sitting shirtless in the sunshine out behind their dugout protected from sniper fire, oiling their Enfields. He never even heard its singing but only saw when he looked up to see Foster's eyes searching the heavens. When Stanton and the others found them, he held what remained of the boy in his lap as he stitched him back together with the sewing kit he carried in his breast pocket. They could do no more than sedate him with morphine at the dressing station and ship him on to Glasgow. So overworked was his doctor, so short of beds was the hospital, he ordered him a three-month convalescent leave.

The Canadians scrounged him passage home aboard an empty grain freighter. Until they in fact docked he harbored doubts they ever would. The rusted boat leaked so that the bilge pumps clanged precarious notes the length of the voyage to keep her pumped out. On deck, even in a stiff arctic breeze, the boat smelled like the months-old battlefield dead had crawled into its hold. He watched from the stern a Z-trail following the freighter as it zigzagged across the North Atlantic. The U-boats, he heard from the sailors, operated that spring with no caution about them attacking Allied ships in marauding packs as they hunted down thinly protected convoys. His freighter, though, arrived in port without event, perhaps because if a U-boat *kapitan* spotted them through his periscope, the freighter he judged to be more of a menace to the King than the Kaiser or because it rode too high up out of the water and he elected to conserve his torpedoes for vessels loaded down with supplies and boys.

    In Saint John's he boarded the Boston bound train where he experienced a little difficulty crossing the border in uniform until the dolt of a customs officer finally understood he was not a deserter but an American who had enlisted to render aid and assistance to his six Cahill cousins native to Cape Breton Island and was making his way home to recover from his wounds. He shaved in the washroom after the train departed Boston and returned to his seat where he slept straight through to Cleveland, waking from his dream of a laughing and broken-toothed Robbie Foster only when the conductor shook him. After he inspected his ticket, the conductor told him this was where he changed trains.

    He wanted only to look from the window in his solitude when they pulled out from Cleveland, but a flock of verbena-scented socialites swarmed into his car. They nested together at one end where they yammered like jays at one another while their thick-waisted husbands occupied the other end, gruffing business and Republican politics through a violet haze of Cuban smoke. He fled to the platform outside the end car where, like a flicker run in reverse, he watched the selfsame farms and villages he had watched eighteen months before, the fields now furrowed and some far advanced into the spring planting. When they pulled into the village depot, he was the only passenger to step down onto the platform. He shouldered his duffle bag and started down the main street, brick paved since he had left, receiving more than a few stares from villagers unaccustomed to seeing someone in uniform not a conductor for the Pennsylvania, Fort Wayne & Chicago Railroad. None in the graying twilight studied him closely save for a peg-legged veteran who tipped to him his faded and moth-eaten GAR cap.

Outside Sally Anne's he dropped his duffle to the sidewalk, and as he stood looking up to the second-story widow's walk where in his dreams he so often saw her keeping watch, the doctor came out onto the porch and stooped to pick up his evening newspaper. He nodded to the thin soldier lost in his uniform who for some reason stood staring up before his house but did not recognize until he was wished a good evening. He squinted down to the sidewalk. A grin cracked his face. He raised a finger to his lips and called in to his wife through the screen door. She at once recognized him without the necessity of his speaking and duck waddled down the steps and wrapped her arms around his shoulders in a great bear hug.

For a quarter hour they stood talking until the iron gate creaked behind him. Sally Anne had finished her spring term two weeks earlier and she now helped out at the sisters' until it too let out for summer. The doctor nudged him with an elbow, giving him a just-between-us-men conspiratorial wink. When he turned he took off his campaign cap and stepped forward. Her mouth dropped open and her hazel, double-sized almond eyes widened. The papers she was to grade that night fell from her arms, and the four of them ran about in the twilight like fox-harried chickens as they collected the exams from the street and off the neighbors' lawns and out of their shrubs, she at his elbow posing him questions and whispering goddamnyous in his ear for not letting her know he was on his way home, for his not writing her a single letter — not one — while he was gone.

At supper they talked first about her half-brother in Chicago because when they came in from the porch the doctor led them into the parlor while his wife set another place where on an end table was a photograph of the doctor's recently married son by his first wife who he had lost in the influenza pandemic of 1892. He had never been to Chicago, and he asked many questions of the doctor who enjoyed impressing a farm boy with the wonders of the big city. The conversation drifted to what became of his and Sally Anne's classmates and from there to her college classes. When she spoke with reverie about this mind doctor from Vienna, her father snorted. Sigmund Freud he contended was so big a quack he deserved at least a pond of his very own if not a lake, and he asked him if he did not agree the allies would be better off if they just lined up all their malingers against a wall and commenced to fire away.

He had laid his silverware crosswise on his china plate and looked straight on at the doctor, as if it was the older man proving himself the innocent. He told them about the mere boys he saw in Glasgow huddled on floors with hands clasped over their heads, crying their Hail Mary's as though still under barrage, sobbing for days without end as they rocked back and forth until exhausted, not even standing so as not to befoul themselves. About a priest who hour upon hour walked the hospital grounds in circles as he stared down at the zeros of his nothingness, now no more than a mere guest on earth, a forever stranger carrying inside within his soul a broken Decalogue he could no longer bear to read. How Stanton, Cahill, and five others had to pry away his hands that cradled Robbie Foster's smoking carcass and hogtie him until an ambulance wagon came to carry him away, he cursing them all the while for now Robbie without a doubt would surely die.

When he finished the doctor was staring red-faced down at his napkin. He lifted it from his ample lap and walked out onto the porch, his hand still grasping a dinner knife that he arced into dark. From a pocket of his tweed coat he took out his pipe, but the evening breeze snuffed out the match and then a second one and after it blew out the third he walked off into the night. The three watched through the screen door until he cursed himself for his lack of manners his mother had taught him and went out. Not seeing in which direction the doctor had gone, he sat on the swing to wait.

Sally Anne came out when she finished helping her mother and sat next to him. She took his hand into hers, and they listened to the night as they swung. After a while he put his arm around her, and she leaned into his shoulder as she had with Mark on another evening that seemed forever ago, the gaslight flame in the streetlamp flickering in the breeze as its small wisps broke and vanished like whispered warnings out of the dark.

She drove him home, taking him halfway down the lane to the farmhouse where he told her she should stop so as not to wake his folks. When she asked if she would see him again before he left, he smiled and kissed her on the cheek. He continued to smile so he could laugh when she slapped him, but instead she pulled his face to hers and kissed him hard. He had no idea girls sometimes kissed so hard. Even the French girls did not kiss so hard. He got out and for a moment she studied him through the windshield with the bold eyes of a bride. The Pierce Arrow disappeared behind the locust grove, and he walked whistling down the lane. After a few steps he stopped. He never whistled. He didn't even know he could.

* * *

No light shone from within the farmhouse. Few farmers then had electricity, and as the wavering coal-oil light soon tired their eyes, most evenings they were in bed soon after supper. He wanted not to wake them, and anyway he was exhausted, so he climbed the ladder to the hayloft where he wrapped himself in his greatcoat. After wallowing in the mud for months on end, he could sleep anywhere, even in stone alleyways, but for the first night since that Christmas Eve the three hags paid him no visit, and he slept the dreamless sleep of the dead, unhaunted by the laughter of young Robbie Foster. When he woke he lay in the sweet-smelling hay watching penciled sunlight fall through the siding cracks, watched his breath smoke in the early morning cold as it drifted into the rafters. He remembered smiling. Today he would not eviscerate with his bayonet some other boy who was as sick of the war as was he. Would not hold in his arms a weeping comrade while the soldier's life bled through his fingers, he reading the boy's life as well as his own in the dilating eyes, their corners blurring when he looked up for Heaven and realized with a final shudder it was nowhere for him to find.

The backdoor banged shut. As his mother crossed the barnyard he heard her singing some nameless Gaelic lament she had sung since he was a child. A song beautiful in its depth that went on for thirty-seven verses plus those claimed from the stories of her life she had added on her own with a melody much like that sung by the hags. Through the floorboards he watched as she pitched hay over the stall walls. He stood with care so as not to sift hay dust through the cracks and crept to the edge of the loft where he crouched low before he sprung into the air, roaring out in his best over-the-top war cry. Molly jerked her head up from the hay. With arms spread wide and his greatcoat winged behind him, he must have appeared to be some mule nightmare of vampire come out to feed because she jerked back, screaming as her egg eyes rolled in their sockets. His mother twirled about, hayfork raised, and as soon as his boots touched the floor she had its tines not a quarter inch from his neck. She ordered him to raise his hands if he wanted not to be breathing out the back of his chicken-thieving throat. He did, telling her he was her prisoner, and asked when they would be serving breakfast to their captives.

She studied with narrowed eyes the boy before her, her breath panting, hayfork upward angled like a demonic Ahab posed on the bow of the *Pequot.* He must have looked as sunken cheeked to her as he did to himself when he shaved in the railcar washroom for some seconds ticked by before the hayfork clattered to the floorboards. She walked to the stall door with her back to him, her shoulders shuddering. With the thousands of heartbreaks she had endured, it was the only time she broke down before him. She reached for the hem of her dress and turned to him, red-eyed and smiling, and told him it would mend his father's heart more than a little if he joined them for their breakfast.

She cooked the same morning meal as was their custom: Cornmeal mush with a slab of butter served in a crockery bowl of heavy cream. Barley bread spread with preserves put up the summer before, and tea brewed from sassafras gathered from her backwoods walks. He carried the tray up the steps, and when she opened the door his father looked up from where he lay propped against his pillow reading the Bible his own father carried from Cork wrapped in lamb's wool. The older man looked grayer at the temples, and the icy blue of his irises had melted some at their edges. His father in turn studied his son's uniform, swallowed, and asked if he'd ceased his senseless Odyssey for good.

He unpacked his duffle after they ate. When he changed into the work clothes folded away in his chifferobe, he discovered his trousers hung off his hips like potato sacking, and it was necessary for him to find a rope to hold them up because his belt lacked sufficient notches. His mother put a hand to her mouth when he came down. She told him she would take them in and went upstairs, returning with a pair of his father's trousers that fit only a little the snugger.

   She had started the spring plowing the week before but not made much progress at it. Mudsinks into which a mule could drop to its belly still spotted the back fields, and Molly and Martha remained weak as newborn colts from lying up all winter. She had loaded up the flatbed from the mountain of cow dung heaped from the previous spring and driven the fields with a parish boy conscripted by Father Michaels. As the child steered the mules in almost a straight line, she shoveled manure out the back, and it since had leached into the soil sufficient to now be plowed under. He put Molly in harness, shivering in the morning cold as he led her up the lane but with the sun bright by afternoon he would be down to his shirtsleeves. He plowed the first row and stopped to allow Molly to blow. Hopping the fence separating their fields from the Rhorer's, he walked into the locust grove. He held his breath and listened. It had been almost two years since he heard a songbird.

\* \* \*

The days warmed as the week advanced, and he had plowed both the front and backfields by early Friday. After he helped his mother finish the sowing he started mending the worst of the fence breaks. It was just grainy light when he headed out the backdoor on Saturday morning. His mother handed him a wicker basket that held his lunch with a dampened flour sack doubled over the top. As much as she would have liked to put up her feet and worked on the pile of sewing, she had not been to the village for a month. She needed to pick up some staples and their mail and intended to be back in time to start his homecoming supper. He kissed her on the cheek and walked out to begin the day's work as the morning's first light rose up over the horizon in a cold magenta of shadow that fanned out across the shallow valley. He made good progress, finishing the west fence before lunch. The north fence that ran along the road, however, had so deteriorated that its rusted staples crumpled into a ferric dust when he pried them out, and more than a few posts had so rotted through that they could not hold a nail and would need to be replaced before he returned.

Late afternoon as he worked his way down the east fence, the bawl from a car horn scurried a flock of nested starlings swishing skyward. A rush of crimson and chrome blurred down the road then U-turned without slowing and pointed back to the village. Sally Anne stepped out wearing English riding boots and a white ruffled blouse with a black skirt creased into a riot of pleats, hands resting on hips as might a plantation proprietress as she surveyed her holdings. Gazing up at her, his heart works spun like a crazed watch.

She had never been more than halfway down their lane, so he made a stirrup of his hands, and she rode sideways as he led the mule about, asking him close questions about farm work as if it were an occupation she was now taking under serious consideration. When they came to the rock dais where his parents had buried his sister and four brothers, she asked him to stop. She read each marker before bowing her head, and when she looked up at him with just such shiny eyes as Merlin might conjure to bewitch the heart of a simple farm boy she asked why he had deserted her.

He told her how on a rainy morning two Novembers before he saw her and the doctor drive by on their way to Mark's college. When he told her what Maude said to him at the Post Office that same afternoon, she fisted her mouth and started to cry. Out on the road a long tendril of ocher road dust snaked behind his mother as she returned in the plodding wagon. He rested a hand on Sally Anne's shuttering shoulder and confessed himself to be twice as dumb as the dumbest mule ever conceived by the hand of God to have left her.

That morning her parents had boarded the train to take in a play at Stambaugh Auditorium, and they planned to stay the weekend with an ailing aunt. His mother asked her to stay for supper with them, and while the two women set the table, his father hobbled down the steps for the first time since the wagon had crushed him. Sally Anne helped with the dishes after they ate while he and his father sat in the kitchen sipping sassafras tea as they debated what needed to be completed the week following, each trying without success not to stare at Sally Anne. When the women were done, she requested him to accompany her up to the road. She asked as they walked if there was not something he wanted to do for himself before he returned. It sure would be special, he told her, if a certain someone volunteered her services to escort him around her college. He had made up his mind to enroll once he got home for good and already had a year's tuition set aside at a bank up in Canada.

\* \* \*

The drive took them six hours. They started out so early that at first they saw no one along the road save for a surly Amishman digging fencepost holes and several hay-loaded wagons pulled by gray-haired mules or sleek-maned Dutch drays, their tales whisking at already pesky flies and lifting their legs like the step dancers he once admired at the county fair. When they reached the college they parked outside the new football stadium and walked to a spreading oak on the main green where Sally Anne spread the blanket she carried. They walked arm-in-arm after lunch down a knoll to the library. Janitor Sam looked up from his sweeping in back when she rapped on the window of the locked door with her class ring. She raised her hand, and Sam smiled a bucktooth grin. With less than twenty women on campus, he had little trouble remembering her. She led him around as he gaped up at the rows of books rising from floor to ceiling. Two floors of books, not just one like the village library, and it was a half hour before she shoved him out the door to look over the rest of the campus.

On the drive home an evening bucket-dropper scudded up behind them, and soon he had the Pierce Arrow buried in mud up to its axles with the village yet another seven miles down the road. He went into the trunk and returned with a brass lamp like those employed on the grand ore freighters that plied the Great Lakes. She found some of her father's pipe matches under the seat, and he went out again, the sideways rain beakpecking his face. He walked up the road with his head down as he leaned into the wind until he came upon the stack of fence posts left by the surly Amishman.

He returned to the car, levering one post under the rear axle and lay the other lengthwise across the road as his fulcrum. When he yelled for her to gun the mighty thirty-six-horsepower engine, waves of mud shot over him as the car sank only the deeper. She locked the doors and made him stand shivering in the rain until she judged him sufficiently clean. After he came inside she wrapped him with their picnic blanket and held him to her to share with him her heat when he continued to shiver. So had they passed most — but not all — of their night.

At dawn he carried the fence posts to where he had found them and walked on until he came to the whitewashed barn where the Amishman was hitching up his plow team. He expressed little Christian charity to a delay in the start of his workday, even when he explained it was their honeymoon, until he offered the Amishman a dollar for his trouble. After he pulled them free and unhitched his team, he asked as he held out his billfold where it was he and his pretty bride was headed to on their honeymoon. Sally Anne's tartan skirt twirled as she turned in a pirouette, hands on her hips and not smiling. He told the Amishman they had better be on their way.

Her parents were not due back from a cousin's funeral in Columbus until later in the afternoon, for which he was grateful. When they reached her house he washed down the car and toweled out the inside. So they would not muddy it anew he walked the three miles home where he found his mother stooping between strawberry rows. He explained what happened as he worked the next row over. She stopped her weeding after he finished, studying him with her brown streaked face. She said she certainly hoped he did not let Sally Anne take advantage of him. She was a town girl after all, and town girls knew tricks that country boys never so much as imagined. She returned to her weed pulling, a co-conspiratorial smile crossing her face as his own burned scarlet.

* * *

On the night before he boarded his train they were swinging on her porch when she asked him for the hundredth time why it was he was he felt duty bound to return. He wasn't Canadian. He told her he had to. He'd made promises. Promises he intended to keep for there was surely a reckoning in whatever hereafter there was for those who did not. How could she trust his promises to her if he did not keep his to them? Should he desert them she would always doubt his constancy. Him staying here with her, she retorted, beat him being over there and constantly dead, her doubts no matter. She slid a little apart, her arms crossed, and in the soft square of light falling through the window, end-of-summer gypsy moths appeared and vanished and reappeared. An ill omen indeed as the month had just turned June.

Neither spoke until he stood to wish her a goodnight. She failed to answer when he asked if she intended to see him off, and when he leaned to kiss her, she would offer him only her cheek. He mounted up his mule and rode out down the street, passing from pool to pool of lamplight. When he reached the corner, he twisted around in the surplus cavalry saddle ridden in another war not all that long ago. She sat on the porch swing as before, looking across the street as she pretended to ignore him. He called out to her that he loved her. Had always loved her since their first day at the Sisters' when he could not stop himself from looking at her. Would indeed always love her. His words echoed on and on in the night and not until they at last died away and the summer silence returned did he ride on into the dark. So great boiled her anger, though, that at the depot she did not let him kiss her, not even a peck on the cheek this time. He tried to remember the last time he did kiss her. He found often now that he forgot what it was he truly wanted so much to recall yet recalled every detail of what he wanted so much to forget.

\* \* \*

Unlike his coming-home crossing, the North Atlantic for his return voyage lay flat as a pond before the storm so the convoy ships stood out like paddling ducks, and the men at the journey's end remarked to one another they were lucky to have lost only the two. The first was a troop carrier sailing just ahead of his. It took two torpedoes when they were but five hours out of Halifax at an hour past midnight as the sky above seemed all moon and stars, the sea afire, the warm summer night filled with the screams of men burning within.

The second they lost as they entered the Irish Sea when they were but a half-day out from Liverpool. The evening was clear with only a scarlet ridge of a half dozen clouds racked along the horizon that chased each other across the sky like a pack of burning rats. The ship struck a mine outside its engine room that burst her boilers and scalded to death dozens of sailors. He and another soldier leaned against the rail smoking as they watched the ship go down, its bow pointed heavenward and surrounded by ship detritus and corpses in red life vests that bobbed in the water like autumn apples until the sinking ship sucked them under with her. His companion remarked this was as bad a portent for them as they could ask for, and so it seemed for three days later as he boarded the ferry at Dover he heard the giant

German eighty-eights though no breeze blew north across the Channel.

He reported to his old unit. When he walked in from the village, he saw as he topped the last rise their line of trenches that stitched back and forth like sutures sewn by a drunken country doctor. He recognized few faces in the lines and was relieved to find Stanton sitting on a cot in their old dugout, staring down at his hands as if in his absence they had been attending some labor not of his doing. In answer to his query, Stanton held them out, palms up, like Christ looking in askance to Thomas.

Their fighting in the summer and long into the fall fell nothing short of butchery, an endless slaughterhouse with his Majesty alone losing seven thousand troops a day. The French, he heard, stopped counting altogether for fear if the true number was so much as rumored they would face another wave of mutinies followed by endless firing squads, and they could ill afford to lose even the most disgruntled of their troops. Recruits who a year before their governments would never have drafted even for administrative only duties now filled the trenches, their training so slapdash their average lifespan slipped to just six months. Many died in their first week. All too many in their first hours off the ferry yet the generals time and again ordered them out of their trenches and across No Man's Land where the greenest of recruits could tell them the machineguners would never allow the Canadians to within a hundred yards of their lines. When again reprieved by the fall rains, their sergeant pulled from his coat a bottle of liberated Napoleon brandy he had saved for the occasion and walked it down the line, letting each man drink his fill until they emptied it and then he pulled another from his coat and when it was gone still another. Something had to give, Stanton told him. Another year like this one and none of them would be marching home.

The something was the United States. He pitied the men soon to be disembarking. Cursed President Wilson as a damned fool of a butcher for sending mere boys into a slaughter he had no real part in save as an armchair philosophizing fart of a far-off observer. As they held out for whatever abeyance the Americans would bring, he waited for Sally Anne's letters that began to arrive the week after she refused to kiss him at the depot. She wrote him a letter a day. Letters she penned in her lapidary hand that spidered across pages of expensive paper posted in alternating colors that reminded him of home and her. Morning-mist gray and sunset rose. Daffodil yellow and forget-me-not blue. After he had been back for some months short of a year, weeks passed without his hearing from her. He speculated she had returned to Mark until his sergeant handed him a great packet of letters bound together with kite string, postmarked Chicago where she was visiting her half-brother and his wife, helping them care for a newborn baby boy. He knew then her letters to be a prophecy from Providence, somehow a contract with their world to come, a covenant irrevocable even by the fickleness of the three sisters Fate in their travels along the back roads through the French countryside as they spread their mischief.

*  *  *

The last time night he sat up in the dead-limbed cherry orchard he nodded off. He woke when he thought he heard from a long way off the sisters singing their dirge. He must have only dreamt it, though, because no one passed along the road, or perhaps he had slept when they had and he was not aware. Perhaps that was when they completed the spinning of his fate. Tossed his coin to begin its final spin. Two days later his sergeant detailed him over to the American company.

He recalled little of what happened to him after the shell exploded. Had no conception of the passing of a day or a year. As agonizing as were his wounds, his dreams tortured him more, and yet like a drowning man he found himself grasping onto them. Often he was again stuck in the mud and holding Sally Anne close to him beneath the picnic blanket. Once he dreamed they truly had their honeymoon, and they were now the couple standing at the American Falls as they gripped the iron barrier with closed eyes, opening them and smiling as they watched the gray fingers of fog whirl above the river like phantom dancers. When they began to shiver from the cold, they strolled back to their hotel room where they stood before the fire and toasted with iced champagne their good fortune. He kissed her downy neck as he undid the buttons at the back of her dress, reminded her that he had told her he would come home. Would come home because now he had something to live for.

Often the dream he willed was of them living on the farm. Sometimes they had two children and sometimes upwards of eight, but no matter the number he doted on each. His folks lived with them, and while he worked the farm with help from his father, his mother took care of the children and Sally Anne taught at the sisters.' In the mornings he kissed her goodbye on the front porch and watched the car lumber up the lane as ocher dust uncoiled behind, and he kept watching until she disappeared behind the grove of locust trees before he walked out to the barn to begin the day's work. One morning his mother came onto the porch as he held his son. They watched Sally Anne fade away, and she asked if he was now not glad he had not gone back for if he had look at all he would have missed.

He hung onto this dream the most now because it was his last morphia dream. He did not dream at all without the morphine, was never even certain when he was awake. One by one his dreams, his memories, ghosted away as though he were dead, or, if not dead, had mostly relinquished the world.

## CHAPTER 29

The Rambler was gone when they got home. Betsy let the engine idle as they sat in the driveway. "Did the folks say they were going somewhere?"

"Not to me they didn't."

"Maybe they left a note on the frig."

"Don't bet the last of your gas money on it."

The refrigerator was barren of any note. As Bartholomew headed into the dining room, the telephone began to ring. "You grab that while I check upstairs."

It was Matt.

"Where are you calling from?"

"Nebraska gas station surrounded by about a million zillion acres of corn."

"How'd you get way out there already? You only left this morning."

"Started out yesterday evening after I left your house. Wasn't going to sleep anyway so I drove all night. Pushed the speed limit a little, but I found them."

"You found who?"

"Your patient's family. Stanton, like I told you."

"Can't be."

"That half-a-picture in Amy Baker's drawer?"

"Yeah?"

"The Stantons showed me the *entire* picture. This one with him in it."

Betsy leaned against the door jamb. On the dining room wall over Nathan's chair hung a photograph from their last family vacation taken with her mother's old Brownie camera from college. The four of them stood before Yosemite Falls, Nathan at the edge with an arm around her shoulder, he ghosting out of focus and blurry, a rainbow arcing over them all.

"This is a great ending to our story. Now we can get your patient home, and I can maybe get hired on up at the *Plain Dealer*. To hell with Congressman Hanna."

Your time will expire in fifteen seconds. Please deposit seventy-five cents for three more minutes.

"Betsy, I'm out of change. I'm going to cop some zees and head back in the morning. I'll see you day after tomorrow."

"But . . ."

A dial tone hummed in Betsy's ear.

\* \* \*

She was reading charts by flashlight in the attic before dawn. Bartholomew hitched a ride out mid-morning.

"We've got to find something that shows he's not Tommy Stanton."

Betsy could have made more progress that summer, but instead of only organizing the charts for shipment while searching for that of her patient, she found it impossible not to read them as she went along. Thoroughly. Their lives sidetracked her. She rooted for their recoveries as she would a paperback hero, elated at their discharges and crestfallen at their deaths. They already had found the charts for 1918 and 1919, and now she searched the stacks for those of 1922. By noon Bartholomew located the ones for 1920 and 1921. These they unstacked but did not organize, looking only in each for the date of the last entry and the signature below. Evelyn Wolf's again stood out not only because they saw it so often but because she signed her name in a shivering meticulous script. Her heart sank when next she found only the 1923 charts. The two searched on. They took no break except for opening their brown-bag lunches, reading as they ate. Bartholomew whined to go home at six o'clock but she made him hitchhike, not stopping for the day until the sun sank behind the cemetery trees. On the road home she fell asleep and came within feet of drifting beneath a semi-truck trailer, waking only when its driver blasted its air horn.

*Crazy bitch driver! Stay off the road if you can't hold your liquor.*

The next morning she left Bartholomew a note, telling him he had earned a day off. She arrived puffy-eyed at the hospital an hour early as the food manager was unlocking the doors of the cafeteria where she bought a cinnamon roll and two large coffees. Filbert came up sometime after one o'clock and hollered down the canyons of boxes if it wasn't a good time for her to be taking a break. When she walked to the door, he stood grinning.

"What's so goddamn funny?"

He ran a finger over her cheek and showed her the dust. "We could pass for brother and sister."

For the first time in days she laughed. "You might even pass for white if you stood next to me."

"No way, Missy. Uh uh. I finds me more than enough troubles all on my own just as the good Lord made me."

She pulled a dollar bill from her apron pocket. "Will you buy me a milk and Snickers, please?"

"That all you be having?"

"I'm not much hungry."

"You keep eating thisaway, you'll be nothing but a spook yourself."

\* \* \*

That evening Betsy found her mother in the kitchen. She had not been outside her room since the night she journeyed the village in her nightmare sleep. She seemed still asleep because when Betsy asked about Bartholomew's whereabouts, she raised her hand holding the silverware toward the door, encompassing the neighborhood within her gesture and returned to setting the table. Her father explained when he came home that Bartholomew's team had made it to the Little League semis and would likely be back late. She was in bed before he came home.

* * *

When Matt came up around noon with two icy cokes, she didn't look up.

"Intuition tells me I've been doghoused."

"He's not from Nebraska."

"Photos don't lie."

"He's not lying."

"No, but he's confused. After being here for half a century, who wouldn't be?"

"If I find his chart, will you not run your story?"

"If you find his chart, I won't run my story *if* it shows he's not Tommy Stanton."

"Deal. Now let me work."

"Are you telling me to get lost?"

She flipped a page. Matt stood.

"See you around then."

* * *

Bartholomew hitched a ride out to the hospital, and the two of them went into the patient's room. He was glad they had returned. He worried whenever they left they would not. Knew such a day would come soon.

"Ask him if he wants us to get him home."

The patient's hand lay still for a long time. *No.* His finger paused for a moment. *I cannot. This is my penance.*"

"Ask him why this is his penance."

"Are you sure you want me to, Sis? What if he clams up on us?"

"It's now or never if we're going to get him home."

# CHAPTER 30

Their sergeant accompanied him and Cahill to the village two miles behind their lines with orders to assist in evacuating its civilians. He left a gendarme and himself at the crossroads and posted Cahill a quarter mile down the rutted track with strict instructions to direct all evacuees towards the crossroads. Quality control in the French munitions factories had grown so slipshod that one in three of their artillery shells either failed to explode or fell short, leaving a score of homes leveled in the past six months alone. Troops were massed in the reserve trenches and rumor had it the allies intended to cross No Mans' Land two days hence in one all-out push lead by the improved British Mark V tank with their attack preceded by a twenty-four-hour bombardment.

A group of villagers approached the crossroads near dawn. When the gendarme directed them to follow the right fork, the villagers insisted they be permitted to take the left. The Allies had shelled the right fork twice that week already, killing half a dozen sheep. From the camions carrying shells they knew when a bombardment was imminent, and camions had rattled through their village at midnight. The gendarme explained they could not take the left because it took them too close to the Canadians where they would draw fire from the bastard Boches. The villagers refused. Some sat on their sheet-bundled packs in the middle of the road. He and the gendarme unslung their rifles and with bayonets forced the peasants up the right fork, following them to the top of the rise and watched until they disappeared over the next where the last peasant turned, shaking his fist and cursing them and their progeny should any mischance befall them.

He and the gendarme returned to the crossroads. As they shared a smoke between them, they heard the death-fugue singing. He dropped his Enfield and ran. When he reached them, the villagers were spread across the road, their sheet-bundled packs blown open and possessions scattered, just out of reach. A pack of war-crazed dogs already surrounded the dead, lapping from pools of misty blood, steam of man and beast mingling in the early morning cold. Fifty yards up the road he came upon four girls who had walked together so as to share their courage. The eldest could have been no older than six. The girls stared back at him with broken eyes sunk in grimace distorted faces like those depicted in the book of Judges. The image of one child snaked inside his heart and burrowed out a nest for itself where it rested yet. A faceless girl with a photograph protruding from her ripped pocket. In it stood a smiling Stanton and beside him a row of peasant children, the girl nearest him grasping hold of his John Brown belt as though it was all that held her fast to this world. He looked again at the faceless child before he slipped the photograph inside his tunic.

After their attack got postponed, his sergeant told him of his reassignment to the Americans, advised him it would be better if he forgot all about what he saw the day before. He packed his kit and found Stanton, telling him of his reassignment but had not the heart to give him the photograph he carried inside his tunic. If the Canadians made little effort to find him, he understood; with him being wounded a week later, losing his family and Sally Anne forever, this was his penance and would always be so. He had no wish to be found, no wish to go home. He deserved all that befell him.

\* \* \*

The worst for him came when the morphine injections ceased and along with his wounds he suffered from the sweats and the chills. Hallucinations that could only have been gifts begot by Satan himself. It was then he truly descended into Hell, which seemed to him only just for it is when we find ourselves in Hell we learn it is there no act is forgotten. Discover that Hell and memory are one.

Months sifted through the hourglass of his life, and he had no way of counting its grains. In time the withdrawals eased, his pain receded. In time he figured out the parts of him missing. Wherever he felt pain that was what was gone, and everything seemed to be gone save his index finger. With it he tapped out letters that would have been Biblical in length if some scribe had but written them down. Some to his family where he asked their forgiveness for the hardship he knew he had caused them. Some to Sally Anne. Letters never written, letters never read, but if he kept his sanity, tapping them out — over and over — is what kept it. So in some way they were right. His learning telegraphy may have been a spot of luck. May have been but it was yet too early to say for certain.

After what he guessed must have been many months, he felt a rolling beneath him, the same sway he felt in his bunk on the ship from Halifax to Liverpool. It excited him. He prayed to God he had at last died. Prayed this to be his crossing Jordan. He had done his time in Hell but apparently not done enough for it stopped too soon, and he was again left to his letters. It was while he telegraphed on his bed sheet that he felt a thump on his chest. He thought it to be a nurse checking his remaining lung until a series of rapid thumps followed the first. Someone was telegraphing to him! It had been so long, not since he and Stanton pulled guard duty together on the night before the slaughter of the French civilians.

The chest thumper was Timothy Samuels, and he said they were patients at Walter Reed. Samuels had cowboyed the ranches north of Santa Fe before he tossed his bindle in with the Army the week after Congress declared war. While he volunteered for the Cavalry, he ended up a telegrapher, more than a little bit daft by the time the Armistice got signed after a friendly-fire artillery shell destroyed the peasant farmhouse where they billeted. The Army shipped him home in 1919, but he did not last long on the outside, which was all right. Here he had three hots and a cot with no worries about some cop nightsticking him on the back of his noggin as he slept off a quart of hobo applejack in a storekeeper's doorway.

Walter Reed, though, had started to shitcan their veterans after Congress cut their funding once again, notwithstanding the veterans had no place to go and no one who would take them in, but why should congressmen care? The veterans had to be slackers if they still inhabited the hospital after all these years. As the hospital shut down a ward, they boarded it up. Samuels, however, remained too confused to be let loose, and administration transferred him down to the same ward as his. Samuels scoped out his bunkmate while he unpacked his duffle and noticed the telegraphing finger. So fast did the finger tap it took him a minute to figure out the finger was Morsing. Morsing almost as fast as Samuels could read. Samuels asked him how he had gotten there. He told him. Samuels wanted to know if he was certain his family had no idea of his whereabouts. He was and he made Samuels promise never to reveal to anyone his true name.

A nurse spotted Samuels telegraphing on his chest and asked him what the devil he thought he was doing. She hurried to a ward doctor who reported the telegraphing patient to a brother who was a major in the Signal Corp. When the major came out, they Morsed long into the night, but he gave the major only the *nom de guerre* he gave the Canadians.

Days passed. Sometime in the spring Samuels tapped on his heart. The major had contacted the Canadians. Because it was Government policy to keep its charges in the hospital most near their families, they were transferring him to a hospital in Ohio. Samuels guessed the Army had tracked down his Canadian unit and they must have given the Army the depot address he put down for his next of kin. The patient said he was glad he had not given the Canadians his true name when he enlisted. Samuels knew and swore he told no one, but who could say for certain because Samuels was a liar. Or so the patient told them.

On the day they moved him, Samuels sat on his bed and the two Morsed for hours until they carried him away to the train station. Samuels said that in the fall he was going to try once again to make it on the outside, and he promised to come to Ohio. He asked Samuels to stop by to see how his folks were doing. Begged him to see how Sally Anne was getting along. It would do his heart more than a little good if he knew she had married and now had a swarm of children frisking in her skirts. Samuels said he would, but he never heard from him. Never heard from anyone again until Bartholomew tapped on his arm years later. No one that is save some long-forgotten telegrapher who sometimes stole into his room. Or perhaps he too was but a dream. Some phantom from out of his past. Who could say for certain?

## CHAPTER 31

The patient's hand ceased its tapping. The muscles in his stick-thin arm relaxed. Bartholomew twice tapped his wrist but the finger remained still. He turned to his sister. "So what do we do?"

"He's not Tommy Stanton."

"I know he's not, but what do we do?"

"His chart. We have to find his chart."

\* \* \*

Near the end of her shift Nurse Baker came up.

"Matt called. Said he has his story written. Before he presented it to Henry he wanted to know if we had any comment."

"Will they even run such a story?"

"I asked him that. He didn't know for certain. Says he's going to call Hanna about moving the patient out to the Omaha VA so he can be near his family. Give Hanna a chance to look like a hero so maybe the *Journal* will run it. If not Matt says he knows of another paper outside the county not in Hanna's pocket that would jump at the chance."

"But he's not from Nebraska."

"I know, sweetie."

"How much time do we have?"

"A day maybe. Two at best."

Betsy looked at the chart she held.

"You two should go home."

"Yes, ma'am."

She put a hand on Betsy's shoulder. "Be back all the earlier tomorrow."

"I told you we keep seeing Evelyn Wolf's name in so many charts. She might be able to help us if only we could find her."

"Fifty years. The woman could be dead. Could be retired in Hawaii."

"Her name wasn't even in the phone book."

"You told me. Twice. Go home, Betsy. You're exhausted. Try to get some sleep."

"Yes, ma'am."

\* \* \*

Matt found her at noon the next day wedged between two walls of fiberboard boxes with an entanglement of angel-haired cobwebs dangling above her and a chart lying in her candy-striped lap. He sat across from her and after unfolding the day's *Morning Journal* he took from the brown paper bag and set upon it a cold Dairy Queen cheeseburger and a now runny milkshake.

"So how long do you plan on staying up here tonight?"

She opened her purse to show him the two large flashlights and the four packs of D batteries she purchased at Hooey Hardware on her way home the night before.

"You making it a sleepover?"

"Making it a weekover if I have to."

He read charts with her until it was time for him to leave to cover a village council meeting.

"You still upset with me for pushing ahead with the story?"

"It's all right."

"I'll be back after work."

She did not answer. He watched her reading for a moment more before he went out of the attic, his footsteps echoing down the stairwell until they died away.

She read through the afternoon until in the failing light at the bottom of a rat-chewed pile of boxes hidden behind the brickwork chimney she came upon a chart with the name of the patient scissored out. She blinked.

"How odd."

She walked to the window, angling the chart up to the light as she flipped its pages. Unlike all the other charts, this one had no date of discharge, no date of death, and the last line written in it was the chilling calligraphic signature of Evelyn Wolf.

* * *

Matt met her on his way up the steps as she hurried out of the hospital.

"I was coming to find you. We need to talk. Now."

"Something wrong?"

"I found his chart. I know I did."

They sat in his Volkswagen as he read. When he finished the last page, he handed it back to her.

"You think it's really his?"

"The date fits. Explains why no one knows who he is."

"If it's really his, Mark's not going to be happy you found it."

"Mark?"

"The Honorable Congressman Hanna."

Betsy looked up at the attic window. She looked at Matt. "Sally Anne's Mark?"

"Who's Sally Anne?"

Betsy leaned back in her seat, tapped her mouth with a fist as she considered.

"Betsy?"

She took hold of his wrist and turned his watch toward her.

"What time does the library close?"

"Eight o'clock I think. Why?"

"Let's go. I have a hunch."

* * *

Mrs. Urbschat led them to the back shelves where the library kept their Saint Paul yearbooks.

"We have them going all the way to eighteen ninety-six when the old sisters' school published their first. Which year are you looking for?"

Betsy ran a finger across the books. 1911. 1912. 1913. She tapped its spine. "This one."

"All right. Now I know you'll be careful, Betsy. The paper they used then contained so much acid the pages tear if you so much as breathe on them and this is the only copy we have. They are truly irreplaceable."

"We will."

She carried the annual to a long oak table. An attic musk twitched their nostrils when she opened its cover.

"Look there." Matt pointed. "Old Ben Cutler when he was a kid."

"And when he had hair."

"That stood straight up."

There was a photograph of Saint Paul's before they added its two wings, cows grazing where the gymnasium now stood. Another of the football team with players holding their leather helmets without faceguards and several of the boys looking out with crooked noses. The next page pictured the class of 1915. Three boys and five girls. The boys wore gray flannel trousers and white collarless shirts, the girls dressed in white-starched frocks with ribbons bowed in their hair and tied around their sleeves. All stared into the camera with the Post-Office-poster eyes of children attending a convent school except for one girl with snow-blond hair who dared smile up at the boy standing behind her. Betsy ran a finger along the line of names.

"It's her. Sally Anne. She's really for real."

She traced a finger beneath the line of names for the second row. "His is Hamilton."

Betsy carried the yearbook to Mrs. Urbschat's desk. "Would you know anything about her?"

The librarian pulled her bifocals to the end of her nose. "You mean Mrs. Hanna?"

"The congressman's wife?"

"Yes, indeed. I'd forgotten she was a Rutherford then. She's Mrs. Hanna now to everyone. Few people even know her first name and fewer dare address her by it. Her people have lived here for donkey years. Town founders and all, you know, just like the Hannas." Mrs. Urbschat smiled. "Wasn't she the sassy one though? Wouldn't know it to see her now with her health and all."

Betsy pointed to the boy. "What about him?"

"James Hamilton? Can't recollect any Hamiltons from town. Not surprising what with the two wars and the Spanish flu and the Depression. Lots of families upped and disappeared. Went to California or died out. Got buried behind country churches or back corners of abandoned farms. Might just as well have never been born for all anyone remembers of them." She ran her finger along a line of names. "There's Mark Hanna standing next to him. Perhaps he remembers."

"I wonder where their farm was? The Hamiltons', I mean."

"Why don't you look in the parish records? The church stores them here for folks researching their family tree. We keep them in the stack next to the old yearbooks."

## CHAPTER 32

Strange how time passes. The years. The lives passing through those of James Hamilton and Sally Ann Rutherford. Five summers went by before Timothy Samuels kept his word he gave at Walter Reed to look in on the Hamiltons and Sally Anne. The summer before she married the congressman. Strange what mischief the Sisters Fate manage to spin for if not for Mr. Samuels, she would never have married the congressman. Or so in later years she often comforted herself.

She was gardening behind her house when he limped down the alley and introduced himself, stammering and twisting his workmen's cap behind his back, shy as a stick-beaten dog. As they sipped tart lemonade on her back porch, he told her that late in the summer after Walter Reed moved James Hamilton, Jamie she called him, they discharged Samuels a second time, giving him enough money to buy a train ticket that would have gotten him to Santa Fe by way of Hanna. His undoing was they also gave him a new suit.

The nuns of neighboring Saint Mary's sewed new suits for all of the veterans so upon their release they would not have to wear their old uniforms years after their discharge and have some opportunity to find gainful employment. Men outfitted in Irish tweed as they wandered the neighborhood streets carrying brown paper parcels under their arms were a common sight. Mothers without a doubt warned their children to beware because as he walked down the sidewalk the younger ones scattered before him. Little girls wailed. The older brats called him Mr. Loony Bin to his back and ran off. It was a pack of their big brothers who rolled him. The first thing he saw a few inches from his nose when he came to was his bloody hair greasing the end of a baseball bat. They had robbed him of his train money and taken the paper parcel holding what little he owned. Stripped him even of his father's gold watch. Night was fast falling. He stumbled down streets, keeping to the shadows, until he came to a park where he laid up, sleeping fitfully in a thicket of mulberry bushes. The next morning he washed the caked blood off his face and out of his hair in a duck pond and rinsed out as best he could his white shirt. He guessed he may have suffered a concussion, but he did not want to return to Walter Reed. They might keep him for good, and he had places to go. Vows sacred delivered from one soldier to another he intended somehow to keep.

He poked through the trashcans until he found part of some kind of a sandwich wrapped in newspaper from the day before. After brushing off most of the ants, he sat on a bench and tried not to look at what he ate as he read the help-wanted ads. A bum searching the same trashcans stumbled along. Though they had never met, each recognized a don't-mean-nothingness in one another's eyes.

Samuels offered to split his breakfast. They talked. His name was Benjamin Franklin Murphy. He too had served in France. As the two ate they reminisced about what they had done in the war, where they had been, what they had seen. Short romances each had savored. Soldier things. Neither talked much about what he'd done since. When he asked about work, Ben said the orchard keepers on the other side of the Potomac in Virginia were looking for peach pickers. A mule-drawn wagon pulled through every day to drop off those who could not go a day longer without a drink and picked up those who had no choice but to try. That evening the two threw their bindles in with the Stratford picking crew.

You can go into remission from shell shock, maybe manage your affairs, yet the war will haunt you until the end of your days. A firecracker exploding on the Fourth of July. Newsreel clips. Certainly the crack of a baseball bat to the side of your head, and once you drop through that rabbit hole again you can wait a long while, if ever, for you to find your ladder out again.

The two veterans followed the harvests until the December rains drove them to Saint Petersburg where an orange grower who had been a captain on Pershing's staff allowed Ben to squatter a shack, and there the two passed the winter. To eat they worked odd jobs. Growers often had a little winter work to get ready for spring. Bean money they called it. Bean money and maybe some bacon fat. Stole when the bean money ran out. Crawled through cellar windows and jimmied car doors. Some days their lives grew as cold and wet as they had been in the trenches so when it grew too miserable to work or to find something to steal Samuels hid out in the public library. There it was dry. Warm. He liked sitting with his back to the clanking radiator and feel the wet steam rising from his clothes. Often he chanced upon something to eat. The crust of a spoiled child's sandwich. A browning apple core. The Saint Petersburg library was open to anyone so long as they were white and kept their zipper up and did not smell of bathtub gin and so long as they looked to be reading. Over five winters he finished all of the Harvard Classics.

The spring of nineteen twenty-two was the first year they contracted out to the Hannas for the strawberry harvest. Once they'd gleaned the fields and were ready to move on to their next job for the Smuckers cannery over in Wayne County, Samuels told the crew boss he had family nearby and would catch up with them in a day or so. He walked the railroad tracks past the depot until he found a campsite to pitch his lean-to. Each morning after he washed himself in Mill Creek he walked into the village where he hung out at Shorty Stevens's pool hall, picking up a little cracker-barrel money at eight ball. Asked the stray question between shots. He told Mrs. Hanna he could not be certain if Jamie was at the local hospital because two days after they took him away a rumor spread of a train derailment. He did not know if anyone was hurt. Did not even know the rumor to be true. The Army might have kept it out of the papers.

She demanded he immediately drive with her out to the hospital. It was her first time there. Since the laying of its foundation stones in May of nineteen-seventeen, the village had ostracized the hospital. A sizeable segment of its citizens were second generation Irish and first generation German with no love lost for anything English and especially anything French. Their outspoken bias held that if war was truly necessary that America had entered it on the wrong side. Rumors propagated of pestilence running rampant with the rats seemed true when scores of villagers succumbed to Spanish influenza. Mrs. Hanna often saw at first light from her widow's walk the sheet-wrapped bodies stacked on the sidewalk of those who had passed in the night. Watched men pushing wheelbarrows haul them away. Few ventured outside their homes. Groceries got delivered to backdoors by schoolboys wearing handkerchiefs soaked in wood alcohol over their mouths. The sheriff nailed up posters prohibiting all public gatherings. Schools shut down. For months churches cancelled services, and while the dead were buried, their funerals got postponed or never held. Several families were wiped out altogether, and all had suffered the loss of some member. After the epidemic ended, even the D.A.R and American Legion would have nothing to do with the hospital.

The hospital in turn kept to itself. Went so far as to have patients come in and caskets go out aboard midnight trains. It could have as well been on the moon for all the village cared, and only its most desperate lowered themselves to take jobs there, and with few exceptions was still true during Betsy's time. While the village depended upon the federal money, workers who lived twenty miles and more away, though still in the congressional district, filled most positions. The hospital even so suffered a terrible shortage of qualified doctors and nurses during and in the first years after the war. Most — the ones under sixty — were in the Army, and upon their discharge they went elsewhere. Anywhere else. Only those exhausting all other opportunities came. Tales spread in the village of dope-fiend doctors. Nurses of dubious reputations and released inmates of insane asylums. Mrs. Hanna's stepsister had worked there since the day it opened.

She told them when they got to the hospital if Jamie Hamilton had ever been there he was now certainly dead. They received dozens of soldiers with little in their charts, some with not so much as a name. Always with severe wounds. Few lasted long, coughing up each day bits of mustard-burned lung. Several months maybe if lucky. Or in their agony unlucky. She walked them out behind the hospital to the cemetery it kept for soldiers with no next of kin. Orphans and runaways filled the Army in those days, immigrants who had left their families behind, and this was where they buried those whose caskets they did not freightcar home. A cemetery for orphans and runaways and those who had come to better their lives in an America known to them through myth. A cemetery for those without charts. For the loneliest of the dead. Nurses called them the Nameless Ones. They had no records save from the day they arrived until the day they died. Men without a past and a finite future indeed. Without Jamie's chart from Walter Reed, the hospital wouldn't know to tell his family. Wouldn't even know to ask the Canadians.

Mrs. Hanna and Samuels were less than satisfied. They looked at what records the hospital did keep for their Nameless Ones. Read word by word until almost midnight. Though the charts detailed the patients' medical care, they seldom held personal information other than the date the soldier arrived and his date of death. The number of the plot in back where he had been buried. Never a clue as to who he was. Never a clue that Jamie Hamilton had been one of them.

Her stepsister said she knew the rumor of a derailment. Had heard the doctors talk of a mystery train carrying patients to hospitals around the country going off track deep in the Alleghenies. No one hurt, but the doors of the Pullman carrying the patients broke open and charts flew. Records ended up scattered through the forest where snow drifted waist high. Some pages got gathered up but most were lost in the blizzard wind of February, and the train could not tarry for it would have been buried in hours. A few of those patients may have come there while others would have gone on to Chicago, Omaha, or Seattle to be nearer their families. No telling at which hospital Jamie may have gone or where his chart ended up. Their last Nameless One died in the winter following the rumored train wreck.

They returned the next day. Her stepsister said she had spoken to Dr. Himes who agreed to write to Washington for authorization to disinter the last Nameless One if they wished. They walked the grounds and talked. Samuels said even if not their Jamie, whoever he was deserved better than to rest in a potter's field for the forgotten. So the two of them buried the Nameless One out at the Hamilton farm in the rock-filled dais that cropped its grasping fingers up out of the earth, his tombstone left blank save for the date of death while they awaited better evidence as to the identity of the deceased.

That same summer Mark Hanna knocked on her door. On account of his flat feet, or so his father blackmailed the effeminate examining physician to attest, the Army deemed him unsuitable for combat. They were, however, ravenous for college boys in administration, and they assigned him to the War Department. Because of his connections the Army put him to work as their congressional liaison. He grew close to the representative for his district, whose election campaigns Mark's father financed, and after his discharge he went to work in Congressman Brown's office. He stayed with him until Brown died of pneumonia in the sub-zero winter of nineteen twenty-two. With the blessing of the Republican Party, he ran for the seat, vowing to leave no stone unturned, especially since he had been absent from the district for five years, and he bragged later how he must have knocked on every door in the county. Late one June afternoon, a few weeks after Samuels took up residence in the loft of the old barn her father had converted to a garage and began to tend her garden, he knocked on hers. She stopped breathing for a good fifteen seconds. Why, he demanded to know, had she not answered his letters?

After she received word about her Jamie, she did not have it in her to answer. Courtship by another she deemed an adulterous betrayal. Hanna's letters she left unopened let alone read. For many months he was persistent. A year maybe. Eventually the postman delivered them less and less often; in time he ceased to have any to deliver at all. She still had them bound with string in a trunk up in her attic, all unopened, but now maybe Hanna could help.

She told him about Samuels, what he had told her about Jamie. Besides Hanna teaching him telegraphy, they had been friends of a sort at the sisters', yet at recess always playing on opposite baseball teams. He said he would use his connections to find out, lying later to her that Hamilton was lost beyond hope and doubtless dead. He went on to win his election, and they married the next June after she graduated. She kept the Rutherford Mansion, teaching a year at St. Paul's before she asked for a leave of absence but found Washington populated by lunatics. Found herself in time taking the train home more and more often, sitting always beside the window so she could look out as she passed through the Alleghenies. She returned to teaching. On his years when not running for re-election and did not need her making an appearance at his side, she saw him but once or twice besides Christmas. She called herself twice bereaved. Her house built with a widow's walk not without reason.

## CHAPTER 33

Mrs. Hanna stood in front of the Rutherford Mansion when they drove past on their way out to what had once been the Hamilton homestead. Matt raised his foot from the gas pedal.

"What do you think? Should we tell her?"

"It's time. She's waited for over fifty years. It's more than time."

They pulled into the adjacent alley. Mrs. Hanna seemed to be studying her rickety porch swing that dangled askew from its one unbroken chain, twisting in the breeze, its oscillating shadow slow and random. Spent brown leaves portending an early autumn littered weed patches where she once tended petunias and impatience and geraniums. Herbs for her special teas whispered by the elderly ladies of the village to cure life's maladies.

"Mrs. Hanna?"

"Good afternoon, Betsy." Her voice cracked, the words faltering at their ends. She frowned at Matt. "I'm sorry, young man, but the Congressman's gone out. A fundraiser I think."

"We didn't come to see Mr. Hanna," Betsy said. "We came to see you."

"Me?"

"I've seen James Hamilton."

The old woman turned to Matt, her shattered marqueterie eyes set in their leathery hollows seeking confirmation. He nodded. She looked again to Betsy. "What did you say, child?"

"I've seen him. He's almost home. He always was."

\* \* \*

She crooked her finger at them and turned.

As the three entered her hallway, Matt leaned to Betsy's ear.

"You're not going to tell her everything, are you?"

"Shush." Betsy raised a hand to the side of her mouth. "She'll . . ."

As if she had walked into a wall, Mrs. Hanna halted before them. She shuttered in a queer tremble, like an old cat carried in from a freezing rain. The tendons in her neck bulged taut in the gray light and her hand flailed the air as though something precious had escaped its grasp. She grabbed hold of a doorjamb, her knuckles white and knees stammering. Betsy and Matt looked wide-eyed at one another. Only after a long minute did the old woman's knees quiet and her fingers let go. She turned to them, smiling an odd half-smile.

"Will you have a seat in the parlor, children? I've a stove burner to turn off."

She walked back to the kitchen, her ankles twice bowing and she touching a picture-framed wall with her fingertips.

"Do you think she's all right, Betsy?"

"I don't know."

"What should we do?"

The swinging door into the kitchen swished closed.

"Do as she asks."

"Maybe we shouldn't have told her."

"We had to. She can help us get him home. She is his home. All he has left."

They entered a high-ceilinged parlor appointed with mahogany furniture that remained a turn-of-the-century room with dark varnished wainscotings. Brown curtains sewn from Indian lace filtered out almost all hope of sunlight. A gallimaufry of horse and dog and cat knick-knacks crowded the fireplace mantle and above it hung a roman-numeral clock, the house silent save for its tick as the silver pendulum arced with the constancy of a hay reaper's scythe.

The kitchen door creaked. A dress lisped down the hall. Mrs. Hanna nodded at a frayed sofa where the three sat, her breath souring now of rum and mint. She opened an end-table drawer and removed a slender spine-broken book. She leafed its pages until she came to a faded yellow envelope and read to herself the poem it marked. "Who lived and died believing love was true."

"Ma'am?"

"Nothing, child. An ancient woman's mumblings. Now tell me what it was you saw."

She listened while Betsy told of her discovery, closing her eyes when Betsy recounted Hamilton's wounding.

"Would you care to see the picture Jamie sent to me after he returned to France?"

"Oh, yes. Very much."

She took from the envelope she used as a bookmark the photograph of a boy who looked to be about the same age as Matt, standing at ease with his campaign cap tucked under his arm and his dark hair combed straight back. He looked like he was trying hard to appear straight-faced and soldierly. Trying hard not to smile or perhaps only not to cry. His image in the photograph had faded through the years to little more than a shadow save for his haunting sepia eyes.

"What do you see?"

Betsy shook her head.

"I see death."

Betsy angled the photograph so it caught the russet light. She nodded.

"I'll get a duplicate made for you if you like."

"Oh, yes, I would. Very much. Thank you"

Mrs. Hanna returned the photograph to its envelope. The mantle clock thrice chimed. "This hour too will soon be gone."

Betsy covered the old woman's blue-veined hands with her own.

"How was it you first heard?"

"A telegram. It took a long while for the Canadians to find the Hamiltons because Jamie had proffered a phony name. Gave them a useless address." Mrs. Hanna shook her head. "He was always such a scalawag. His sergeant wrote a lengthier letter saying no one knew what happened. Perhaps something would turn up."

"It must've been hard not knowing. Always holding onto some hope."

"Harder all the more for if not for Jamie, I would never have become a teacher."

"Because he tutored you in geometry?"

"Oh, my." Mrs. Hanna blushed. "So he told you that whopper, did he?"

"It's not true?"

"Though Jamie was mule-whip smart, my falsehood was but a schoolgirl ruse to get him to pay attention."

"How did he help you become a teacher then?"

"I didn't have it in me to continue after the telegram. You see I sleepwalked through a world where life and death were memorized. My awakening came when what I dreamed should transpire in my life did not."

"The telegram. The letter."

"Those, of course, and more. Life happened. Real life, Betsy, not storybook life. Not life where it all makes sense on the final page, but as it's truly lived, where there is no sense but the sense with which we delude ourselves so we can keep going on for one more day. It was well after the Armistice before I was well enough to return. Then I could not."

"Why couldn't you?"

"The influenza epidemic claimed Daddy first. He treated so many. Dozens and dozens. Then Mama took ill on the afternoon we came home from his funeral, such as we had, just the two of us and Father McCray. I was alone. I knew nothing of investments. Didn't know there was a time to sell as well as a time to buy. I lost everything except for this house in the big Panic. My college fund sank along with the old Union Bank."

"So how'd you finish?"

"I was swinging out on my porch one afternoon in the summer of nineteen twenty-two, hiding in one of the storybooks I yet read. Mrs. Hamilton pulled up in their wagon. I'd not seen her since she drove in to let me read the letter from Jamie's sergeant five years before. She ceased to come in for Mass, and even if she hadn't, I stopped attending. She looked grayer, thinner, yet she still looked out upon the world with the demeanor of a Celtic brigand.

"We chatted for maybe an hour until she told me she had better be getting back. Said that Mr. Hamilton was . . . waiting for her to return. Yet she didn't go but sat studying me. Tried to make up her mind this was the bridge she in fact wanted to burn. Finally she reached into her apron pocket and handed down the passbook for an account up at the Royal Bank of Ottawa endorsed over to me. She said Jamie had given them strict instructions it was for me if he failed to return."

"Why did they take so long?"

"He never said any such thing. They needed his money, needed it desperately, but they couldn't bring themselves to touch a penny of it. It was blood money to them, yet by giving it to me, a bit of him would live on. In me, in . . ." Her thumb brushed the back of the envelope she held holding his photograph. "Well, in me."

"Whatever became of the Hamiltons? Did they move?"

Mrs. Hanna looked away. Three late afternoon shadows stretched across her threadbare carpet.

"Upon her return that afternoon she and Mr. Hamilton walked out to their barn where he wrapped around the center beam a heavy gauge rope and noosed each end. They slipped them over their heads and . . . stepped off. Constable O'Neil determined at his inquest that they had jumped at the same moment for when the bank's auctioneer found them the next morning they dangled in the breeze holding hands."

The clock pendulum arced. A minute passed before Betsy found her voice.

"W-Why?"

"Better for you to ask why not? Their lives turned from difficult to beyond impossible. By the thinnest of margins they managed without Jamie. Then with the signing of the Armistice, crop prices collapsed. The bank was to auction off their farm the next day. With it gone there would be no place left in this world for them."

"Except the county home."

"The Irish are a proud people."

"They could've saved themselves if only you'd known."

"No, child. They had enough."

"Why didn't they try? If you don't try, you don't do."

"You are so young." She lifted a strand of Betsy's chestnut hair from the girl's shoulder and rubbed it between thumb and finger. "As young as I was once. You've not yet learned how life drives you down, hammer on nail. How you await death's calling with the impatience of a debutante watching the clock. You have time yet to learn. The Hamiltons lost the will to try, grown depleted as the land they worked by a life of heartbreak, a cemetery filled with dead children, their last running away and losing him for good. Mr. Hamilton little more than a cripple. The bank selling off their farm out from under them."

Betsy looked across the hallway into a dining room where a handsome farm boy all one winter and spring sat at a table as he tutored a sassy-eyed girl with snow-blond hair still sleepwalking through life.

"Those illusions of youth life does not steal from us, death will. I'd not yet lost mine. I went back. Finished what

I'd started. Returned to the sisters', by then Saint Paul's. Married the congressman."

The mantle clock ticked. Betsy squeezed the old woman's hand.

"Will you come to the hospital to see him? Come tomorrow?"

Mrs. Hanna sat quiet for a moment, her eyes searching the feint blue-gray shafts of light dancing with brown motes slanted upon raw cords in a worn carpet. Her lips quivered. She looked at Betsy.

"I cannot."

"But why?"

"You may come to learn in your old age that there is no evil in this world more evil than that of aloneness. No man so evil. To be so alone as to be excluded even from the love of God. No price is too steep for me to pay not to be so alone."

"I don't understand."

"Do you believe in revenants?"

"I heard Nathan use that word once."

"Likely he heard it from me. It's an old fashioned word I sometimes heard from my grandmother. A revenant can be someone long forgotten and now remembered. It can also be someone returning after a long absence."

"Yes, ma'am. Sort of like Mr. Hamilton."

"Indeed for it can also mean a ghost."

"A ghost?"

"Jamie is one of mine. I cannot help you. May God somehow find it in his mercy to forgive me for adding yet one more sin to my already interminable list, but I cannot."

"Spend an hour with him, Mrs. Hanna. Just an hour. Half an hour even. Please. Who can it hurt?"

"Someone very precious. So precious as without them would be to leave me truly lost in my aloneness." She raised a finger to her temple. "Listen to me, child. Even with these old and failing eyes I read too much. Nights when I cannot sleep I wander my attic. Open musty trunks from my girlhood and read until dawn from college texts only now I can appreciate. Roadmaps for life I should have followed when I yet had the opportunity. Wisdom is wasted on the old. In our youth we lacked the time to listen. We believed we had no need. Believed we would invent it as we stumbled along in our blindness. Somehow run into it head on by accident. After we have lived our lives the wisdom of the centuries once at our fingertips does us no good. So listen to an old woman now learned in the lessons of life when I tell you to take this quest no further. You have years to go before life breaks your heart. Wait. Don't rush to beak it now."

"I can't." Betsy stood. "I'm sorry. I can't. I've come too far."

## ACT III
## CHAPTER 34

"This has to be it."

Matt pulled off Old Salem Road onto a rain-gullied lane barren of telephone pole or bellied electrical line that ran on down for an eighth mile between two rows of crippled fence posts laced with rusted barbed wire fingering out of the earth. A two-story farmhouse shingled with peeling asphalt and roofed in rough-cut slate stood at the end of the lane. The front porch had lost a support post so that its roof slanted at a precarious angle and half the floorboards were missing. A storm made up to the west in the last of the troubled sunset. Betsy lifted her door handle. "Might as well take a look around."

A wobbly barn rose on the other side of the lane. Rat gnawed holes spotted a rotting floor. The east wall had collapsed and the roof was falling in. A solitary crow perched in the middle of a sagging center beam blinked at them and when they failed to leave flapped its wings and with outstretched neck screeched its high-pitch caw. Matt grinned.

"All we need now is for the headless horseman to come galloping out."

"Don't go giving anyone ideas, Ichabod."

The ozone-charged air grew sharp as angel hair with a cold wind that rose out of the approaching storm. Betsy pointed to the two rows of tombstones near the backwoods at the far end of long unplowed fields. "Might be one of those family cemeteries Mrs. Urbschat spoke of. The one he told us about."

A failing light spread pools of shadows between the rough-chiseled limestone markers and one granite marker.

Three stood in front. Oliver Hamilton and Corinth Hamilton had died in 1922. The granite tombstone set a little apart from the others barren of name bore a date in 1921. Black clouds with their dark tendrils following crossed the horizon.

"Come on, Betsy. It's fixing to storm on us. I've seen enough. Let's go back to the paper and get started on rewriting our story."

\* \* \*

Matt was reading aloud as he typed with Betsy seated across the desk and flipping through the pages of her notebook when his nostrils twitched. The musk of Jade East cologne snaked into the room as a shadow darkened across the office floorboards. Matt raised his eyes mid-sentence. Thumbing his vest pockets in the doorway with Oliver grinning behind him stood Mark Hanna.

"Muckraking away on your big story are you, McLain?"

"Just polishing the final touches."

"We were on our way back from a country club fundraiser when Oliver here spotted your Volkswagen parked at the curb and a back office light on inside. Couldn't be good, I told him. Young man working away on a summer evening. Couldn't be good."

"You knew his story would get told. Someday. It pretty much had to."

"Yes, though I prayed it wouldn't be until after I'd long been feeding the worms."

"You never struck me as much of a churchgoer."

"Oh, you'd be surprised how often those sleepless from a troubled conscious find a need for prayer."

"You knew all along then?" Betsy pointed her notepad at him. "You knew it was Mr. Hamilton out there. Up in that room. Alone."

"I must confess I did."

"For how long?"

"Since the afternoon when I was walking the wards with Evelyn Wolf . . ."

"You knew her?"

"Don't be a goose. Of course I knew her. She was Mrs. Hanna's stepsister. They nicknamed her Maude. Mad Maude she came to be called. Anyway, we were walking the wards when I recognized Jamie."

"How could you?"

"Because a telegrapher's touch is as unique as his signature, and I was the one who taught him."

"So it was you! You were the one in his room telegraphing to him. He wasn't just imagining it."

"No, he wasn't. I knew Jamie immediately and while the dolts they had working out there wouldn't recognize telegraphy from their pedophile retard of a janitor picking his nose, one of the patients who'd served in the Signal Corp might. Should Sally Anne find out, I never would have convinced her to marry me. Not with her outsized sense of loyalty. I would have lost her again. This time for good. So Evelyn moved him to a private room with only her having a key. I got her named as head nurse so she could keep him under wraps, and I could keep her quiet. Ordered her to destroy his chart."

"She didn't."

"Yes, I know. To keep her job after her habit came to light she tried using it to blackmail me with Mrs. Hanna."

"Mrs. Hanna knew?"

"Oh my, yes. She's known for years."

"She knew? She knew and she never tried to see him?"

"Maude didn't tell her until after we were married."

"She still could've done something. Gone to see him."

"You will learn soon enough, young lady, that everyone has their price." Hanna smiled. "Anyone can be bought. Anyone."

"Not everyone."

"We will likely see which of us is right before the curtain falls on our little evening drama. I think, though, you are destined to be disappointed."

Matt rotated the typewriter roller holding the last page of his article. First one way, then the other. He looked from Betsy to Hanna.

"You were still taking quite a risk that her sister wouldn't rat on you to someone else."

"Not so great, though she did have quite the nasty streak in her. Addicts can be like that. She would have gone far in Washington. Sadistic sometimes even but she was an asylum graduate after all. Her family called it a boarding academy, but it was really a coo-coo school. Her father somehow pulled professional strings to get her into nurses training. A wonder student in dissection, I'm told. Manic depressive we would call her now, which she self medicated with laudanum. Should she talk to anyone outside her family, she would have had zero credibility. Zip. Old Doc Himes could make certain of that. Really only a matter of time before she overdosed. So sad but Doc Himes ensured the hospital kept a ready supply on hand and put Maude in charge of keeping inventory. Never did find where she hid his chart. That was my only real concern. Jamie had until this summer been all but forgotten except for the few staff necessary to keep him alive. Once in a while by one of the patients."

Thunder rattled the front plate-glass window. Hanna reached into the coat of his black silk suit. An embargoed Cuban cigar no more than reached his lips when Oliver held a gold-plated Pierre Cardin lighter to it. "That Brindle boy, Roger . . ."

"Randy," Betsy said.

"What's that?"

"His name was Randy."

"That What's-His-Name Brindle boy didn't know all that much. Heard some scuttlebutt maybe. Snooped around some. No doubt he told your brother what he suspected, but I'm certain if Nathan had gotten home, I would have had no trouble convincing my new press secretary that whatever he heard was mere delusions. No trouble at all." Hanna smiled at Betsy. "Everyone has their price."

"Of course since Nathan didn't make it home, you never had a chance to risk his lack of integrity."

"I'm not much of one for taking risks, young man. Should I ever come across some saint owning up to a crumb of grit, I will have you on the phone in two seconds flat. Now that would be one humdinger of a story."

"Only in the world of Washington."

"In anyone's. You hicks out here in boonieville think you're oh so special. So righteous." With a little finger, Hanna tapped cigar ash onto the floor. "No need, though, for you to be sitting by your phone like some dried-up spinster prune. You will never receive such a call from me. Never. Every man, every woman, can be bought. One need only find his, or her, price."

Matt looked over Hanna's shoulder.

"Oliver? No camera tonight to memorialize our conversation?"

"Evening's young yet, McLain."

"Now you take your Nurse Baker as a prime example."

Betsy's eyes widened. "What about her?"

"After spotting McLain's wrecked excuse for transportation, we drove out to the hospital. Had us a real heart-to-heart wet-hanky talk. Now she's a sad case if ever I saw one."

"Sad how?"

"Well, her job — her entire career as a nurse in fact is so . . . tenuous, you know, what with the suicide on her watch of that Brindle boy."

"That wasn't her fault."

"The Nurses' Board of Review — more than a few of whom I'm responsible for their appointments — could be persuaded otherwise. Then there's her making zilch of an effort to find the family of the village's favorite son when it was right under her nose."

"But you ordered her not to! You ordered everyone not to so much as try!"

"Know of any witnesses, young lady?"

Betsy looked across the desk to Matt. Matt shook his head.

"As I said she makes for a very sad case indeed. Baker wants to hold onto her career. Word ever got out any further than it has already about her losing a patient, let alone the other, why she would find it difficult to find a new position. With the news coverage I'm certain would follow, maybe impossible. She will pay any price to hold onto what she has, for word not to get out, because what she has now is all she has and ever will. Was that not your impression, Oliver?"

"Yes, sir. It was."

"Everyone has their price. Without exception." Hanna turned to Betsy. "Now I take it, young lady, reuniting Jamie Hamilton with his childhood sweetheart means a great deal to you, does it not?"

"Yes, sir."

"Exactly what Baker said. Would make up in some little way for your brother not coming home."

"Some. Maybe."

"Some, you say. Maybe, you tell me, but it's as close as you are going to come in this world. This, though, is the nutcracker you find yourself within. Should your story ever get out, my life — my political life I have struggled to build over the course of half a century– is over. Finished. Forget about capping it off by darkhorsing in as the presidential nominee at the convention in two years. Should your story see the light of day, I won't be able to so much as keep my congressional seat out of the lecherous hands of a child molester like Thomson."

"Well, you should lose it."

"Should I really? Do you think for one minute anyone filling my shoes will be one lick better? For all you know, I could be something of a saint in Washington. My colleagues may refer to me as Saint Mark the Magnificent." Hanna snorted. "Sometimes I forget the ignorance — no, make that the arrogance — of youth. Not only will you have destroyed my political life, I will lose my marriage as well. Have you considered those consequences? Would Jamie Hamilton want you to destroy the life of a dying woman for his sake?"

"It's you who lost them for yourself."

"Do you really think so, Miss Snippet? Well, let me enlighten you as to the facts of political life. Should your story get out, I'll lose, but you will lose more. That I can promise you."

"Lose what?"

"Forget saving my marriage, it'll be gone. My only hope for salvaging a political life would be to destroy the evidence."

"How can you destroy the evidence? Mr. Hamilton's out at the hospital."

"Where Jamie is can change," Hanna snapped his fingers, "in the blink of an eye for I can move him tonight."

"Move him to where?"

"Who can say?" Hanna smiled. "We now have several hospitals in Japan with this war dragging on and on. Or maybe one of those in Australia. Germany is definitely on my list. It would take some string pulling, I'll grant you, but I'm an expert string puller."

Matt glared into the doorway. "You slimy son of a bitch."

"If I wasn't, son, I would not have survived in Washington for as long as I have."

Betsy turned to Matt. "What should we do?"

"What do you want us to do?"

"You've worked so hard on your story."

"It's more yours than mine. I'll have others," Matt again glared into the doorway, "and I'm going to make it my life's work to write every sonofabitching one of them."

"Come, come, Betsy." Hanna pulled on his cigar. "You know deep-sixing your story is the right move. Reunite for however briefly two childhood sweethearts torn apart by a hard-hearted world just as your brother was torn from you."

Betsy looked down at her notepad, Hamilton's words written in their pages.

"Surely you can see it's the right move to make. More important than wrecking your revenge on an old man. Besides. Running your story will kill Mrs. Hanna. Simply kill her. Her heart's not been good for some time. Her doctors give her a year. Two at most. Anything could kill her sooner. Anything. Certainly a broken heart. More importantly, should not Jamie at long last have his hour of happiness after everything he's gone through? Know he has paid his penance and can now receive his redemption he's told me so often he wants so badly."

"Everything he's gone through with no small help from you."

"All water under the bridge, young lady. I can't change any of it even if I wanted to." Hanna pulled his watch from his vest and clicked it open. He showed its face to her. "Time is something for you to consider. How are you going to live with yourself every ticking moment for the next fifty, sixty, odd years knowing you took away his last chance for some happiness in a miserable excuse for a life? All for the sake of your selfish gratification at getting even with an old man for some imagined slight."

"Imagined!" Matt leaped up out of his chair. "This girl imagined you secreted Jamie Hamilton away. A virtual prisoner for over fifty years. She imagined you tormented Randy Brindle into sailing a swan dive off the hospital roof because he was almost on to your secret? She imagined?"

Hanna puffed on his cigar. Studied the two before him through its shifting haze of blue smoke.

"You've left this girl with very little left to imagine. She has more than a fair picture after listening to Hamilton of how her brother died as ignoble a death as you drove Randy Brindle to."

"I've no time for your youthful sentimentality. There's another important function I'm already running late for. Young lady, I haven't all night. What's it going to be? Where do you want Jamie spending the night?"

"Betsy." Matt placed his hand on hers. "Mr. Hamilton wouldn't want you to sell your soul for him. He traded away his own when he enlisted. He knows the steepness of its price."

"Congressman Hanna is wrong. It's not for something selfish. It's not about getting even. I don't care about getting even. It's about giving Mr. Hamilton some piece of happiness before it's too late."

"Like his not dying alone. Like his dying beside someone he once loved. Someone he still loves and who still loves him."

"Yes."

"It's about his not dying as Nathan died, isn't it, Betsy. Far away. Alone. With no one to remind him of how special he was to her."

"Yes. Goddamn you. Yes."

"Your brother too would tell you not to pay the price."

"I can't." Betsy lowered her head. Her voice broke. "I can't betray him. Not after everyone else has."

"You've made the right decision, young lady. The magnanimous one. Forget what bull pucky McLain's pandering to you. He wants his story is all. I know your brother would be proud of you for he was one who knew how to make hard decisions and then carry them out."

Hanna pointed his cigar at Matt.

"You see, son. It's just as I told you. We all have a price for which we're all too happy to allow ourselves to be sold. Money. Power. Soothing our conscious. I should know. I've devoted a half century to extracting a deal by unearthing a person's price."

"I can't say a proclivity for corrupting men, let alone children, is a character trait to be proud of."

"It's a hard lesson to learn, I'll grant you. Once, believe it or not, I was as much a naïve do-gooder as you, McLain. It took some time for me to wrap my head around it, but if you want to not just thrive but survive in this world it is better to learn its lessons sooner rather than later. Far less heartache to eat away at you. Better she learn now, unlike her starry-eyed brother. Like you, he wouldn't believe me either. For a minute there while you were talking, I thought Nathan had returned from the grave. If he had made it home, though, I would have squeezed it out of him like you wring a washcloth."

Betsy raised her head, her face burning and eyes afire. Matt studied Hanna. "You found Jamie Hamilton's price, didn't you?"

"I guess you could say I did. I had no choice. There was always a risk despite my precautions that someone who should not would enter his room or because of his health he might need to be transferred to a larger hospital. Always a risk that someone would recognize his tapping for what it was. What to do? What to do?"

"What did you do?"

"I cautioned Jamie that he should only telegraph to me. Warned him of a similar instance in New Orleans where the poor patient ended up in a carnival freak show."

"I never heard of that."

"You never heard of it, son, because it was a story I made up. I told Jamie that should he meet a similar fate it would break his mother's heart."

"But his mother was dead."

"He didn't know that. I did tell him they lost their farm — which only deepened his guilt at deserting them — but his father was now an overseer of my properties. Should someone recognize his tapping as telegraphy, should word ever get out of a war-damaged patient, that would change. Then his parents truly would be destitute."

"Of course because of his guilt he never asked to see his family."

"I comforted him when I visited his room with their made-up messages. From my wife as well. Even if he had asked, Jamie had no idea they were so close. I told him he had been returned to Baltimore after the derailment. He knew in any case what he looked like and wanted no one from that life to see him. At least no one he had been close to. I had no problem carrying out my charade. With no sense of sight or hearing he had no sense of time. No sense of the year unless someone told him."

Matt looked at Betsy and back to Hanna.

"We never even thought to tell him the year, but why would he telegraph to us after you warned him never to do so. Not with anyone?"

"I had overlooked the propensity of the dying to tell their story. The need to be heard one last time. Tell it to anyone who will listen. The dying and the old soon to be dying. Our need to tell our stories. Unburden ourselves when perhaps we should remain silent. To be understood. To at last understand ourselves. Perhaps it is one of the early symptoms signaling the onslaught of our dementia to come."

Oliver nodded. He may have smiled. Hanna clicked open his watch.

"Children, I'll bid you goodnight now."

Hanna and Oliver backed into the darkness. The brass bell jingled on their way out.

Betsy turned to Matt.

"I can't."

"I understand. If you can't, you can't."

"No, you're not understanding me. We can't let him keep getting away with it. He has to be stopped. He's destroyed enough lives. You have to get your story out. Somehow."

Matt smiled. "He doesn't control every newspaper in his district."

"What do you mean?"

"Ever since Hanna canned me for a week, I've been working on a Plan B."

"What's your Plan B?"

"I know an editor who's sick of Hanna's embarrassing shenanigans and will be all too happy to run it. Front page this Sunday."

"Who?"

"Feldspar at the *Times Leader* down in Martins Ferry. His son served in ROTCy with me. Took us both pheasant-hunting last fall. Promised me over the phone yesterday that he'd run it in a heartbeat. All I have to do is hand him my copy."

"You have to get it to him then. Hanna must be stopped. We have to try. If we don't try, we won't do. Mr. Hamilton would agree his seeing his Sally Anne one last time is too high a price. So would Nathan."

"That's my girl."

Betsy sat back in the chair. She tapped a pen on her notepad, Matt watching her.

"What is it, Betsy?"

"Something's not right."

"What?"

"Something my dad told me once. There are people out there who when they want something from you they'll tell you what it is you're desperate to hear. What you want too much to hear." Betsy looked into the darkened doorway. She looked at Matt. "He makes promises too easily. We know too much now. His word can't be trusted. He's tricking us. Buying time to destroy the evidence."

## CHAPTER 35

Matt had left his keys dangling in the ignition, and it was Betsy who climbed in behind the wheel. She leaned over and rolled-down the passenger window. "Get your slowpoke butt in here if you're coming!"

Even before they were outside the village limits, she had the gas pedal floored, the speedometer needle arcing toward Matt.

"You better hope Durkin's not out on patrol."

Betsy glanced down at the speedometer. "Come on, come on. We don't have all night."

"If you want this puddle jumper to get us out to the hospital, you need to ease up some. You'll smoke a rod. This isn't Nate's 'Cuda you've been busting around town in all summer."

She again glanced down at the speedometer, but kept the gas pedal floored. Shafts of car headlights illuminated the lead drizzle of rain within.

"With the road as slick as it is, you're going to put us in the ditch."

"Yeah, yeah, yeah."

Gravel pinged the undercarriage when they fishtailed off SR 14 onto the township road. Red and blue beams strobed the tree branches a half-mile on just inside the wrought-iron gate where a squad car straddled the hospital drive blocking its entrance. Sheriff Durkin in his Smokey-the-Bear hat was standing beside the open driver's door as he spoke to a pot-bellied deputy, his words rising in gray bouquets, their arms folded over their chests and looking like circus clowns as the roof-rack LED lightbars flashed the plastic rain slickers. Their arms dropped as Betsy pulled off onto the shoulder.

Durkin parted his slicker and stood thumbing his holster belt. The deputy aped him. Matt shook his head.

"They must've called Durkin before leaving the hospital earlier. Wanted to be certain no evidence got left behind that would substantiate our story. He had no intention of letting Mrs. Hanna see him."

"What should we do now?"

"I've a strong suspicion of what Lying Larry is going to tell us." He pushed his door open. "Let's play this story through anyway."

They crossed to the cruiser.

"McLain." The sheriff tipped his hat. "Miss."

"So what've you got going on tonight? Inmates staging a breakout?"

"No. Nothin' as exciting as all that. Rendering some assistance in the transportation of a patient is all. Nothin' for members of the press to be concerning themselves with."

Above the copula of the hospital hung the nacre paring of a dying moon shining through the parted clouds. Betsy rose on her toes to look over the cruiser's roof and up the hospital lane. "Transporting him where?"

"I ain't at liberty to say, Miss."

"Didn't know transporting a patient from a federal facility required a county sheriff's escort," McLain said.

"It got special requested."

"Special requested?"

"Also got especially special requested to keep all elements of the news media out by the road should any of you all show up makin' a nuisance of yourselves."

"Nuisance? Hell, Larry, I'm just a hardworking reporter earning his way back to college."

"Gettin' to be a damn contrary one at that."

The cruiser radio squawked. Matt nodded.

"Nice unit."

"She gets the job done for us. To protect and to serve. That's our motto."

"Looks new."

"Does she?"

"Oh, now I recall." Matt clicked his fingers. "Commissioners paid for it from that earmark Washington sent their way. Let me think. Now whose committee did that come out of again?"

Durkin centered his holster belt about his ample girth. "Think it'd be a right smart idea if maybe you and your girlfriend here waited in that Bug of yours. Wouldn't want to deal tonight with no traffic fatalities should that ambulance comes barreling through."

Betsy still looked up the lane. The ambulance had backed to the side of the hospital, its rear door swung open, and four men now lifted in a gurney. The drizzle was turning to rain.

"Betsy?"

"Can't we wait here until his ambulance goes by?"

"You can either wait inside that dilapidation of a vehicle, which my deputies are fixing to start citatin' on a regular basis from here on out, or you can wait in the backseat of my new cruiser that McLain's taken such a cottonin' to, in cuffs, after which I'll be transporting' you all up to my jailhouse. It'll 'bout make your folks' summer for 'em, I reckon."

"That's not right."

"Miss, you ain't near old enough to decide what's right and what ain't. You need to be letting your elders make those kinds of decisions for you."

"You mean the kind that got my brother killed? That kept Mr. Hamilton locked away for the crime of letting someone else make those decisions."

"Miss, I don't know nothin' about no Hamilton, but you better be makin' up your mind right quick. You can either wait over there in McLain's car or in the back seat of this here cruiser, but there ain't goin' to be no waiting any place where the Congressman can eyeball you."

"Come on, Betsy." Matt touched her shoulder. "We're getting wet."

"Hell, you are wet, and what're you doin' out so late anyway, McLain, carousing the back roads with a minor? Now get along, both of you, before I start seriously considering' about what all it is I can charge you with."

They returned to the Volkswagen, this time Matt behind the wheel, their breath steaming its windows as rain thudded the roof. Matt wiped at the glass with the sleeve of his blue chambray shirt. "Here they come."

The lights of the long Lincoln Continental beamed down the lane followed by those of the ambulance, catching in them the poplars bordering it, their quicksilver clash of leaves. When they reached its end, the two vehicles stopped, and the sheriff and his deputy walked to the rear of the limousine. Its back window lowered. The end of a cigar reddened and faded. Oliver stepped from the driver's door. He opened an umbrella and walked out to the road. Matt cranked down his window.

"A dirty piece of business, Oliver."

"I've witnessed worse crimes committed in the name of democracy."

"Your boss wins again."

"One can never tell for sure in these matters, McLain. For this performance I'd venture the fat lady may yet have one more tune left in her lungs."

"My guess is every scrap of paper proving the existence of James Hamilton, once upon a time an honored member of his Majesty's Royal Canadian Expeditionary Force, is in the back of the ambulance."

"Don't be silly. The Congressman had me load every scrap of paper into the trunk of his Lincoln."

"I suppose Nurse Baker had a come-to-Jesus talk with him while you were loading."

"Oh, yes indeed. The Congressman promised to find her another hospital. Somewhere less stressful. Maybe in

Hawaii. Keep it hushed up about her negligence contributing to Brindle's suicide."

"There wasn't any negligence!" Betsy's fist pounded the dashboard. "There was only Hanna's baiting."

"Quite right but the Congressman has risen dissembling to an art form, even by Washington standards. He also agreed to sweep under the rug about Filbert's dealing to the patients. Retract his tip he'd made to the DEA."

"So even after the *Times Leader* runs our story, we have no backup for it. Only a wild tale imagined by a vengeful reporter who lost his job. A grief stricken candy striper."

"Maybe not."

"Meaning what?"

"The Congressman's getting up there. Part's beginning to go. His bladder is starting to give out on him. Could be cancer. He needs to be considering retirement, make way for new blood, and not in the next election. This one. When Nurse Baker let us into Hamilton's room, he had to go downstairs to use the restroom and left me alone with him."

"Bad bladder or not, he wins again."

"Like I said, don't sell the fat lady short."

"Come on. You know Thomson hasn't got a snowball's chance."

"Especially after I walk little Shirley into Durkin's office tomorrow morning."

"Who's little Shirley?"

"Twelve-year-old that Thomson gave a ride home from the school playground this afternoon after a disgusting degenerate detour." Oliver smiled. "You can never tell when the guy tailing you's got a camera equipped with a telephoto lens. Her parents are livid. More than mad enough to sue as well as hungry for a pretty good payday. Gave them a name of a good lawyer. Should keep the Thomson name in the *Journal* for at least a year. Longer with all the appeals sure to be coming."

"I guess the sixteenth congressional district will have to muddle it through the next two years like it has the last fifty."

"Like I keep telling you, Matt. Maybe not. The congressman as you know likes for me to keep my camera handy just in case, but he's getting so distracted in his old age he doesn't notice when instead of my Leica I have the Polaroid strapped around my neck."

He reached into his coat and handed to Matt a photograph of what looked to be an eyeless, noseless, mouthless mannequin lying in bed with two sets of IV tubes running out of drip bottles and into its one stick-thin arm. Matt looked up, but Oliver was already returning to the limousine. He raised a hand.

"When you write about me in your next gig, McLain, say something endearing me to the voters."

He opened the front door of the limousine and got in. Its rear window rose. The sheriff and his deputy climbed into their Washington-paid-for cruiser and turned onto the township road. The LED lightbars flashed red and blue beams through the trees that swayed in the wind. The window-darkened limousine followed. Betsy raised her hand as the ambulance drove by.

"There's nothing more you could've done, Betsy."

"Doesn't make it any better though." She looked at him. "Does it?"

He shook his head. "Your car up in the parking lot?"

"Was when we left."

They started up the lane.

"Time for you to be getting home."

"Why? I won't be sleeping."

He pulled up alongside the Barracuda.

"I'll let you know when our story's going to run. We're sharing the byline."

"The story *and* the photograph."

"You're goddamn right. The story *and* the photograph."

"Goodnight."

"Goodnight, Betsy."

She leaned over the gearshift and kissed his cheek. "Thank you for trying."

"We're not done yet."

"You mean the story?"

"That too."

Betsy didn't answer. She got in her brother's Barracuda where she sat looking in the rearview mirror as white sheets of rain harried down the lane like phantoms unloosed until the Volkswagen disappeared into the rainy dark. One by one the lights inside the hospital went out, and only when the last one darkened did she lower her face to her hands.

\* \* \*

At the long roll of early-morning thunder, Matt turned around in his driveway. His nostrils twitched. A burnt-iron tang of fast-coming rain burgeoned in the cold wind. He trotted down to his Volkswagen, but not until he was unlocking the door did he spot Betsy asleep beneath a sycamore planted in the devil strip of grass growing between the sidewalk and street, her long cheerleader legs curling to her chest, her head resting on arms folded across her knees. He hurried to her, placing a hand on her shoulder.

"Betsy. You okay? Betsy."

She opened her eyes, looked at him, and closed them again.

"What are you doing out here?"

"I couldn't sleep. I told you I wouldn't."

"Why didn't you come to the door?"

"I didn't want to wake everyone."

The windshield of the Barracuda parked at the curb grayed with dew. "How long have you been out here?"

"Not long,"

"How long's not long?"

"Three-thirty. Four." She wrapped her arms around her shoulders. "It's getting cold."

He draped his canvas sport coat over her shoulders. "Tell me what's wrong."

She pulled the coat tighter.

"Betsy. Please tell me."

"I can't believe he's gone. After all these years. After all He's put him through, God couldn't give him an hour of happiness. Why is that so much to ask?"

Matt sat beside her. "I'm sorry."

"Me too. Doesn't do him much good, though, does it?"

He picked a leaf of grass, ripping it into halves then quarters then eighths and held out his hand, the wind swirling them away. He looked at her.

"You gave him your comfort in his last days. Brought him as close to home as he could come if only for a few weeks."

"It's not enough."

"Life never is."

"He should've died *here* with somebody holding his hand. With somebody telling him he was the one who made all the difference in her life. He should've been buried on his farm beside his family." Betsy shook her head. "I should've been allowed to say goodbye. It was my chance to make it right."

"You made it as right as any person could."

"You don't see. He's not home *now*. He was so close. For fifty years. So close and he didn't know because no one would tell him the truth. Now he'll never be home."

Thunder guffawed in the distance.

"God, you are truly a trickster." She laid her head on her arms. "I'm tired of His tricks."

They sat. After a while, her stomach gurgled.

"Are you hungry, Betsy?"

"I guess I forgot about supper last night."

"You're in luck then because I conjure from scratch the best blueberry flapjacks in the world."

"What about the hospital?"

"Isn't this your last day?"

"Maybe." Betsy shrugged. "I don't know. What about you?"

"Henry no doubt already has a box setting on my desk."

"I'm sorry."

"Don't be. Now I've got one hell of a story. With that photograph, we might even break the AP wires. *Plain Dealer* here I come."

He stood, pulling her to her feet, and as they walked to the house for the first time since she received word about her brother Betsy held hands with a boy.

Part way up the drive, a raindrop splashed her face. Then another. Matt looked up.

"Weather's turning foul."

"No." Betsy smiled. "It's not."

"You could've fooled me."

"It's turning inclement."

"What?"

"The weather. It's turning inclement.

"Inclement?"

"A wonderful word, don't you think?"

"Don't hear it used much."

"No, not much. Only between people special to one another. It's a long-ago lover's joke between Mr. Hamilton and Mrs. Hanna."

Matt leaned and kissed her on the temple. "Maybe I should add it to my vocabulary."

She took his hand again. "That would be nice."

## CHAPTER 36

The summer of 1974 was not Betsy's last at the hospital. In addition to enlisting the help of Mrs. Urbschat to begin her unearthing of early village history and of World War I — a study that would consume her for the next decade — she continued to return each afternoon following classes all through her junior and senior years and to drive her dead brother's Barracuda out early every Saturday morning. She continued to sit in on the Friday night poker games.

"So I can be certain not one of you malingerers stays on for so much as an hour longer than when I can run your skinny butts out of here." She spread her poker hand before her, all hearts, taking the measure of each pair of eyes circling the table before she pulled the twenty-dollar pot toward her and tossed in her ante for the next. "Not for so much as a minute even."

She slid the deck to Johnny Handsome who held up a hand, his fingers spread, and began to flick his deal around the table.

"Five card stud," Betsy said.

Captain Kidd studied the face cards showing. "I think she means it, fellows."

Johnny Handsome nodded.

Every afternoon that fall and winter Betsy practiced with Quickdraw until he mastered his yoga. A culinary school up in Youngstown accepted him the next spring into their special needs program. Encouraged by Matt, who had switched his major from journalism to business administration and acted as his investment promoter, Quickdraw opened his own restaurant following graduation, backed by Dr. Barnes and the other physicians at the hospital.

"It'll be a great tax dodge for you," Matt told his uncle. "The best part is you won't have to shoot it behind the stables like you had to with Cleveland Slew last racing season."

She found for Hawkeye a teacher of Braille willing to drive out to the hospital, and the two of them helped him earn his GED. After he was admitted to the Education Department at Youngstown State, she escorted him around campus for the first two weeks of the fall term until she was certain he could find his way back to his apartment without her. Betsy researched plastic surgeons in the library while he sat in class. She found at Saint Elizabeth's a Dr. Rees, who had served in a MASH unit in Viet Nam, and cajoled him into attempting a restoration of Johnny's lower jaw for the pittance of a surgical fee the VA paid. He would never speak, but at least he could eat solid food at Quickdraw's and not be gawked at. Johnny too earned his bachelor's and found a job teaching the mute in Cleveland's inner-city schools.

Betsy and Matt dated some. He escorted her to the spring prom at Saint Paul's notwithstanding the ribbing inflicted on him by his fraternity brothers about robbing the cradle, and they remained steadfast friends. Matt finished up at Case Western Reserve in another year and got hired on as a stockbroker down in Akron at E.F. Hutton only to quit less than two years later to move out to California where he earned his MBA at Stanford. On one of his few visits home, he explained to her that a single winter out of the cold and snow had ruined him for life. They exchanged Christmas cards and photographs. He married a Malibu beach beauty, and for seven years each card came with one more child crowded into the family picture.

Betsy continued serving as a volunteer out at the hospital after graduating from Saint Paul's until she earned a nursing degree and got her first job at Walter Reed. Between Christmases she received an assortment of correspondence from her Ward 7 patients. A wedding invitation from Hawkeye. From Johnny Handsome a baby announcement. Snapshots of Stud and his paraplegic wife with the little Cambodian girl they adopted.

She was as good as her word she gave at the poker table. She got everyone home. Everyone save Jamie Hamilton, late of the His Majesty's Royal Canadian Expeditionary Force. Everyone save herself. Some nights when she visited her parents she found herself walking again along the Penn Central tracks down by the abandoned depot. When she heard the far-off whistle or saw the white bore of light, though, she would step off the tracks. She had unfinished business yet to attend.

After a year at Walter Reed she grew restless. She drifted from job to job as a sort of itinerant nurse at Veterans' hospitals in New York, Chicago, Dallas, Phoenix, and then on to lesser-known ones in Missoula and El Paso and others in still smaller towns. The hospitals as always were so understaffed that no one asked about her choppy work history. She stayed on only long enough until she got acquainted with any who might have been on staff in the summer of 1974 or might remember anyone who had been on staff, but none knew of — none had even heard of — an eyeless, noseless, mouthless patient with no legs lying in bed with two sets of IV tubes running out of drip bottles and into its one stick-thin arm with only a single twitching finger.

*You've gotta be shittin' me, honey.*

With the high turnover in VA hospitals, she found fewer and fewer staff at any of them who had worked there when Jamie Hamilton might have been a patient. There was only an aging radiologist and an alcoholic orderly in San Francisco. When she made her way down to Los Angeles there was no one, and at the end of her shift she took to hanging out evenings at Captain Jack's being bought drink after anesthetizing drink by airline pilots claiming to be divorced and on Friday and Saturday nights in the dimly-lit seedy clubs lining Sunset Boulevard. She quit nursing full time and only temped for a few days when it came time to pay her dealer and the rent on the first of the month. Temp jobs in time grew more irregular as agency clients complained about her forgetfulness on the job. Her tardiness. Her not showing up at all or looking red-eyed and haggard when she did.

*Have you had her drug tested?*
The years passed.

\* \* \*

*December 1983*

Her father never spoke to her about the journal her brother kept during the three weeks when he was home on his last leave. Look as she may she never came across it on those nights when she wandered into his room after everyone was in bed. Not until ten years following his death did it drop again into her life on the afternoon of her father's funeral.

She and Bartholomew lost their mother only three months before, and it fell upon them to make the arrangements. Family and friends crowded into the living room following the services and, the blustery cold notwithstanding, out across the front yard and into the yards of their neighbors. Their guests had not eaten since lunch, and Betsy stood at the kitchen sink putting together another tray of vegetables and her mother's tin-box recipe for dill dip when the door behind her squeaked open.

"Bet you don't remember me."

A paunch-stomached and balding man dressed in a Armani suit stood in the doorway.

"I know your voice." Betsy's eyes narrowed. "I can't though for the life of me put a name to it."

"The last time you heard it would have been ten years ago on a rainy summer night outside the hospital."

"Oliver?"

"Your memory's amazing."

"What are you . . .?"

"Your folks always stopped by my congressional office whenever they came to visit you while you still worked at Walter Reed. Thank me for my support in getting the War Memorial through committee."

"They never told me, but thank you for taking the trouble to come in from Washington."

"No trouble. This is my real home now."

"Oh?"

"I married Congressman Hanna's grandniece, Sarah Anne."

"Yes, I'd forgotten. Is she here with you?"

"No, home with a cold. She didn't want anyone else to catch it."

"She's sweet. Like her aunt."

"I had an ulterior motive for coming today."

"Same old Oliver."

"Your father told me more than once how close you had grown to your patient that Hanna and I moved away that night. One reason I came today was to say how sorry I am for my participation. My only excuse is I didn't know and I was young and too ambitious at the time to ask."

"Thank you. Thank you for saving Nurse Baker's and Filbert's jobs."

"He needed to be stopped, and they were good people."

"The best."

"I heard Filbert quit a year or two later. Never heard what became of him. Amy retired last year. We threw a huge going-away party for her. Twelve years out there had to be some sort of record."

"Yes, indeed."

"Again, I'm sorry. If there's ever anything I can ever do, please do not hesitate."

"Flowers."

"What?"

"I've always wanted to lay flowers on his grave. That's the main reason I took my first job near Washington. That and the Library of Congress. I often walked through Arlington on my days off or summer evenings. I thought I might someday, somehow, stumble upon his grave."

"But he's not buried in Washington."

"He's not?"

"He died before Hanna could get him loaded that night on the plane headed for Guam. He had him buried out in back of his family farm in their little cemetery."

"Hanna wouldn't have told him he was being moved."

"Not that I saw. Couldn't take the strain for some reason. I'd no idea he was so weak. The poor guy's heart must've given out at being moved."

*I warned Jamie of a similar instance in New Orleans where the poor patient ended up in a carnival freak show.*

"Being moved and not knowing where to."

"He had Durkin and his deputy dig the grave themselves with him watching. I thought you knew."

"No." Betsy dabbed at her eyes with the hem of her apron. "I didn't, but at least he did that much for him. Got him home. Did Mrs. Hanna know?"

"Do you think he would ever have told her?"

"No. Not in a million zillion years."

"He knew Hamilton was the love of her life, and he loathed being second best at anything. Certainly in love. He never forgave Hamilton. Never forgave her. It took me a long time — too long — to realize the depth of his hatred. I wish I had then. Imagine. Keeping another man prisoner for over fifty years for the sake of pride."

"So in the end we made the right decision. Even if Matt and I agreed not to run our story, there was never any chance of reuniting them. He would've been dead before she came to him."

"Again, I'm sorry."

Betsy nodded.

"I'll see to it flowers get laid every Veterans' Day."

"We both will. Does he have a stone? One with his name on it?"

"I'll find out."

"No, I'll take care of it while I'm home. Do you think the owners would mind?"

"I'm sure Sarah Anne won't mind."

"Sarah Anne?"

"She inherited it from Mrs. Hanna."

"She bought the Hamilton farm?"

"It was left to her by the congressman. Mark, Sr., was a founder of the Hanna Bank and Trust. Hanna appointed himself to the board of directors when he died. As Durkin and his deputy dug Jamie's grave, Hanna admitted to me that he suffered from nightmares of word ever getting out of a nameless patient at his hospital. It was he who pressed the bank to foreclose when the Hamiltons fell behind on their mortgage. He told me he intended to grubstake them to a farm in California's Central Valley once they were homeless, but they — had other plans. As the Hamilton farm is adjacent to his family's property, Hanna purchased it anyway at, of course, a very good price."

"Tell Sarah Anne that I said thank you."

"I will. I had a second ulterior motive for coming. Always liked your dad; your mom too. I wished we'd heard in time so we could've made it back for hers. Sarah Anne and I were on a fact-finding mission in South Africa, what with the uproar we'd been having over apartheid. Mandela."

"I read about it in the *Times*."

"We stopped in to visit your dad when we did make it back a few weeks later."

"Oh, thank you."

"Don't thank us. We enjoyed it, but we stayed much longer than we'd intended. As we stood to leave he asked us to wait a minute and went upstairs. He gave us this." Oliver fished a tarnished key from a coat pocket. "He made us promise to hand it to you. Personally. He meant to when you were back for your mom's funeral but forgot in all the hustle and bustle. He said he was entrusting it to us because he was afraid something might happen before he saw you again. I suppose he thought if he mailed it that it might get lost."

Betsy stared at the key lying in her palm. Warm, almost burning, so much like another key placed there by a pawn-shop proprietor in her long ago.

"Do you know what it might unlock, Betsy?"

## CHAPTER 37

Betsy had walked by Nathan's footlocker every time she entered his room. Often she sat on it so as not to rumple the bedspread because her mother would have guessed in a heartbeat who it was, and she thought of his room as her own sacred sanctuary. A refuge for her to go where she felt closest to him, where she could be restored and gather up her strength to go on one more day.

*Just one more day, Lord,* Betsy sometimes heard her pray under her breath. *Just one more.*

Yet Betsy too needed her strength to go on, she too needed to know. Needed to understand, yet at the same time she did not want to understand. She tried to open it a couple of times, but always it was locked. She could have asked about a key. Maybe jimmied the lock with a clothes hanger. Yet if they kept it locked, there was a reason. Her father protecting her mother. Betsy knew when Oliver handed her the key that what was inside her father never wanted her mother to see, but knew Betsy needed to see, and as she stood looking down at the key it gave her the goose egg shivers.

All keys to the unknown now frightened her. While the key to Jamie Hamilton's room without a doubt saved her life, it forever changed it too. Sent her careening down roads she never expected to travel. For like Mrs. Hanna she had sleepwalked through a dream where life and death seemed memorized. It had taken her a decade to sink as far as she had. What new door would this key open up for her? Upon what road would she now find herself afoot? Her hand trembled while she stood in the kitchen looking down at it. Another key to the unknown that burned as if anointed with acid. She pocketed it in her apron and thanked Oliver and returned to chopping carrots and celery for her guests. The key could wait for now. Though not for long.

She had other keys in her life. The key to her brother's Barracuda. Other kinds of keys with their own locks to open. Books mostly. Books had been her great keys in opening up the past. In opening up Betsy to Betsy. The nineteen-thirteen yearbook that she and Matt found in the Hanna Public Library. Stacks upon stacks of books first in the Library of Congress and then in the Imperial War Museum that helped her so much in putting together the unknown parts of Jamie Hamilton's story. *The Odyssey* in unlocking the impossibility of our ever coming home, yet it is a journey the gods will never permit us to abandon. The predestination ordained by the three sisters Fate. It seemed to Betsy after a score of readings that old Homer made John Calvin sound like a flaming free-will Bohemian.

To Betsy the *Odyssey* above all was the story of a soldier's journey home. A journey that took him ten years because the gods willed it to be so. Willed it because of the atrocities the Greeks committed both before the war with Troy and after even though the gods willed those atrocities as well, starting at the very beginning when Agamemnon sacrificed his daughter so the winds of war would blow their ships out of the harbor bound for Troy. Sacrificed her solely to placate his honor. Then at its end the gods willed the Greek slaughter of King Priam as he prayed with head bowed before his household altar. Willed the rape of his daughter, Cassandra, in the temple of the virgin goddess, Athena, the girl's protectress. Willed Agamemnon's sacrifice of Priam's other daughter, Polyxena, to the ghost of their dead hero, Achilles. When he returned home, the god's willed their revenge on Agamemnon by his wife taking his life for his slaying Ifphigeneia. Twenty-five hundred years before, Homer managed to rhyme his story with that of Nathan and of Jamie Hamilton. With that of Hawkeye and Johnny Handsome. Stud and Captain Kidd.

Odysseus was lucky, though. He made it home after only a ten year journey; it took Jamie Hamilton over fifty. Luck, as he well knew, is but a spinning coin. What are the joys of life today can turn into our sorrows tomorrow.

The justice of the Greek gods on her first reading, or even her fifth or tenth, seemed so cold. So brutal. A justice where good intentions meant nothing. Where all that mattered are actions and the consequences of actions. The Greek war with Troy, like Jamie Hamilton's, like Nathan's, was inevitable, and the gods sanctioned all of the atrocities committed. The Greeks could with justification in her eyes claim the defense of necessity. Yet its necessity did nothing to mitigate the horror of their actions. Did nothing to spare them from retribution for their actions by the same gods who willed their commission. While the justice of the Greeks differed from the one she had learned, she could not now say with certainty their conception of life, about actions and the far-reaching consequences of actions, was in error. Yet how could Nathan see the consequences of his enlisting on those he loved? How could Jamie Hamilton, late of His Majesty's Royal Canadian Expeditionary Force? How could they see the wrecked lives their decisions would leave in their wake? Betsy's. Her family's. Especially Mrs. Hanna's.

She and Betsy became the best of friends. When her time came, she refused to walk her first step out into that good night from a hospital bed. Betsy took two weeks leave from Walter Reed to sit with her in her upstairs bedroom at the Rutherford mansion. Blind by then, she had her read aloud Millay's poetry, and when she read the last poem on the last page she gave to Betsy as a keepsake her book and its photograph of Jamie Hamilton she used as a bookmark. They talked between readings, or rather Mrs. Hanna talked while Betsy listened. She took her old stenographers pad out from her purse while Mrs. Hanna slept and made notes. She told her more stories of early Hanna. Directed her to the local old-folks' homes where the veterans of the War to End

All Wars lived out the end of their days and were more than happy to have a young girl listen with patience and eager questions as they recounted for her as best they could recollect with their shadowy memories what they had seen. Their tales took on a tone of insistence, though they never told her what they themselves had done. Or perhaps they had. Many received regimental newsletters, and they would write to tell her about upcoming reunions, invited her to attend in their stead, which she did whenever she could get away.

Hoping to impress a pretty girl with their once-upon-a-time virility, the soldiers boasted to her about their own houses of entertainment and more. She learned from those reunions of others in Toronto and Ottawa. Alberta and Vancouver. She showed around the plastic-wrapped photograph that Mrs. Hanna used as bookmark, and with politeness they studied the boy pictured and tried to be helpful but shook their heads. Their eyesight failing. It had been so long. Their memories of what was but eddied mists of cemetery fog. One or two seemed maybe to recall a Jamie Hamilton, or was it a John Hamilton or maybe a James Hanson or maybe he was only known to them by his *nom de guerre*, but there were so many dead, acres and acres of them, he now but one more revenant to them.

4Always centerpieced at the head table of their reunions where any surviving officers sat, stood a black-ribboned bottle, always of a 1918 vintage from a French vineyard near where they had served. To be opened by the lone survivor. A nurse at one the old-folks' homes run for veterans admitted to her that only once had the last man standing ever opened such a bottle. Or rather had it corkscrewed for him for by the time he was the last man standing he could do little more than for a few minutes maybe sit up in bed. Drink and eat and piss through plastic tubes. Any alcohol would kill him so a group of doctors and nurses gathered around his bed and filled their Dixie cups and smiled as they tried not to gag on a wine soured to vinegar. So Betsy's notebook pages filled.

The day before she died, Mrs. Hanna rallied as Betsy had seen the dying do so often. Always a reserved woman, she was more talkative than Betsy had ever seen her. School-girl giddy like her old Gang once was. Impish perhaps for that day she told Betsy of her all-too short courtship by Jamie Hamilton. Of her conspiracy with Mrs. Hamilton.

On the Sunday after Sally Anne and Jamie had their picnic over at Mount Union College, his mother for once did not wake him for Mass. She drove herself in to Hanna, leaving early, not pushing the mules but allowing them to plod along at their own pace, she lost in her thoughts. When they reached the outskirts of town, she stopped for a minute to watch the swirl of runoff from the recent rains carry away leaves and limbs beneath Mill Creek Bridge. The carcass of a spring-born rabbit floated by. For a second its fur snagged on a tree branch that overhung the bank not twenty feet from where she sat in their wagon. One of its eyes had been sucked out, the other raisined up and loose in its socket, rolling with the creek flow and pointing toward her. She could not look away. After a minute the current pushed the rabbit free and out of sight downstream, and she watched where it disappeared until she heard the toll of church bells. Tolling she now sometimes thought she heard when she walked back to her children's cemetery.

Father McCray celebrated his first Mass in his new parish that Sunday. Her mother following the services as Sally Anne stood waiting at the bottom of the steps cornered him outside to schedule an evening when he could come to the house for supper. When Mrs. Hamilton came down the steps, she cocked her head to where Mrs. Rutherford stood before the church door and smiling at the priest like a schoolgirl engaging the new boy in class. She told her she suspicioned Sally Anne might have a wee bit of a wait. Sally Anne said she suspected her to be correct, in which case she had better be getting home to be certain dinner had not overcooked or worse. Mrs. Hamilton told her she always enjoyed coming into the village this time of year when their tulips and crocuses came into bloom and asked if she might not walk home with her so she could better inspect the flowerbeds before she returned to prepare her own family's Sunday dinner. If she had the time she would have liked to keep a flowerbed, but with there always being one thing or another more important on the farm, she had never gotten around to it. They talked about the service. Both agreed that because of his youth and vigor Father McCray would be a grand addition to the parish. When Sally Anne told her it was a shame he had sworn an oath of celibacy, Mrs. Hamilton said it did seem she heard more than one sighing heart that morning.

The two walked on in silence after exhausting Father McCray as a subject of conversation until they had almost reached the Rutherford house where Mrs. Hamilton told Sally Anne about her drive into the village. About her seeing the spring-born rabbit floating in the creek. Sally Anne said she had suffered similar premonitions and worse. Told her she wished there was some way they could make him stay. Maybe hog-tie him and hold him captive in the Hamilton barn loft until it was over or until he came to his senses. The two looked into each other's eyes for a moment before Mrs. Hamilton reached out a hand to Sally Anne's shoulder. She told the girl though there was nothing more she could do as a mother, Sally Anne could, and it would be no sin blighting her soul.

Mrs. Hanna would tell Betsy no more, and it was Nathan's diary that would be the key to finishing her story of James Hamilton, late of His Majesty's Royal Canadian Expeditionary Force. The key to seeing actions and the consequences of actions.

## CHAPTER 38

As Bartholomew eased himself out of his old bed in his old room, the radium dials circling Nathan's clock read 4:57. He tread bare-footed downstairs clad in only boxer shorts and T-shirt to the kitchen where he put a match to the burner beneath the stained coffee pot his parents had lit every morning since the day after their wedding night. While Erin had another three months to go, her stomach hung low so she looked more like she was going on nine. Their doctor down in Morgantown was a five-hour drive away. After the coffee perked, the burner flaming full blast, Bartholomew carried two mugs upstairs without taking the time to add sugar and milk.

Erin sat in the cab of their Chevy pickup an hour later with the window rolled down and talking to Betsy who stood in the driveway dressed in the ratty bathrobe Nathan had given his dad so many fathers' days before while Bartholomew packed their suitcases into the truck bed. She reached out to take Betsy's hand when she asked her if she did not mind that she and Bartholomew wanted to name their son Nathan. Betsy watched her younger brother for a moment as he roped down the suitcases. She was destined never to have a son. Someone should carry on the name. Someone had to, and she gave Erin's hand a squeeze.

"I'm so happy for both of you."

Bartholomew jumped to the driveway after he finished tying down the tarpaulin and pecked his sister on the cheek as he hurried past her. "You take care."

"You too, Hotrod. Remember you're driving for three now."

The truck tires chirped on the cold concrete in the sharp winter air. Betsy cupped her hands to her mouth.

"Show off!"

Erin reached across the seat. The truck bumped to a stop. Bartholomew frowned out the window past his sister. Erin spoke to him again. He rolled down the window.

"I'll be back late evening to help with the sorting."

"No. That's okay. You need to stay close to Erin now."

"You sure?"

"I'm sure. Have a good trip. Call me when you get there."

Bartholomew rolled up his window. Erin waved. The pickup taillights all too soon disappeared within the foggy dark, and Betsy went inside to begin.

It was late afternoon before she carried the first of the garbage bags out to the row of trashcans lining the alleyway. She let the porch door slam shut behind her when she came back in, jingling the row of keys that dangled from their brass hooks her father had screwed into the plywood wall alongside the door. The key to the Barracuda hung at the end. She looked out the window to the shed where it had sat since she finished nursing school, now rusted through in dozens of half-dollar size holes, its axles resting on cracked cement blocks, the tires and battery long since rotated, nesting families of mice snuggled into its rotting upholstery. Nathan's last pack of Marlboros with its last cigarette she could never bring herself to finish waited in the glove compartment.

She touched each key in the row of keys in turn before she sucked in her breath and went into the living room where she had left her purse setting on the piano and took out the key Oliver had laid in her palm. Twice she dropped it as she climbed the stairs. She dragged Nathan's footlocker from his closet across the carpet to the foot of his bed. When the lid opened with a soft pop, a silver cloud of familiar smelling attic dust drifted out. She peeled away the layers of young-man memorabilia with the same care as she would unwind bandages from a burn-scarred patient. She laughed when she came upon a box of unopened condoms. Hummed old tunes long forgotten as she shuffled through her brother's collection of scratched forty-fives until she uncovered his journal in a bottom corner.

She ran two fingers along the cracks crisscrossing the leather. Front. Back. Up and down the spine. She leaned her back against the footlocker, propping her knees before her and opened his journal. For a moment she closed her eyes and held it to her nose, breathing in the lemongrass scent of its paper before she thumbed its pages, their fountain-pen ink faded to robin's-egg-blue, his handwriting more difficult to read than she remembered, only the first couple-of-dozen pages filled. No photos secreted between them. No letters unsent. She returned to the beginning.

October 6, 1972

Well, here goes nothing.

I'm riding this rattletrap Greyhound that most likely saw its best day's thirty-some years ago when Dad was coming home after his getting mustered out. We're maybe an hour away from the Youngstown depot, on my way back from Fort Bragg at the end of jungle training. Good God, though, my handwriting looks like some geezer who's come down with a serious case of the D.T.'s. Another dose of the shakes. They keep getting worse. Coming more often.

I've had lots of time to kill on this long old ride. Made good headway through *The Odyssey*. Read last month's *Playboy* I don't know how many times, even a couple of the articles. The war news in the *Time* I purchased at the bus station was just too depressing. Just a matter of months before Hanoi's tanks are rolling down Saigon boulevards. I ripped the article out and shoved it through the window. So much for my new found environmentalism. The woman behind me 'rassed on me about being a litterbug. She was right, and I apologized.

Okay, I've procrastinated as long as I can.

I began writing in here this late in my trip because I'd no idea of where to begin. I'm not certain if I know now, but I'd better hop to it anyway. Like the old man's always carping at me, you'll never get to where you want to go, boy, if you don't start someplace. Even a bad place is a better place than a no place.

* * *

The sun's setting behind the last of the Alleghenies before we dip into the Ohio dairy country. I caught in the glass me smiling back at me, imagining how Betsy will turn out in a few years. Maybe by the time I'm home again. I hope I'll be around to see for myself. Sometimes, though, I'm not so certain. Not so certain. I probably will. It's just these damn shakes, but I didn't have them the last time before I shipped out. Why now?

The first one hit me some weeks ago. A few days later as I was standing in the checkout line when I bought Bartholomew his radio at the company PX, I saw this journal up on a rack next to the *Playboys*. Last one they had. Journals not *Playboys*. The troops would mutiny in a minute if they ran out of *Playboys*. Not even any journals out back in inventory. They'd trouble keeping enough in stock, she said. Soldiers and their journals. You hear planeloads of them taking off every day and all night every night, probably every last sumbuck packing a journal in his kit if not already spread open in his lap.

As I handed it to the clerk to ring up, I hadn't a clue as to what I would write in here. I thought, though, if I got started something might come to me what it was I should tell Betsy. What I could say to make right my not coming home if I don't. If such words could even be written. Where to begin? As good a place as any is to tell her sometimes families deal with the death of a child and move on. Somehow they find again the sweetness of life through its mysteries. Sometimes though — perhaps even most of the time — they don't.

She's too young I'll bet to remember the O'Neils who lived a couple of streets over. They never did deal with let alone get over their little Franky breaking his neck after a rung gave way from the jungle gym he was hanging from upside down at the playground. His death ate away at them like acid on flesh until nothing remained but the bleached-white bone of anguish. He wasn't dead a year before Mrs. O'Neil filed for divorce right after her husband let out for the territory ahead and never was heard from again.

Even before Judge Thomson signed the decree, she took to devoting her evenings to philosophizing amongst Dorothy Brindle and her other disciples up at Perry's Tavern, advanced into the afternoons after her decree got signed, and when the ink had dried some she started in the late mornings. Some days when Elwood pulled in he found her waiting for him in the parking lot. The door of her Caddie would be open, and she'd be sitting sideways with her Keds splayed out on the gravel as she worked the crossword in the *National Inquirer*. Often she helped him open up. She'd mop down the floor and pull garbage cans filled with empties out to the curb as he worked the parts of the crossword she couldn't get.

Perry's closed early on the Christmas Eve of 1966. Through the whiteout blizzard and the haze of the vodka salty dogs she was partial to, it's possible she didn't notice the flashing red lights where Court Street crosses the Penn Central tracks. But then again maybe she did. Durkin recounted to me how law enforcement procedure required him to photograph Mrs. O'Neil before they lifted the body out. Even now it gives him the goose-egg shivers. Wakes him up at night drenched in a sweat, the season notwithstanding. An anguished face staring back at him through spider-webbed glass. Bloody and fisheyed, the last-gasped question on her lips, why?

I don't know which way we'll go if I don't come home. I thought, though, if I can figure out how to make it right with Betsy, it'll keep her off the railroad tracks in a Christmas-Eve whiteout, asking herself why.

* * *

My bus has pulled into the terminal. Passengers are collecting their bags. Fast-asleep children are getting waken who don't want much to be waked. Getting off and going on. I'm still in my seat, but I can see Betsy waiting with the folks. Arching up on tiptoes. Dad's hand is resting on her shoulder, holding her back. For now. She hasn't spotted me yet, though she looked right at my window, blinked, and looked on as though I wasn't here. Must be the fresh Army-buzzcut. Guess it does give me sort of a Mr. Potatohead look. It'll again give her something to 'rass me about. I'll stand soon, but for a moment I want only to look. Look so I can carry her memory with me.

October 7, 1972

Sure is swell to be home. Mom, and especially Dad, asked me lots of questions. Seems the Army hasn't changed much. Still infested with moronic officers. Wished I could've paid more attention to Betsy. She said about zippidy zilch. Just sat watching me. Like she was working on her own memories to backpack out with her someday. Definitely out of character for this one. I mean, talk about your normal giggling chatterbox. Sometimes she makes my ears tired. I was too worn out to say much when we went upstairs, what with our drivers stopping at every cottonseed town and coalmining hamlet we drove through, I was one beat-up Army dude from my twenty-hour trip.

Had fun going with the folks this evening to the football homecoming. Watching Betsy cheer. She sure has grown up since I came home last. Or maybe with my time short before shipping out I'm taking the time to look. Nothing so concentrates the mind. I went down to get us some Cokes at the concession stand during halftime where I bumped into Sarah Anne Hanna of all people. She's a senior now over at Mount Union and plans on teaching next summer in a one-room schoolhouse somewhere in the hills of West Virginia south of Morgantown. Her great-aunt retired from

Saint Paul's a couple of years back and has been in poor health. So Sarah Anne comes home every weekend or every other weekend to look in. Her husband is Congressman Hanna but he seldom pries himself out of Washington unless there's an election coming his way. The years he's in the batter's box, though, are another matter, and I see him everywhere all the time, or so it seemed the summer I worked on his paper. Sarah Anne said she needs to find someone to check in on her great aunt come summer after she's run off to the land of the hill jacks. Maybe I can talk Betsy into it, but good luck on getting Mrs. Hanna to go along. Maybe though. She was once her favorite piano student. One she told me she had the highest of hopes for ever making it to Carnegie Hall.

Sarah Anne told me as we stood in line that the guy she threw me over for in turn threw her over the month after I reenlisted. Talk about timing being everything. Not one to bear a grudge, we're going out tomorrow. Like our moronic drill sergeant used to tell us, smoke 'em if you got 'em, girls.

October 8, 1972

Betsy, shall I say, was less than overwhelmed with me again seeing Sarah Anne. She evidenced her displeasure by marching into my room after I got back from our date and making a choking face with her hands around her neck. Should my time in the Army had lobotomized my senses to the level of our moronic officers so I might have missed her point, she thrust a finger down her throat. She put a little too much English into it and started to retch. I thought she really would puke when she ran out, slamming the door to the bathroom. Too bad, Sis, because next Saturday I'm driving over to Alliance to see her again. We had a lot of fun tonight, and yes, though I may not be an officer, I was a gentleman. Well, sort of. No more than a peck on the cheek when I left her at her door with only a very casual-almost-accidental brush of the back of my hand across her oh-so-sweet behind. Smoke 'em if you got 'em, girls. Maybe my drill sergeant wasn't so moronic after all.

Drove out to the hospital to see Randy Brindle this afternoon. Their head nurse told me he wasn't in, which seemed odd. Very odd, in fact, because besides his burned face, Randy's a Section Eight patient. A nutcase. Baker got called away on a patient emergency but said she'd tell Randy that I'd dropped by. She was sure he'd be happy to see me. She also said to be prepared because he was much worse than when I'd seen him before I left for my last tour. Great. How much nuttier could he have gotten?

October 11, 1972

Sure was quiet around here today with the two squirts in school. Dad at the shop. Mom says the war's been giving him lots of overtime with time-and-a-half Saturdays. I carried the picnic furniture up to the garage attic for her, and while up there I found some old family albums. What a trip they were to flip through. Betsy's got to be the spitting image of Grandma at her age right down to her impish smile. If she pulled up her hair and put on a high collar blouse, you'd have Grandma Addison as a teenager.

Hosed out the old grill when I came down. As I was getting a wire brush out from under the kitchen sink, Sarah Anne called. Change of plans for the weekend. She wants me to drive over *early* so I can pick her up at twelve o'clock on Friday. She has only the one afternoon class, and she figures cutting it won't irreparably harm her GPA. Poor woman just can't bear being away from me. I must admit being a man in uniform does have some benefits. It'd better because the draw backs can be a real killer.

Again drove out to the hospital, and Baker again said Randy was out walking his perimeter. She said after she had told him that I'd stopped out, he said it still wasn't too late for him to talk me into going AWOL. The shakes I've been having tell me that Randy may be right.

October 18, 1972

What a wonderful weekend this turned out to be, but it sure started out strange. I was beginning to think Betsy was right about Sarah Anne being weird. She's not. Just different as Betsy is different. Women of depth, I've been discovering, often are.

Left in the old 'Cuda for Mount Union late Friday morning. Sarah Anne's dorm is an older building, surrounded by an ivy-covered brick wall. Same one where Mrs. Hanna lived when she was a student there. After the mongrel monitor guarddogging the front door of her dorm and the chastity of her charges sent up for her, Sarah Anne showed me around. Pretty campus. Started back for Hanna about 3:00. We talked some about her classes on the hour drive home. What it was going to be like for her teaching in a West Virginia hollow to ringwormed kids who maybe didn't wear shoes in the winter let alone summer and lived in tarpaper shacks without plumbing. I said it might do her a world of good. I shared with her Grandpa Addison's philosophy that he'd yet met a woman brought up on indoor plumbing who turned out to be worth a barn-owl hoot, at which she slugged my arm and accused me of possessing Neanderthal ancestry.

She asked about Army life, but on the drive over I'd come down with a bad case of the shakes. The worst ever. So bad I needed to pull off onto the side of the road and sit there for a good five minutes gripping the wheel, all the while wishing I'd never heard of the goddamn Army and Green Berets. Didn't want a relapse to spoil our day, so I directed the conversation back to her. Listened without hearing and didn't have a clue of what she said until we came up on the Always Fresh fruit stand where Dad used to take us for pick-your-own strawberries and corn-on-the-cob and apples for Mom's cobbler. Sarah Anne asked me to turn into a dirt lane. Strange lane. No telephone poles. No electrical wires. Turned out to be a farm the Congressman had bought years and years before at auction and then just let it sit fallow, which no one could ever figure out why because he knew how to squeeze a penny until President Lincoln screamed bloody murder. She said there was something she needed me to do for her. So after we stopped I scooted over and put my arm around her. She pushed me away, accusing me to in addition of possessing Neanderthal ancestry of having a one-track mind, which slander I vehemently denied. I told her it had two-tracks, they just both played the same song in stereo. She laughed, and we got out, but when she took my hand, she got dead serious. We followed a footpath past a collapsing barn to an abandoned cemetery in a back corner. Mrs. Hannah had asked her this past August to drive the two of them out there where she showed Sarah Anne a tombstone. Strange tombstone. A date but no name. What kind of a remembrance is that? Mrs. Hanna told her she once suspected she and her old gardener might have buried there a James Hamilton. Then she told her the oddest story. She is not Sarah Anne's great aunt, but her grandmother. This Hamilton was her grandfather!

This cemetery was on the now abandoned Hamilton homestead. Turns out that Mrs. Hanna and this Hamilton were classmates at Saint Paul's when it was a sisters' school. He and Mrs. Hanna ended up being more than mere classmates visiting one another to pass the time while he was home on leave from World War I. Prim and if nothing proper, she found herself with child after he'd gone back, whereupon she quit college and went to Chicago to live with her married half-brother. Sarah Anne asked her if she ever wrote to Hamilton that he had a son. She had not. After she saw him off at the now abandoned Hanna train depot, she never saw him again. Never wrote about their son. Of every sin she regretted in her life, not telling him — not giving him something to carry with him — weighed on her the most.

Sarah Anne asked her why it was she's not known as a Hamilton. Mrs. Hanna told her it was because on her son's birth certificate she'd foolishly listed the boy's father as Mark Hanna. This was before he became a congressman.

She did so because he might believe he owed some obligation to her son in case something should happen to her and Hamilton. She didn't tell him until after they were married, which was her second biggest regret for it was a father's say-so that then carried the weight of law. A father who determined who raised his child if he didn't care to. Women had zilch in the way of legal rights. Had only recently gotten the right to vote. It was his knife, like the one affixed to his watch chain, and he'd held it to her throat. Held it there still.

She returned to the village following the birth of her son, leaving the boy to be raised by her half-brother and his wife as their own. He reached his majority without interference from Hanna and married. Shortly after Sarah Anne was born, they divorced. Neither wanted to raise a child alone in the big city. Sounds like there's something more to the story, but it's all Sarah Anne could tell me or all she would. So Mrs. Hanna brought her to the village to keep her company in her middle-age loneliness. To keep watch with her from the second-story widow's walk. She raised Sarah Anne as her grandniece, the conventions of the time and the village being what they were and remain. Parish opinion would force the school board to fire her if word ever got out of her youthful promiscuity, her being married to the congressman notwithstanding. Worse, Sarah Anne would be known as that grandchild of the town whore who once taught in the parish school. She knew firsthand the cruelty of Hanna, the village as well as the man.

She told Sarah Anne she saw much of Hamilton in her. Sometimes she seemed to be not so much a grandchild as one of the children she and Hamilton should've raised. Then again maybe she was only ripening into a foolish old woman. Sarah Anne asked her why she was telling her this now. Why hadn't she either told her as a child or not at all? After the calamity of telling the Congressman, Mrs. Hanna promised herself never to breathe a word of her child to anyone. Not even to Sarah Anne. What compelled her to break her promise was that two nights before she'd dreamt of Hamilton. She paced her room until dawn when she woke, emptying a half bottle of rum in the bargain until she fell back into a fitful sleep. Troubled because she hadn't dreamt of him in years, or if she did by morning she'd buried her dream so deep it was forever beyond her reach.

She saw him only in shadow, shrouded within a cyanic fog where his voice seemed as though it came from far away, his words Delphic when only after a long while come they did. When she asked if she in her unhappiness could join him, he told her she could not. The world he occupied was separate from hers, one outside the ordinary world of men. His world was one of penance. A world to watch the suffering he had caused, the suffering caused by others of his kind. To watch until he made it right. She asked him why his suffering alone was not sufficient penance. Everyone in life suffers, he told her, but if he was to receive his absolution, he had to do more than suffer. He somehow had to make it right. When she asked him what it was he must do to make it right, he faded so deep into the fog that when again he spoke she couldn't hear his words. His voice drifted away until all that remained was an awful and dead silence, an enormous emptiness without echo.

I asked Sarah Anne as we walked back up to the car why she'd brought me there. Why was she disclosing to me family secrets she should be loath to reveal? She said it was because after I dropped her off last Saturday, she too had a dream. She could remember little of it, but what she could had something to do with Hamilton and something to do with me. She said she'd tried in her sleep to will the dream to return. So far it had not. I drove her home, neither of us speaking. She asked me inside to say hello to her aunt, but Mrs. Hanna was sitting on the couch in her parlor, asleep, her chin resting on her chest, a slender spine-broken book in her hands. Sarah Anne whispered that I should go but to call her later. Then she kissed me and pushed me toward the door, her hand on my butt.

October 20, 1972

Another strange day. One adding another chapter to the strange story of James Hamilton, late of Hanna, Ohio, recently revealed true grandfather to the woman who is once again my girl. Started out by me once more driving out to the hospital. Freezing rain, which made keeping the old 'Cuda out of the ditch a real challenge but also kept Randy inside. When I walked into his ward, he was lying on his cot, dressed in a shift and laceless sneakers and reading *Huckleberry Finn*. I stood in the doorway a moment studying him, remembering him as he once was, as we once were, until he looked up. He raised his hand and grimaced a smile guaranteed to scare the bejesus out of any and all trick-or-treating children come Halloween. He closed his Twain and asked me if I was ready for him to whump my ass in chess. Said he'd been practicing since the last time I was home. I told him that'd be the day when he could whump my ass no matter how long he'd been practicing. He got the chessboard out from under his bed and suggested we go down to the cafeteria where there wouldn't be so many distractions disintegrating my powers of concentration. Said he intended to give me every advantage before he thoroughly whumped me.

The cafeteria was mostly empty. Only a doctor and nurse eating a late breakfast with each seated at opposite sides of the room and their backs turned to one another. It was quiet as Randy promised. The clatter of dishes in the kitchen where a faint hillbilly falsetto played on the radio. Rain hissing on the cafeteria window behind me. We played the first game without talking. There wasn't much time to talk. Randy, true to his word, whumped my ass in under a dozen moves. His spirits picked up. He handed me back my pieces and grew more talkative. We started a second game. Randy asked how I enjoyed Special Forces. When I told him I didn't see how anything could possibly be worse, he said to give it a few weeks and I would. Said from what he'd seen the Viet Cong took a sporting interest in whumping on the greenies. Then he asked me if I'd ever gotten the straight dope from Congressman Hanna about the secret patient upstairs. I reminded him it was only a supposed secret patient. One suspicioned by a Section 8 patient, and no I hadn't.

Randy won our second match as well as the third and the fourth and then it was time for me to leave. He walked me out to the 'Cuda, the freezing rain notwithstanding. He told me that by the time I got back again from the Nam, he'd have the patient figured out. Maybe get hold of Baker's keys somehow. We had to spring the old guy. Had to. Some day it might well be him locked up behind that door. If you didn't fight the bastards tooth and nail with every breath you took, that's what they did with Section Eights. Lobotomized their brains and locked up their butts.

Then Randy did something he'd never done before. He hugged me. Told me whatever else I did, not to pull a John Wayne over there. There were people back here who needed me. He turned and went inside, his hospital shift soaked and plastered over his emaciated hips.

I rode along with Mom in the afternoon to the A & P where I gossiped some with Mrs. Warner at the checkout while Mom shopped for my farewell dinner. My Last Supper as Betsy called it at breakfast. I've got to say she's been one relentless twerp in her campaign to get me to desert to Sweden. Go AWOL in Canada. Maybe she'd be satisfied if I just disappeared up in our own attic. Last night she woke me when she cried out, but when I stood in her doorway she seemed asleep. When I asked her this morning if she'd been having a nightmare, she looked at me kind of funny. So maybe she hadn't or maybe she'd forgotten. At least Mom bought chicken at the A & P and not lamb.

We spotted Mrs. Hanna on our way home, out on her front porch collecting the late mail delivery. I said my old teacher might get a kick out of visiting with me once more before I left. Mom thought so too and dropped me off at the curb. Mrs. Hanna was all smiles when she saw me coming up the walk. She set down the mail on the seat of her ancient swing and wrapped me in a great bear hug. An unusual display of affection for so reserved a woman. She said she'd only lit the burner under the teakettle but knew enough of soldiers not to ask me to join her. She took me into her parlor, and when she returned from the kitchen she carried on a pewter platter two cut-glass tumblers and a half-empty bottle of rum. By the time I left, she was only a tiny bit less tipsy than I was, though she must've put away twice as much. She'd do the Army right proud.

I told her after our second shot that I'd made my peace with maybe not making it home this time, but I worried about Betsy. As Mom and I drove home from the A & P, we passed the courthouse, Themis on the roof holding the scales of justice in equal balance. I wondered which way would the justice of life dip for Betsy if I didn't make it back. What I wanted most for her was for her not to lose the sweetness she now had for life. Her sly sense of humor. That smile and silliness and her endless giggle fits. What Dad called her Betsyness. I wanted her to know life's sweetness often comes from its mysteries, and she would always have its mysteries. If I could make her see this before I left, I would've made it as right as I could.

She walked over to her bay window where she looked out at an autumn-brown lawn. Her garden of weeds she called it now. It'd started to rain again since we came in, and the window panes rattled in their frames. She stood there for a long time, hands posed in the small of her drill-sergeant-straight back, before she turned to me. She said the lesson I wished to teach was not so little. In a half-century of standing before a classroom, she'd learned that arithmetic could be taught. The lessons of life, though, were something else entirely. They had to be learned. No matter the wisdom of the teacher; no matter how willing and perceptive the student. Few mastered them. A teacher might show the way or a way but at best that was all. At best.

The mantel clock tolled the hour. She told me that this past August she'd driven out to the Always Fresh fruit stand, intending that evening only to purchase their early Jonathans so she could put up her winter applesauce and was heading home down Old Salem Road. Since the day they buried whomever it was she and her old gardener had buried out there, she must have driven by the rutted lane leading down to what once had been the Hamilton homestead a thousand times. Always she looked straight ahead with her windows rolled up even in summer. She wanted to see nothing, to hear nothing. Revenants were known to roam the premises. Rumors eddied through the village in the years between the great wars of this century about supposed goings on out there. John Fitzpatrick for instance recounted at the Country Kitchen when he came in from hunting pheasants at dawn and his hands still shaking that he'd heard a woman crying. He searched and searched but found only a ragged bandana snagged on the limb of a long-dead sassafras bush. Shirley Johnson, a woman reputed for her sobriety, swore she saw while driving by shadows hanging from a barn beam. Her husband Dean just as adamantly swore he'd looked to where she pointed and saw nothing but a collapsing barn. There were others but whatever someone reported hearing or claimed to have seen came always at the hour of the half-perceived. On mist-filled mornings or in shadowy twilight. Mrs. Hanna had pulled into the lane and walked along the path to the little cemetery. Once more she read the names and dates of the dead Hamilton children as she first had that afternoon when Jamie led her back on Molly. That night, for the first time in years, she dreamt of Hamilton.

November 5, 1972

Well, this is it. Tomorrow I'm off once again to lunacy land. When I finish writing in here tonight, I'm dropping this not-so-old journal in my footlocker and leaving the key on Dad's dresser. My hope is should I not make it back this time it'll give them something more to hold on to than faded memories and yellowing Kodak moments. I can say little more anyway. No matter how much I draw this out, I won't come to any truth I can bequeath Betsy, though I must remember to tell her before I leave not to worry about cheering at the game, about not going to the airport to see me off. Her life must go on.

Dad and I talked out on the porch for so long this evening after she went to bed he started to shiver from the cold even though he wore a Donegal sweater over my old Buckeye sweatshirt. Beginning to show his age. Said he'd go inside. I told him I wanted to look over the old neighborhood one more time before I turned in. Ended up outside of Mrs. Hanna's. I sat across the street in the 'Cuda, hoping to catch a glimpse, if not of her, then of something. Heard the bawl of the Penn Central far outside of town where it crossed the trestle at Mechanicsburg. When her light at last darkened, I too found myself drawn to the Hamilton farm where I stood among the tombstones beneath a pale moon and a gauzy swarm of stars. Markers in silhouette. My gray breath pluming. There I too heard an awful and dead silence. My own enormous emptiness without echo, snagged in the trap I'd constructed with the strings of my own heart.

I know now Betsy will be all right. She will again see the sweetness of life through its mysteries revealed to her for we do not live our lives in straight lines but in circles bewildering to us as a maze, our present lives circling our past, all the while circling the present and past of those we love, which, with luck, is where mine and Betsy's will converge. Then we two will each in turn have completed our own Odysseys home.

*  *  *

Betsy raised the cracked leather of her brother's words to her lips and for a long time sat looking out the window where the sun was setting beyond the fields that Jamie Hamilton once plowed eighth-mile long cornrows. Along Old Salem Road the lights of tractor-trailer rigs passed each other random and indeterminate. The whistle of the Penn

Central sounded. As forlorn as a heart breaking. In a minute it sounded again.

## CHAPTER 39
Epilogue

*The silence of this night makes me marvel at what Jamie Hamilton endured. Except his silence lasted for better than fifty years, to say nothing of his having no sight and he couldn't speak. Probably not much of a sense of smell either without a nose. I don't know if he could taste — I don't recall ever seeing a tongue and he may've chewed it off years ago when they coldturkeyed him off the morphine — but it didn't matter since he couldn't take in whole foods. All he had was his finger and a prayer someday someone somewhere would listen. Those someones turned out to be us, and I was as greedy as a Sunset Boulevard wino to drink in every word his finger cared to tell me. Not only because it would get him home, but if I would never know Nathan's story at least I could know his, and in knowing his I would come somehow to know something of Nathan's.*

*My old stenographers pad lies on the desk beside me, its pages yellow and well worn from the years and the reading and re-reading. I add a note now and again when some revelation creeps up on me. Not a week goes by that I don't slip it out of Nathan's footlocker. I don't read it all in one sitting, mind you, which would take me hours, but maybe a page or two some nights before I go to bed or when I can't sleep because I'm again* running that summer frame-by-frame over and over in my head.

It was Mom who made me take shorthand. I was eyeball deep in the academic courses then: Calculus and physics and headed for some highbrow college. Who knows, maybe even the Ivy League. Depending on what week it was, I wanted to be the scientist who discovered a cure for cancer or the first woman to run General Motors. A hotshot criminal lawyer freeing the innocent from the jails of injustice. Shorthand was for girls sleepwalking through commercial studies with the ambition of a slug who would be secretaries for a couple of years until they snagged a husband and started pumping out babies, the more desperate homelier ones well inside of nine months of marriage. Mom said shorthand would give me something to fall back on. Definitely old school, Mom was, not quite accepting of women having careers other than as housewives and mothers, but maybe a schoolteacher if the girl was a real go-getter. She made me take home-ec too, I guess so I could take care of my husband and his children if my dreams didn't pan out. Well they didn't, but except for my signature peyote recipe I've not baked a cookie since. Like shorthand I saw it as a distraction from my destiny with glory.

Mom in her own way, though, was right on because my shorthand sure came in handy that summer as my brother dictated the patient's telegraphy. I wrote on only one side of the page. On the reverse side of nearly all the pages, though, are my notes of what I've filled in the years after or guessed at from the history I've studied. Talks with other veterans of the War-To-End-All Wars and the elderly in rest homes. Wandering the stacks of the Library of Congress during the year I worked at Walter Reed. What I read about for almost a week when I camped out in the Imperial War Museum. Well, not the museum itself. They bounced me out when they switched off the lights, but I did spend more than one night in my sleeping bag on benches along the Embankment when funds got light and I hadn't finished my research. Brushed my teeth in the Thames until a rubber floated by, but I was the first one back at the stacks when they threw open their doors the next morning.

 My notes from that first afternoon are the exception as they're pretty much spot on what he told us with only a little later guesswork on my part. I'm amazed at their detail whenever I look them over. I've asked myself how many hundreds of times — how many thousands of times — did he tell this story to himself before he told it to us? Enough to get it right I guess. Or did it get embellished along the way over the years through the mist of memory, the fog of sanity? That's the other thing. Never was I certain how sane he truly was. I mean, how sane could he be after being alone with his thoughts for more than fifty years?

 The one thing I am certain of is that salvation can sometimes only be found in extreme and doomed commitments. I read Nathan's journal for only the second time when I came home this evening from the VA over on Wilshire where Mr. Wagner died this afternoon. After I flew into LAX from Daddy's funeral a couple of months back, Mr. Pringle told me his agency had this patient who turned out to be a real pill. Drove away every single nurse he'd sent over, some within like only a couple of hours. I was perfect for the job he said. Because of all the complaints the agency had gotten about me he was giving me this one last chance to redeem myself on account of he didn't much care if Mr. Wagner complained because whatever inept care he got out of me he had coming to him in spades.

 Pill turned out to be putting it mildly. Mr. Wagner was more like a butt-busting suppository. He'd been throat shot during the waning days of Iwo Jima, and so I needed to take this crash course in signing and reading lips at L.A. City College. Caring for Mr. Wagner took me back to ten years ago to my days at the VA in Hanna. I'd learn then that once you let them blow off their head of steam they've got against the world, all they really want deep down is for someone who'll listen. I gradually cracked his shell some, and after a few weeks of his being pretty pissy to me, he'd sign something about his war, and I'd asked him a question. He gave me the silent treatment at first, but then he began to lip a word or two, and from there he worked his way up to signing whole sentences and then on to his stories. I came to enjoy my time sitting bedside with Mr. Wagner, but he suffered from a smoker's heart, and this afternoon when I went into his room carrying his lunch tray, I could tell the time had come to call the ambulance. He died holding my hand, and I thought of Jamie Hamilton dying all alone in the back of his ambulance. Thought of Nathan dying face down in a shit-filled rice paddy with his heart ripped open inside his chest.

I was in bad need for some comfort when I got home. I'd no friend I could talk to, so I dug out Nathan's journal and let him talk to me again. When I finished the last entry, I got the vodka bottle out of the freezer and watched The Fall Guys and Dynasty until I drifted off. A tossing, fitful sleep until I sat again in the Hanna cemetery beside his tombstone in the dewy grass, the tombstones gleaming gray in the misty moonlight. Fog eddied through the trees, and from within the fog the shadows of thousands of boy-soldiers walking in mile-long lines passed me in silence. Some smiled. One pointed behind him. In the last line walked Nathan between two others, his arms falling from their shoulders as I stumbled to my feet. He mouthed something to me, and the three continued on out of the cemetery. After they crossed the tracks, he turned back and raised his hand, and again before he disappeared into the woods he mouthed his words to me, words this time I could see: Live for both of us, Betsy. I'm counting on you. You've got to live life for both of us.

*Tonight as I write this with candle burning, giving voice again to the teenage girl I once was and forever ceased to be, I'm the same age as Nathan was. Now a has-been Valley Girl, tramping out in a Hollywood hovel, gold watch and diamond earrings he gave me that Christmas long ago hocked, vodka bottle drained in the sink and crack baggie flushed down the toilet.*

*Beginning tomorrow, and with each day given me, I vow to live every one of them for both of us. Me and Nathan.*

We at Moonshine Cove Publishing knew when we finished reading the manuscript of *Revenants,* that Scott Kauffman's novel is something special, a novel that would stick with us for a long time, one that might haunt us from time to time.

If you feel the same and you'd really like to read something else by Scott, you're in luck.

On the next page, we proudly present the opening chapter of Scott's forthcoming novel *Last Call at Last Chance* coming soon from Moonshine Cove Publishing, LLC.

Chapter One

She finally fell asleep on my couch. We – she – talked on for the better part of six hours. I hadn't taken a leak since I'd come in from the airport and wasn't out of the living room for more than a couple of minutes, but when I came back she's sound asleep, cradling a pillow that Sophocles likes to use for a chew toy when he can't go out to molest the neighborhood cats on account of the rain.

    Soph won't go near the couch. He's sitting straight up beside me, like he would if he stood watch over his flock with a she wolf culling the perimeter. Strange. Old English Sheepdogs are aggressively friendly. I've watched him escort our postman from door to door all the way to the end of the block just to see him safely out of the neighborhood.

    She was sitting on my porch step when I pulled into the driveway late this afternoon. "Hello, George," smiling as I came up the brick walk. "Your bedroom window was locked. So here I sit."

    I asked her inside and fixed us both double Irishes. Lighted the fire. She seemed not surprised when I told her my brother was dead. I think she knew. Said while she had loved Jude, she saw it coming. Coming for years. Death snaked one step behind him like a second shadow. I didn't say much. Just listened. Why hadn't she told me all this before?

When I came back from the bathroom and saw her asleep, I switched off the floor lamp. There's just enough light from the street and the dying flames in the fireplace for me to write. I'll give her a bit yet. If she doesn't wake soon, I'll bring down the blankets and pillows from the spare bedroom. I haven't yet fixed the lock to my bedroom, so I'll need to wedge a chair under the doorknob. Now that she's here, I don't know how I'm going to get her out. We can't stay together. We can't.

I should wake her. Tell her she has to go. Dump her at a motel across town. I know she's got money. But it's raining out. Well, if she's developed a hankering for life in the Pacific Northwest, she'd better get used to it. Maybe I should wake her anyway. It'd be too easy for her to get comfortable here in my Craftsman bungalow. One I've spent almost every weekend and all of my vacations restoring since I came out here five years before after I ran away from the rumors, Washington Park behind me on the hill, boat lights bobbing out on the Willamette, bells tolling up from Saint Matthew's Passion. Too easy for her to stay, too easy a woman to fall in love with. I know that. Jude knew so too and paid dearly. It was the two of us who killed him. If only he hadn't begged me to go back. For how could Jude, Jude the insatiable student of Greek tragedies, of the Oresteia and Antigone, not know I could only save her by destroying him.

CPSIA information can be obtained
at www.ICGtesting.com
Printed in the USA
FSOW01n0528141216
28426FS

9 781937 327811